Torn

Torn

Book Three of The Awakener Series
by
R.E.S. TIDMORE

RUTHLESS WRITERS PUBLISHING

Other Titles

The Awakener Series
Awaken
Oblivion

The Verbecks of Idaho
Midnight's Dream
Delicate Dream
Unbroken Dream

Managing Mayhem
Bliss

D is for Defective

Coming Soon
Book 4 of the Awakener Series
Redeemed

Dedication

To all my readers, thanks for all your support. I couldn't do this without you.

Thank You

Prologue

Lifetimes painted in blood had flickered through his mind, along with glimpses of his abilities and heightened senses. Chad stretched out his fingers in front of him, trying to come to grips with a reality in which he could see anyone's past with a mere touch if he opened to his energy and allowed it to flow into them.

Chad rocked forcefully, balanced on the edge of his bed, his fists pressed against his temples, unable to breathe. *All those lives can't be mine. They can't be!*

One lifetime after another, all peppered with images of a girl with light-blue eyes scorched his mind. An unbearable weight crushed him and viciously yanked at his heart. The coupling bond compelled him to rise and leave the room, but he fought against it; the thought of his present life and what he was willing to do in order to keep it helped him remain rooted to the spot. His rocking slowed, and eventually, his hands fell to his sides. A cold emptiness touched his heart, as if a witch had cast a spell on it.

The bedroom door opened and his mother's round face and soft, brown eyes popped into view. Her curly, mocha-colored hair swung over her shoulders as she opened the door wider.

"Everything okay in here?" she asked, brows stitching

together.

Chad straightened. He missed seeing her every day: her happy smile that could light up a room, her cooking. The chow hall had nothing on his mother's cooking. It was hard to believe it had been years since he'd lived at home.

His father's tall, lean figure appeared behind her. "We heard a commotion and wanted to check on you," he said, ushering Chad's mother into the room so he could follow.

She gently took Chad's hand. Instantly, the dread that had filled him so completely along with the sudden awareness that there was much more to the world than most people knew vanished like a layer of dust.

"We know you're just here for the weekend, and we shouldn't be nosy now that you're a fine Marine, but I can't help it. I'm your mother."

His father pulled a Kleenex from the box on the nightstand and handed it to his mother so she could dab the sweat from Chad's brow.

"I'm all right. I was just having a bad dream." Those words couldn't have been more true.

"You know you can talk to us, Chad. Returning from another deployment overseas can be . . . stressful. We're here for you." His father rested a firm hand on his shoulder and squeezed, pulling Chad back to the present. "I've been there. I know what it's like to have to adjust again."

"Thanks, Dad, but I'm fine—really. It was just a bad dream."

Sam, his younger brother, strolled out his open door, chewing on a piece of beef jerky. He stopped, turned, and poked his head into Chad's room. "What the heck's everyone doing up in the middle of the night?"

"I could ask you the same thing," their mother said.

Sam's eyes widened. "I was . . . waiting for butt-face to wake up. He said we were going to pull an all-nighter gaming."

"Sure you were," their father said.

Chad took pity on his brother as he squirmed under their father's steady glare. Sam was in his second year of college and settling into his life. Man, he'd missed that little shit; moreover, he'd missed out on watching him grow up and become a man thanks to nine years in the military, including five deployments. Chad stood up, walked out into the hall, and slapped Sam's shoulders, causing him to flinch.

"Let's do this. I'm going to kick your butt," Chad said.

"Yeah, right. I'm way better than you."

"I'm sure you are. As long as we're talking about gaming and not studying for exams, that is."

Chad put Sam in a headlock, winked at his parents, and walked him down the hall toward the den, but paused to look over his shoulder and watch them walk back to their room, their arms wrapped around each other's waists. None of his other lives were as normal as this one. He loved his parents and his brother, and they loved him unconditionally. They supported every decision he had ever made, whether it was breaking up with Sarah Watts in junior year or turning down a lacrosse scholarship to join the Marines. They trusted him to know what was best for him because they had raised him that way.

This was the first lifetime in which his awakening had come so late. In others, he'd awakened to his past lives and his power at sixteen or seventeen years old. Old enough to be happy for the time he had been given to lead a normal life, but young enough to be intrigued by his power and seek out the Seer as soon as the coupling bond pulled him to her. But at twenty-seven, he had a career and plans for the future. He wasn't so willing to walk away from it all out of a sense of duty to the Creator as he might have been years ago.

He and Sam sat down next to each other on the worn loveseat. The controller felt heavy in his hand, and his skin felt tight. Chad knew everything was going to change now that he was awakened. The pull in his chest would grow stronger until he sought out the Seer and reintroduced the coupling bond in this life.

As he played with his brother, laughing and heckling each other, his mind wandered to Leora and Darron. Were they still out there? Had they managed to live a good life after the cabin burned and the Seer died in the bloodstone circle? His protective instincts rose to the surface. They would need him to complete the Awakener's High Council. He was an Advisor to the Awakener of Souls—his daughter from his most recent life.

He clenched the remote so hard it broke in his hands. Sam blinked at him.

"No need to rage out just because I'm smoking your score."

"Sorry, bro." He placed the pieces of plastic on the coffee table in front of them.

His brother left the den and came back a minute later with another remote in his hand. He held it out to Chad.

"You break this one and you owe me a hundred bucks."

Chad sucked in a breath and forced a smile. "Read you loud and clear."

They went back to the game, but Chad caught himself glancing at his brother out of the corner of his eye. Would this be the last time they were together? Now that he was awakened to his power, he would not age. He would be frozen in time until he died, most likely at the hand of the Hound. How many years could he pull off the ruse before they noticed he wasn't getting any older? Ten at most, he figured. Or, would he never visit them again in the hopes of keeping them safe from the Hound and the Council of Souls?

·●○﹏○●·

The weekend flew by in a wave of laughter, and sooner than he would have liked, Chad exchanged goodbye hugs with his family. He was back on base at the shooting range, belly down in the dirt. What the hell was wrong with him? He wasn't hitting shit. He glanced down the row of shooters and then scanned their targets. They were all making their shots, so why the hell couldn't he?

Stretching his neck from side to side until it cracked, he tried to shake off the pulling sensation in his chest, but it was getting harder and harder to ignore. The fact that his current situation had been created as a means to pass the time until he awakened pissed him the hell off. This life was better than all the others. He couldn't walk away knowing he would be unhappy for yet another lifetime after he opened to the coupling bond. He didn't understand why the Creator had chosen him to bond with the Seer. It was clear she didn't love him and never would, even though he had tried to make the most of every lifetime together.

He took a deep breath and let it out slowly. Then, using his power, he heightened his senses. Smirking, he bent his head and peered through the scope, ready to fire—until a man appeared in front of his target. *Shit.* He glanced at Williams next to him, but he didn't seem to see the man. Fear exploded like a grenade inside him when Chad turned back to the scope, thinking maybe he was seeing things.

Marcus's massive body blocked out the sun. Crossing his arms over his wide chest, he bent at the waist to glare at Chad, his black-and-red eyes glowing.

Chapter One

Three months had raced by since Chad's awakening to his countless past lives, as well as the ability to see others' memories with a simple touch. As an Elapsed Seer, he could see the patterns that governed the soul and the pain of their choices, but he could not unlock memories from past lives like Leora could. His ability was tied to the current life of a soul, nothing more.

"Thanks for the ride," Chad said, his feet crunching down on the hardpack by the side of the road.

He slammed the passenger door shut and waved goodbye to the Good Samaritan who gave him a ride to the Sequoia National Forest in California. He watched the battered truck meander down the road until its taillights disappeared. Snow drifted around him like ashes from the gates of hell. Dressed for the cold and with a backpack full of supplies, Chad set off on the hike to the Cavern of Souls.

The cavern had several hidden entrances and tunnels that plunged into unnatural darkness so heavy and thick that it clung to the skin. The best flashlights couldn't cut through the heavy, black veil, but it called to him, and the destiny mark's answering burn on his right pec muscle caused him to grimace. He closed his eyes and recalled the path that would take him to the eastern entrance. He saw the two large, gray boulders with an ancient sequoia tree shooting up between them in his mind. To almost anyone else, the tree appeared to be a few hundred years old and counting; however, in guarding the entrance to a place where time stood still, the tree stopped aging just like all who lived within the cavern.

He opened his eyes. Sequoias towered above him like powerful warriors covered in white armor, ready to hold the souls of this world back from the next one. He took in the beauty that was once his home, having forgotten how awe-inspiring the land was. There was a time when he found himself at an entrance, watching, wondering what the outside world would be like. It seemed promising when the Creator chose him and Rachel to be the parents of the Awakener, but that was more than two thousand years ago. Back then, he was naïve, lost in the idea of love. He was a fool.

Clenching his jaw, he massaged his burning right pec. The irritating pain had begun the day he made it back to Kaloosh and stayed at Darron's cabin after Leora's awakening in the sacred circle. He had known the cost of his betrayal would be the destiny mark; or rather, he had gambled on it. He'd seen the curiosity etched in the Hound's sharp features the day he made the deal, and yet the Hound had not asked why he'd so willingly made such an arrangement.

Now that the Creator had marked him for eternal death because of his betrayal, he wished to see Stephen the Gate Keeper and High Priest to the Council—his mentor and friend—one last time. It seemed fitting to end his life where it began. After that, there would be no going back. There was no reason to.

He set his jaw and tromped through the snow beyond the tree line at a brisk pace for miles, desperate to shake off the guilt festering in him like a splinter. Leora, the Awakener of Souls, had taken her power from the Council and sealed their souls in the cavern, making them unable to travel to the spiritual plane to guide mortals, who saw them as angels. The Council of Souls was not happy with that, and had found a way to fight back using the Hound.

Leora was safe with her husband Gavin in Kaloosh, not far from the bloodstone circle. Gavin was both a Leecher and an Amplifier, unlike the Leechers still in the cavern. He could drain a person's life force to a single beat of the heart, or jack up their power until they exploded. Gavin was her protector, and Chad knew Gavin's love for Leora was stronger than the ripples of time itself. Chad had watched Gavin take his own life upon Leora's death just so they could be reborn together. It was an undying devotion that Chad had never witnessed before.

He paused at that thought, placing a hand upon one of the giant sequoias as he closed his eyes. There was something—or someone—out there. He could hear its heartbeat. He continued, but kept his eyes peeled.

Darron, Leora's brother and the Soul Hunter, would soon be off to retrieve the Seer—or Rachel, as she was called in this life. He didn't go to help awaken the Seer as he had in the past. He hadn't spent time with Leora or checked on the growing baby he sensed inside her. He didn't want to connect in this life; didn't want to see or know them. He stayed one day with Darron to catch up on what had happened since Marcus took him and used his blood to get past the bloodstones and enter the sacred circle. His time with Darron was a vicious reminder that a cycle of death surrounded this path that the Creator had chosen for them. He found his way out and took it.

Exhausted, Chad sat on a fallen tree. He pulled out his phone and checked the battery: five percent. With a tap and a swipe, his finger hovered over Darron's contact info. He wanted to know if he'd acquired the Seer, if she had awakened safely. His brow furrowed as he frowned. He had no right to ask. Turmoil rode through him like a Humvee under heavy enemy fire. He put the phone away and then ran a hand through his shaggy hair on the top of his head; his curls were almost as prominent as his mother's. How long would it take before Darron and the others realized he was not coming back? His heart hammered against his ribs as shame threatened to suffocate him. He had no honor, and his courage had failed him in this life. He was not the man he thought he was.

A branch snapped, pulling him from his thoughts. He searched for the source of the noise. The hair on his arms rose. Someone was there; he felt them. Then, he saw them.

A bear of a man with no whites in his eyes, no pupils, and no irises—only black ink swirling like a dark storm—stared at him from behind a tree no more than thirty feet away. Chad sprang to his feet, but the man was already barreling toward him.

Chad pulled the knife from its sheath at his waist before their bodies collided; the man slammed him against the fallen tree he'd been sitting on, and his head hit the rough bark. Dazed, he barely registered the knife dropping into the snow as meaty fingers wrapped around his throat, squeezed, and lifted Chad from the ground. He tried to break the deadly grip as the man attempted to crush his windpipe, then quickly lowered his hands and shoved them up between the man's arms before yanking his elbows down. The man leaned toward Chad, and he slammed his forehead against the bridge of the man's nose. The man stumbled back; Chad clutched at his throat as he found his feet once more, gasping.

Chad spotted the knife in the snow and lunged for it.

Before he could get a grip on the handle, the large man knocked it away and landed a solid punch to Chad's jaw, but not before Chad hammered an uppercut to the man's face. Chad saw stars for a moment and quickly blinked them away to retrieve the knife. The man fell back into the snow, and Chad jumped on him before sinking the blade deep into the man's side three times. He pushed away to kneel beside the man, who stared up at Chad with blood running from his nose and his side. Steam rose from the snow where his warm blood stained it crimson.

"Who are you?" Chad ground out through the intense fire in his throat. The man only grinned sinisterly at him. This confused Chad, clogging the pathways of his mind like pond sludge. He held his knife to the man's throat. "Who are you?"

The man laughed and coughed up blood. When he spoke, his voice hissed like an echo layered upon an echo. "So good to see you, Elapsed Seer, and so close to home. We missed you."

Home? We? Chad blinked. A Council member?

The man was nobody he had seen before. Chad pressed his lips together. Then again, he hadn't been to the cavern in years. Perhaps the Creator had called forth new members? But what was he doing *outside* the Cavern of Souls? Members were held by the bloodstones of Adam. And how did he know who he was?

As the life drained out of the man, his stormy, inky black eyes faded to a flat, lifeless gray.

Shit!

Chad tugged up the man's jacket sleeve and touched his arm. There was still time to reach into the man's memories and piece together what was going on. He closed his eyes and unleashed his power. Gray, blurry images surfaced, along with the dual emotions that accompanied them: panic, fear, loneliness. The memories were months old, maybe even years. How could a man not make new memories between then and now?

The answer came to him slowly, as gradual as an ember becoming a flame. Once, just before Chad and Rachel left the cavern, Stephen had told him about his theory that Council members could possess humans who were weak in spirit. Stephen had called them the Lost. Could this be yet another corrupt thing the Council had learned to do over the centuries? The Council had enabled Leora to help weak souls find their purpose after so many lifetimes of failing to obtain her power because of the Hound hunting and killing her and Darron. There were many lost souls wandering the world.

The Council could get to Darron and Leora without the use of the Hound; they could still be in danger. Chad pulled out his phone and called Darron, but it went straight to voicemail. He hung up and dialed Gavin.

"Hello," Gavin's deep voice answered.

"Tell Darron, the Lost are being possessed." The connection crackled. "The Council is using the Lost."

"What? I can't—"

The signal dropped. Chad stared at the phone for a few seconds.

"Fuck!" he screamed into the trees.

The air popped and crackled with his anger. He stood up to march back the way he came, but his feet wouldn't move.

His phone rang, and he wasted no time before answering. "Gavin."

"Darron and Rachel made it back. They have a girl with them: Tabitha. She was working with Marcus, and she says she's Stephen's daughter. Be care—"

The phone went dead again, this time because the

battery died.

Darron has Rachel.

Chad's relief was quickly followed by concern. Stephen didn't have a daughter. Council members couldn't have children. He frowned. If she was working with Marcus, that couldn't be good.

Snow swirled around him. His chin dropped and his shoulders sagged; Chad suddenly felt weary. He couldn't go back. There would be no more reincarnations. No more being the father of the Awakener and the Soul Hunter. His time for that was over.

Chapter Two

A day had passed since his encounter with the Lost. Chad steadily climbed the mountainside, searching for the eastern entrance to the Cavern of Souls. The wind whipped around the giant sequoias and scraped at his face like shards of glass. The chill in the air froze his lungs, making the climb more difficult, but he was close; he could feel it. Every hair on his body stood at attention, picking up on an energy source that was not far above him. The wind picked up, as though the elements themselves wanted to keep him away. He flipped up his hood and kept climbing.

Unwanted thoughts of Rachel plagued him. The dull pull of the coupling bond had morphed over the last several hours into a sharp pain that radiated out across his entire chest like short-circuiting wires. It dwarfed the constant burn from the destiny mark. He wondered if Rachel had awakened to her past and her power, and if that was why the coupling bond was beyond irritating by this point. Was she trying to reach out to him?

Her name passed through his lips for the first time, only to be swept away by the icy wind. "Rachel."

The Creator had chosen him and Rachel to sire and parent the Awakener and the Soul Hunter because of their abilities and their innate loyalty to the Creator. He knew the bargain he struck with Marcus would devastate Rachel, and that the coupling bond would then be severed. Although, he doubted any love would be lost due to its unraveling. They had already spent many lifetimes doing the Creator's work, trying to find a balance between purpose and duty, and look where it had got them.

He recalled the first time he laid eyes on her. Diligently serving Stephen, Chad sought out Serena on behalf of his mentor, but was surprised to find a new Seer wandering one of the outer caverns near the healing spring. The water glowed in soft, iridescent blues and cast an unworldly glow on the cavern walls. Her long fingers had reached into one of the pools, curling and stretching. The sensation of the water on her skin caused her mouth to round in an O shape and her round eyes to open wide on her beautiful face. He had paused, remembering his own arrival in the cavern and to this world. It was overwhelming to see, but not know, to try to understand one's surroundings as well as the feelings and senses that accompanied them.

He hadn't wanted to disturb her. Her thin red brows pinched together, her large, pale-blue eyes narrowed, her full lips pressed together, and that wild red hair of hers cascaded over her shoulders to skim the surface of the water she played with. He enjoyed watching her learn about their world, and did so from afar for many years.

During Stephen and Serena's love affair, the new Seer and himself were often left alone or given tasks separately to fill their time. He had seen the curiosity in her eyes every time Shamus—Stephen's protector and head of the Leechers—was near. He'd seen the subtle touches, the small smiles exchanged when they thought no one was looking. Chad knew the new Seer and Shamus were in love, and he'd been glad for them.

But when Serena and Shamus vanished, Stephen was

inconsolable, and the Council got out of control. Stephen never explained what happened. He only said that Chad and the new Seer were to be bonded and leave the cavern in order to sire a new light in the world. Chad had no expectation for love to grow between Rachel and himself.

In this life, however, his parents had showed him what true love was, and he could not force himself to place duty bound in death above the prospect of finding true love. He tossed the thought away like a piece of trash soaked in bitterness. He would not open to the bond because he knew he would never have Rachel's love, but it would still prevent him from seeking out another. Regardless, he was done trying to prove himself. The Seer could reach out to him all she wanted; it would change nothing. What was done, was done. He'd made his choice.

He zigzagged around one tree after another, his mood heavy and dark. The underbrush grew thicker and clung to his pants, making his climb through the snow that much more cumbersome. Minutes turned into hours, and daylight began to wane.

In the distance, two boulders flanking a massive, ancient tree came into view. It was the eastern entrance to the cavern; the boulders represented the Council, while the tree was a symbol of the Creator. An unexpected burst of energy caused his skin to itch, which could mean only one thing: power. The scent of sweat, blood, and earth filled his lungs. He stopped and narrowed his gaze as he soundlessly moved toward the entrance.

Stealing a look around one of the boulders, he froze when piercing emerald eyes locked on him and the tip of a sword aimed at him. Chad stepped out into full view of the large man he once knew so well: Shamus.

Many had speculated that Shamus died or the Creator had called him back to the heavens when he vanished all those years ago, but Chad never believed it, even when Shamus was nowhere to be found on any of the several occasions that sent him to the Council for help. Shamus was too strong and too smart to be killed so easily. And the Creator would not leave Stephen unprotected. Clearly, the others were wrong.

Centuries had passed since he last saw the leader of the Leechers. Leechers could drain the power of any immortal, or steal their last breath if they chose to do so. They served as bodyguards to the members of the Council of Souls. There was a time when members fought, tore apart each other's bodies and hid the pieces so that the soul couldn't return. The Creator sent each of them a Leecher for protection. Shamus, the best fighter of them all, was assigned to Stephen.

Shamus remained loyal to Stephen, and as he was Stephen's devoted mentee, Shamus also protected Chad. Chad had always viewed Shamus more as a brother than a protector, though, which was another reason why Chad never actively sought Rachel's affection. He wanted her to see him and to *want t*o love him rather than Shamus, but that had never happened.

Shamus wore the traditional black leather pants and chest armor with the gold insignia of two crescent moons facing each other, but separated by the tree of life. His head remained shaved on the sides, but with a black warrior's braid running through the center and down to his shoulder. His chest was as wide as Chad remembered, and he loomed half a foot taller than him.

Shamus lowered his sword and returned it to its sheath, narrowing his eyes as he studied Chad. The wall of energy holding the Leecher at bay thickened around Chad like glue as he stepped forward and then easily passed through it. As a Learner, or mentee, to Stephen, Chad was created and sent to the cavern as a man, same as Rachel as a woman. They were not born into the world. They didn't come from the bloodline of Adam. The cavern couldn't hold them, unlike the current Council members, whose bodies were bound to the cavern by the bloodstones. And now, with Leora awakened, their souls were bound too—or so he had thought.

"Where have you been?" Chad found himself asking.

"Working," Shamus said matter-of-factly, as if that explained everything.

Then he reached out and grabbed Chad's right arm, pulling him into a bear hug that lifted him right off his feet.

He'd forgotten how strong Shamus was.

After several seconds, Shamus dropped him to the ground and slapped him on the back a little too enthusiastically, almost knocking him over in the process. "You look different, Lapse. If I hadn't recognized your energy signature, I wouldn't have known you. Brown hair, scrawny arms and legs: where's the powerful body you once had?"

Chad grinned at hearing the old nickname Shamus had given him when he was a Learner in the cavern, but couldn't keep the bitterness out of his voice or the memories from flooding his mind as he replied, "Gone with the life the Council stole from me."

Chad's skin itched as if he'd been bitten by a hundred mosquitoes. *He walked to the living room window of the cabin. Something was out there, just beyond the bloodstones, prowling. It could have been Gavin needing something, but not wanting to bother them so late at night. Darron sat by the fire, playing with Leora. Rachel rocked in her chair and repaired a dress Leora had torn that afternoon. He lifted his jacket from its hook by the door and slipped it on.*

"I'm going to check on something. I'll be back," he

said.

Rachel rose, her pale-blue eyes darkening with fear. "Is everything all right?"

"Lock the door and hide the kids in the cellar. It could only be Gavin, but I'm not sure."

She nodded and squeezed his arm. Chad slipped out the front door and onto the porch. He slowly made his way toward the disturbance based on the itching's intensity; the more irritating it grew, the closer he knew he was. By the time he reached the bloodstones, his entire body felt as if it were on fire. Gavin's power had never caused such a reaction, so someone else was definitely there.

In the distance, he heard rustling in the underbrush and made sure to stay within the protection of the bloodstones. Only those of his blood and his bonded could enter the sacred circle. The hum they emitted calmed him, assuring him that neither the Council nor anyone else could sense his family with any kind of gift. The sacred circle was a void.

As he reached the weapons hold, Chad pulled out a sword: his weapon of choice, despite the evolution weaponry had undergone since he first learned to defend himself. Armed, Chad stepped out of the circle's protection. Whoever was out there would certainly be able to sense him now. He took one step and spotted Gavin crouched behind a boulder; his face was scrunched in pain. Chad moved toward the youth. Just before he reached Gavin, a man stepped out in front of him, and the fire that had coated Chad's skin stopped burning. The black-and-red eyes of the Hound greeted him.

Chad lifted the sword. "You will not touch my family."

The Hound laughed into the cold, clear night. Chad stepped to the side so he could begin working his way between the Hound and Gavin.

The Hound narrowed his eyes. "I will leave my mark as always, compliments of the Council."

"No you won't." Chad lunged and swung at the Hound. "Gavin, run!"

Chad spun and cut Marcus's arm; he hissed as his eyes grew redder. Chad took a step back and then swung the blade high. Marcus rolled out of the way, pulling a short blade of his own from his boot. In a flash, Chad felt a stinging sensation across his ribs, but he didn't stop coming for Marcus, cutting and hacking at any part of him he could reach. Before long, both were bloody and panting.

From the corner of his eye, Chad caught a glimpse of Gavin running toward Marcus with his own sword. Using his momentary distraction, Marcus cut Chad down. He fell to his knees, blood spilling from his throat. Chad clamped down on the wound as Marcus dragged him to the edge of the bloodstones. He reached down and gathered blood from Chad's bared throat, then poured it over his head and smeared it across his face. Marcus smiled at Chad before he stepped into the bloodstone circle.

With no small amount of effort, Chad suppressed the memory of the end of his previous life.

Shamus's expression fell sharply, lips pressed tight, and darkness touched his features, leaving deep lines around his mouth and eyes. "I heard about what happened when Marcus reported to the Council. I'm sorry. I didn't wish for you or your family to die."

Chad moved out of the shadow of the tunnel and into the remaining rays of sunlight, just beyond Shamus's reach. "Yes, well, I didn't make it easy for him to kill me."

Shamus studied him for a moment, and then the corner of his mouth turned up. "You left a few scars. I felt great pride in the battle you waged against him. It is not easy to scar a man like Marcus. His ability to recall every life from birth and every battle he ever fought makes him a true adversary. Your training served you well."

Chad took the compliment as a peace offering and changed the subject. "What are you doing here? Where's Stephen? You never leave him for long."

"I'm waiting for someone's return."

."No one from the Council can leave the cavern," Chad said. He folded his arms over his chest. "If you're waiting for Marcus, he's not coming. The Awakener has contained him, both body and power."

Shamus's green eyes widened a fraction. "She is awakened? I had my suspicions since the Council has been growing more agitated over the past few weeks, but they do not speak to me of such concerns as they know I'm loyal to Stephen and do not care about souls leaving the cavern."

"Stephen didn't tell you she was awakened?" Chad asked.

"The Awakener taking her power from the Council does not affect Stephen and his duties in any way. You know this."

"I haven't forgotten he is bound to the cavern; that his soul can't leave his body as those of the other members can. My fight has never been with him, unless you count disagreeing with how he fails to govern the others."

Shamus flexed his jaw at the truth of his statement. "Stephen has grown numb to their whining. He tells them to pray to the Creator, but they do not listen." He frowned, then growled, "If the Awakener has Marcus, where is Tabitha? What has happened to her?"

Tabitha! That was the name Gavin said before his phone died. It must be true, then; she's Stephen's daughter. Interesting.

"Is she the 'work' you spoke of?" Chad asked, knowing that only someone as important to Stephen as his daughter would pull Shamus away from his side like that.

Shamus stiffened. "What have you done to her?"

Without waiting for a response, he rushed to grab Chad, but hit the wall of energy and was blown back. He landed in a heap about five feet away. It took him a minute to gain his bearings.

"I want to talk to Stephen." Chad didn't know this Tabitha's story, but clearly, she was important.

"If you want to talk to Stephen, you know where to find him. Go get him yourself," Shamus said, climbing to his feet.

"I will not repeat that mistake." Those words were like a branding iron on his soul, and he closed his eyes in a futile effort to escape them. Many years ago, he and Darron had gone to the Council to ask them to stop sending the Hound to kill his family. He begged them to let his children fulfill their purpose and help souls reach the awareness they needed to in order to learn and grow and leave this world permanently. The Council had killed him, though not before Darron managed to escape.

"Bring Stephen to me if you ever want to see Tabitha again!"

It was a dick move, but it would be safer for Shamus to get Stephen than for him to do so.

Shamus puffed up his chest. Chad leaned against the boulder, curious to see if his old friend would call his bluff. He watched the emotions playing across the man's face, marveling at how quickly the atmosphere between them had turned sour. Tabitha clearly meant a great deal to him. Again, a spark of concern for Leora, Darron, and Rachel arose. If this Tabitha was working with Marcus, she could want them all dead too.

Shamus walked away, his footsteps echoing off the tunnel walls. Chad felt a touch of shame and regret. He wasn't behaving like the man his parents raised. He would honor them one last time.

"She's safe! She's with my son!" Chad shouted.

Shamus's footsteps stopped for a few seconds, then resumed until they faded away completely. Chad clenched his jaw, fighting the man he'd become since awakening.

Engrossed by his thoughts, he almost missed a small movement by a nearby tree. A tall woman stared at him with inky, black eyes. Her brown hair was in knots, and her face was smeared with dirt. Her skin was littered with cuts and scrapes as if she had wandered the mountains for days.

Chad sent his energy out to get a read off of her, but felt nothing, just as he had with the man who tried to kill him the previous day. A white haze licked at her pale skin, much like Darron's black mist did when he was losing control of his anger. With a sinister smile, she opened her arms wide. Chad doubled over, feeling as if his body were being torn apart. She drew power to the center of her chest, formed a white ball of light over her heart, then slapped her hands together. The energy shot from her fingertips with a loud crack and stabbed him through the heart. He dropped to his knees, his jaw hanging open in a soundless scream. The woman rotated her arms and yanked them back, opening them wide again. The white light wrapped itself around Chad, pinning his arms at his sides.

Satisfied, the woman strode to Chad, and the white mist around him turned a deep purple. She circled him, running a finger over his shoulders and across his chest. The purple mist responded to his anger and burned his skin. Finally, he cried out.

"What has brought you here?" The woman's voice was an inhuman cacophony of multiple entities.

Chad struggled to breathe, and grunting noises clawed their way from his throat. The woman snapped her fingers, and the energy holding him loosened an inch.

"Why are you here?" the woman asked once more.

Chad trained his eyes on the ground. He didn't know which Council member was possessing this body, but he had the feeling more than one of them was involved if they were able to wield this kind of power with Leora awakened and the Council's collective power gone. *But how?* Casting his eyes down was a show of respect Chad knew wasn't genuine—just a formality.

Chad lifted his eyes and stared at her, but said nothing. She tightened her hold on him until one of Chad's ribs gave way to the pressure.

"We asked a question, boy. Why have you come here? Your horrid daughter has stripped us of our power. We are no longer a threat in the Creator's eyes." Hate twisted the woman's face like a cyclone. "Not going to talk, we see."

The woman peered down the tunnel. An invisible force smashed into Chad's jaw and his body fell to the ground with a thud.

"We will get the answers we want."

The woman conjured an invisible rope and dragged him toward the eastern entrance of the cavern.

Chapter Three

A chilly sense of unease drove Rachel from her bed to the lone window of her bedroom. Delicate rays of moonlight snuck between dark, unforgiving clouds slinking across the night sky. The meager bit of light did little to combat the goose bumps rising on her pale skin beneath the white, cotton T-shirt skimming her knees. The warmth of Gavin's home could not reach her tonight.

It had been three days since Leora and Tabitha restored the bloodbond between Gavin and Marcus, linking them once more as blood brothers in an effort to stabilize Marcus's gift of recording time with Gavin's leeching ability. Marcus's power hindered his means of functioning individually and often made him unpredictable. His presence in the home made it impossible to let her guard down.

She glanced toward the bedroom door, hugging herself; she just couldn't shake the feeling of dread curling around her spine like a snake. Needing to be certain her family was safe, Rachel sent muted gold tendrils of her power toward Leora's and Darron's rooms, where they were tucked away, snuggled up to their lovers. The tendrils were met with even breaths and steady heartbeats.

Satisfied, her power retreated and she turned to the bright and beautiful world laid out before her on the other side of the window. Several inches of snow had fallen quietly during the night, enfolding the town of Kaloosh in an icy, white, barren land. Smoke puffed up the chimney stacks, creating lazy clouds above. Rachel remembered when there was no town, only trees and the humming of the Payette River. She tucked a strand of blonde hair behind her ear. That was so very long ago she could hardly recall it, but it was there in the muck of memories splattered throughout her mind.

Her conversation with Tabitha about Marcus's reaction to the baby after the bloodbond was reestablished, and about how everyone in the room was knocked unconscious except him and Tabitha circled and circled like a Ferris wheel in her mind. Tabitha had said Leora's belly glowed with a pale-blue light when he touched it, and, as if in a trance, Marcus had said Sapphire would change everything.

Rachel shivered at the thought of Marcus touching Leora in any way after the things he had done to her in this life. Her arms tightened around her waist and her lips pressed together. She wanted to kill him. She wanted to fracture his soul into a million pieces and bury them around the world so he could never be reborn again. She sighed.

So weird—wanting to kill someone I don't even know from this life.

Why would Marcus be intrigued by the gift to erase time, as it seemed Leora's baby, Sapphire, would be able to do? He, in essence, was time, and tasked with recording the events of the lives of all those in the circle of Advisors. Shouldn't he be afraid of her? They were missing something vital. With every day that ticked by, she watched her daughter's belly grow. She'd seen this in so many other lives too, but Leora's children never breathed life outside her womb…death had always found her first.

When Darron had questioned her about a vision she'd

had on their journey from San Deigo to Kaloosh regarding Leora's child, she had no recollection of any such thing. And yet, as the days passed after her awakening, her mind became clearer, and the memory of that vision breezed forward in her mind as a fragile wisp. She often saw the future as sheer and delicate as a cloud, and it was just as hard to hold. With every choice one made, the vision could become thicker, clearer, or dissolve completely.

Rachel took a deep breath, closed her eyes, and pictured Darron's panicked face. When she recalled a vision, she could observe it outside of herself, move around it to analyze and process it better. Time rattled through her mind in a cyclone of events before it took shape. It was enough to make her swallow hard against the urge to vomit.

"What year are you in?" Darron posed the question tentatively as he knelt before her.

Sweat beaded his brow, but his calm voice grounded her in the moment, and the cyclone dissolved into one place and time.

Her hollow, distant Seer's voice responded, "I'm in the present."

"What's happening?" he whispered.

Rachel could see the vision clearly. A tiny child rested in her arms, beautiful and perfect. Red curls adorned her scalp. Power swelled from her like magma overflowing from a volcano, suffocating and threatening to destroy all in its path. Rachel shifted against the memory and the way it wanted to tear through all that she was and would ever be, to wipe away every memory she had.

"A child is born. She's beautiful. Love flows into her from many others. My blood is her blood. She's the strongest soul."

Darron swallowed. "Who's the mother of the child?"

An image of Leora, pale and unmoving, gripped her

mind. Blood and sweat marked her body, and her eyes were open wide in shock as she lay in the hospital bed, but she was no longer breathing. Gavin was beside her, his eyes just as wide as he took long, slow breaths. He was a void of power and memory, as were Darron and Tabitha, who were also present for Sapphire's birth.

She swiveled her head toward him. "She will erase time. The light will be extinguished."

Darron stopped breathing. "Holy shit. Who does the child belong to? Tell me, please."

She kept her ghostly eyes fixed on him. No iris, no pupil. "The Creator."

She understood the frustration she saw cross Darron's face. She often wished her visions didn't sound so cryptic, yet knew it was the Creator's way of giving them a chance to change what was to come through conscious choices.

Darron slapped his hands to his face and scrubbed it several times, growling under his breath.

"Are you okay? What's she talking about, Darron?" Tabitha asked in a shaky voice as she moved closer.

He held up a finger to silence her. "How will the light be extinguished?"

Rachel swallowed hard. Leora would not live once she touched her daughter. Her gift of revealing one's purpose would unleash Sapphire's truth, and then she would wipe clean the memories of everyone on Earth; every soul would essentially be reset. Leora would not be needed any longer. She would die, never to be reborn.

"Eternal death." She began to twitch, and the white in her eyes began to turn brown as the vision faded.

"Can I stop it?" he asked.

"Only the Keeper can find redemption and save the Light. The Circle will betray the Light."

Rachel rubbed her temples as she released the memory

of the vision. Betray was such an unforgiving word. Darron's interpretation of the vision and what Tabitha had seen through Serena's memories painted a grave picture indeed, but reinforced their belief that separating mother and child at birth was the only way to save them both. Sapphire, like Marcus, would wield her ability right away, and would not be allowed time to simply live and learn to love. Her gift would not be suppressed until her power called to her, as was the case with Leora and the others.

But how they reasoned that the Keeper to be redeemed was Marcus, she wasn't so sure. Many Council members over a millennium had been given such a title. That Marcus could use redemption was certain, but there was a troublesome feeling in her gut that it could refer to another, someone who hadn't stepped into the light of her gift and been seen.

Her hands dropped, and she gazed out at the white world once more. So many moving pieces, so many things she had to understand and yet didn't know if she ever would. She did not think that the circle that would betray the light referred to the Advisors, but the theory the others had that the light was not Leora, but a symbol of life itself, also gave her pause.

Rachel began to pace around the full-size bed that all but filled the room. Back and forth she wandered, worrying her hands together, stopping occasionally to send out another tendril of power to check on Leora and Darron. She gazed absently at the picture hanging on the tan wall beside the window. That she had not noticed it before concerned her. It showed a half-burned cabin with large boulders in the distance. She stepped closer. The bloodstones, the sacred circle: it was haunting in black-and-white. Before she admitted herself to the hospital several months ago, she had dreamed of that place; she just didn't understand its significance. The second-story, back bedroom was where she died in her previous life. The Hound had come for Leora, but was willing to kill anyone in his way. She'd tricked him by hiding Darron and Leora and making him believe she held Leora as the fire consumed her. This gave her children the chance to run from the Hound. She glanced at the wall where Marcus prowled on the other side. With his gift and power bound by Leora, she could grip his mind, tear it to shreds. But, thanks to their bloodbond, Gavin would know, would feel it. She growled low.

She caught a glimpse at her ghostly reflection in the window. The body she occupied was nothing like the last one. Gone were the full, red curls that matched Leora's; they'd been replaced by long, silky, straight, blonde tresses. Warm chocolate eyes stared back at her instead of cold blue ones. Her body was lean and missing the full curves of her hips and breasts that she remembered.

Rachel's fingers slid over ribs that were even more prominent now than they were just a few months ago. She noted the hollowed cheeks, the dark rings under the eyes; that much had not changed. She'd never carried the weight of the past and an unknown future with ease.

Her stint as a patient was a gray smear of the past, the present, and the future. Shifting between memories of past lives and visions of the future always made her unstable during her awakening, and often pushed her almost to the point of fracturing her mind. If that were to happen, she would never awaken, would never control her gift or remember who she was. She would become a shell, much like the lost souls of this world Leora tried to help.

Prior to her awakening, she'd worried about her outfits, getting her next coffee fix, showing Lily (aka Leora) that she was skilled at her job as an assistant on the psych floor. She'd complained about needing a movie night with ice cream and Oreos on a regular basis, and about how she was going to balance her next semester of classes for her master's degree with work.

That girl seemed at odds with the wise Seer she had been in previous lives. In this life she was upbeat, outgoing, and an optimist to the core. She let out a breath she hadn't realized she was holding. She no longer felt that optimism. Her gift was no longer warm and steady, but cold and foreign inside her.

She leaned against the window and rubbed her chest where the magnetic pull from the closed coupling bond linked her to Chad. He left a week before she arrived in Kaloosh and awakened to her past lives, to her gift. It made no sense, but with the coupling bond still unopened, she could only sense a vague idea of the direction she should head toward in order to find him. There were no emotions filtering through the bond—not that she ever let her walls down to allow that kind of intimacy between them. Still, she couldn't ignore the restlessness she felt. After all they had endured to get to this point—all of them awakened and wielding their gifts—Chad's choice to leave felt wrong.

In their previous life together, they were cloaked by the vibrations of the massive bloodstones, which created a void in time and space that hid them from the Council of Souls. Chad's dark-brown hair was shaggy then, and his body had been honed into tight cords of muscle from centuries of wielding a sword. She wondered what he was like in this life. How had he been brought up? Did he have a good life before his power began to stir? Hers was. She had loved her mother and father fiercely before her mother died of cancer when she was a teen. All the years after her mother's passing were spent with her father, and would be cherished for lifetimes to come. Her heart still throbbed painfully for her father, who had been dead these past two years after a car accident.

She didn't take for granted the time she had before awakening. Every life was different, but they all made her stronger, ready to face what came her way. She didn't linger on the heaviness the continual process brought her. To do so would go against everything she was.

"I don't know why you would go to the Cavern of Souls," she mumbled to the full moon. The clouds had broken up and scattered across the sky to reveal it. She sat on the edge of the bed. "It all feels like a very bad dream."

She flopped down on her back and stared at the ceiling. It had been a week since her awakening, and it was quite the adjustment. Every time, she had to slowly wrestle the memories of countless past lives into their own mental boxes. If she kept the past in the past, she could work through the present with a clear mind.

At the age of twenty-seven, she'd learned that she had children, but not from this body. Leora was thirty and Darron was forty. She held all the memories of giving birth and watching her children grow until the Hound murdered her. She sighed heavily. A new life made the past feel distant, less smothering.

Thank God for that.

Suddenly, uncontrollably, Rachel's body tightened; she panted from the involuntary strain. Beads of sweat broke out over her pale skin, causing her T-shirt to cling to her body. What wasn't absorbed by the soft cotton trickled down her bare legs. She clutched the sheets beneath her; she knew the sensation all too well.

Smoky tendrils billowed up and tumbled over the edge of the fountain flowing within her that held her gift at bay. She had tried for centuries to control the flow of its power, but it had not yielded yet. The tendrils crept through her mind, glazing over every crack and crevasse to close off her instinctual defenses. She had no voice to cry out, and her body was paralyzed. Rachel's heart raced; no matter how many times visions took her under, the fear of being so vulnerable never abated.

Torchlight flickered against onyx walls. A lean, male body was suspended above the stone floor. His powerful arms were chained above his head, the muscles in his torso stretched to their limits. His upper body was smeared with drying blood, his boxers sagged low on his narrow hips, and his manacled ankles dangled inches above the floor.

The man's eyes were closed and his head hung low. In the dim light and under all that blood, she could make out smooth, olive skin, high cheekbones, and the shadow of a beard that gave his features a hint of ruggedness. Brown curly hair stuck to his forehead.

Her heart beat against her ribs with such force that she could hardly focus on the vision that trapped her body. Disoriented, Rachel prepared herself for whatever she was about to witness.

The man's chest rose and fell faintly. His face was etched with agony. Rachel had the urge to smooth away the lines caused by his suffering.

His eyes moved beneath his eyelids. Slowly, he opened them, unveiling the same green eyes that had haunted her since she checked herself into the psychiatric ward.

"Chad," she whispered. "The Elapsed Seer."

Something caught his attention, giving him the strength to lift his head. The green of his eyes vanished in a wisp of angry black ink consuming his irises. A tall, slender, female figure dressed in black leather pants and a white tunic stepped out from behind a heavy wooden door. Brown, straight hair skimmed her shoulders, causing the pale-gray skin of her face and neck to look sickly. Her lifeless expression drew a direct contrast to Chad's clenched jaw as a growl rumbled from his throat.

"Come back, have you?" he said.

"Watching you suffer is the kind of entertainment we seldom get now that Tabitha has left with Marcus." The woman's voice sounded as if a thousand bees swarmed in her throat. She tapped a leather flogger in her hand and a wicked smile stretched across her face. "Shall we begin? We do love hearing your screams."

"Rot in hell," Chad spat. "I can't believe what monsters you have all become."

"Feisty tonight, are we? Let's see if we can help you work off some of that energy."

The woman circled Chad, the leather flogger trailing across his body as she went. Chad hissed as pieces of flesh were torn from his back. Bone peeked through the deepest gashes over his ribs. The woman stopped and tapped the flogger against her palm so that the ends of the leather strips slapped and clinked together.

Rachel's stomach rolled; she knew that sound. Shards of glass were anchored to the tips of the flogging strips.

Chad's hands flexed and gripped the chains above his shackles, his body tensed and prepared for the impending strike. The flogger whistled as the woman swung it over her head, then cracked it against Chad's back, ripping into his body. An agonized scream left his dry, cracked lips. She yanked the flogger back and the shards of glass cut through his muscles like a spoon dipping into pudding. Fresh blood trickled over his older wounds; he wouldn't survive long at this rate.

"Is that all you got, you sick fucks? You're getting soft in your old age," Chad taunted between his gritted teeth and labored gasps.

The woman stepped closer to the light, showing Rachel that her eyes were as black as Chad's. She bared her teeth,

*and red dotted her eyes, but then she smiled. "You're a fool
to think we will simply kill you so soon." She yanked Chad's
head back by his hair and pressed her lips to his right ear.
"We would not say such things if we were you."*

*"The stress of your job has finally gotten to you,"
Chad ground out.*

"Really?"

*The woman viciously raked her long fingernails over
Chad's gnarled back, eliciting another scream from him.*

Chapter Four

Rachel's scream blended with Chad's until the smoky haze of her power pulled back and her body was free of its hold. She clutched the fabric of her shirt over her chest and sat up as she struggled to breathe.

Holy shit! Chad is going to die. She raked a hand through her damp hair and bit the corner of her lip. *Why did that woman sound so odd? It was like she was more than one person.*

The bedroom door swung open and a bare-chested Darron rushed in, followed by Leora in a bathrobe, her red hair tousled from sleep. Still unused to the size of her round, pregnant belly, Leora awkwardly scrambled onto the bed and pulled Rachel into her arms. Rachel didn't protest. In that moment, Leora was simply her best friend and had seen her through countless meltdowns; not her daughter, not the Awakener. That was exactly what she needed and wanted.

A dark mist danced around Darron's tan feet and curled over the edge of the bed to taste and touch Leora and Rachel's skin. He'd said that his power was easier to call upon since giving himself over to become Death.

"Was it a vision?" he asked in a rough voice as he placed a hand on her knee, sending tremors from Rachel's head to her toes.

"Rachel . . . please," Leora said, resting her cheek on top of her head.

Rachel's mouth was so dry she couldn't swallow, but after several deep breaths, she managed to croak, "Yes."

"Of what?" Darron asked.

He blinked his cloudy white eyes that looked much like hers when she was taken by her power, except his was a predatory stare. She wondered if he could see her aura, or perhaps even the exact spot in her body that housed her soul. She hadn't asked him about the changes that had come along with becoming death. She tried not to flinch at the implications.

"It was Chad," she finally said. Leora stiffened around her. Maybe telling them was a bad idea, but they deserved to know. "He was strung up and someone was flogging him."

Darron's white eyes widened and Leora gasped. Rachel extricated herself from Leora's embrace to face them and lean against the headboard.

"How long before the vision is fulfilled?" Darron asked.

Her gift was not an exact science, although her mentor, Serena, had taught her a few ways to gauge certain details based on the clarity of the visions. The future was influenced by many choices, paths taken or avoided.

"There was no haze around him or his location, so a few days maybe. A week at most."

"No," Leora whispered, fear evident in her eyes. "Do you know where he was?"

"Somewhere in the Cavern of Souls. The person hurting him was a woman I have never seen before," Rachel said, still trying to work out who she was and why she was with Chad.

"Damn. I knew I should've gone with him to the

cavern," Darron grumbled.

"Don't say that! You have no clue why he went there in the first place," Rachel said with a scowl at Darron, whose eyes were pale blue once again. "Don't start blaming yourself for things you can't control. If you had gone with him, you wouldn't have met Tabitha, I would have fractured, and the bloodbond between Marcus and Gavin wouldn't have been reestablished."

A moment later, Gavin's wide shoulders appeared in the doorframe and blocked the light coming from the hallway. His not-so-happy expression was directed at her.

Rachel gave him an apologetic shrug and smiled. "Come on in, Gavin. Join the party."

His dark moods rarely affected her. All Leechers wore similar expressions. The scar that ran from his right temple to the corner of his mouth pulled up slightly, but he was still formidable.

"Why would he go there in the first place? We have been hunted by the Council for centuries," Leora said.

The question weighed heavily on Rachel's mind. "I don't know. Many of the Council members have hated your father since the Creator brought him from the heavens as a Learner for High Priest Stephen to mentor. It has never been a safe place for us."

Leora shuffled off of the bed to enter Gavin's waiting embrace. The second she leaned into him, he wrapped her in his scarred arms and held her protectively. He glanced at the wall that separated them from Marcus. Even with the bloodbond restored, Gavin was as leery as Rachel was about his presence.

"What is a Learner?" Darron asked, his brows stitching together.

He pulled a chair out of the corner of the room and tipped it back against the wall on two legs, seemingly more relaxed. Even the black mist was vanishing.

Rachel gently retrieved one of her mental boxes from its place in her mind to answer his question. "A Learner is an apprentice. When a Council member was diligent in their work for the Creator while still within the cavern, they would receive an apprentice. I believe it was the Creator's way of giving the member a child, even though the Learner came in the form of an adult."

"You mean Dad wasn't born? Just, *poof,*" Darron snapped his fingers, "and there he was?"

When Rachel nodded, Darron gaped and let the chair drop back to all four legs. The urge to grin caught Rachel by surprise. He had never cared about the Council or what her and Chad's time had been like before they bonded. Tabitha—who was newly bonded to Darron—was rubbing off on him. Tabitha was a new soul; everything was a wonder to her.

"In the beginning, the Creator sent down men and women. He watched to see which souls would become the smartest, kindest, and most courageous. He tested the souls in the most heartbreaking ways to see if they would remain steadfast in their purpose . . . and to him. Over the centuries, he assembled the Council. Learners were sent directly to the cavern and had no experience with the world beyond it."

Darron moved to the window. His eyes had darkened, so she knew he didn't like what he was hearing. "So every Council member had a life before they were chosen?"

"Yes. Some lived many lives in an attempt to achieve his or her higher purpose, just like all souls on earth."

"So they're trapped," Leora said, brows pulling high onto her forehead, eyes going round.

"It depends on how you look at it. Some see it as being trapped, but I guess others see the ability to help guide other souls without aging, dying, and being reborn as a gift."

"Don't get so worked up over them," Darron ground out to Leora. "They don't deserve your righteous anger. Even if they were once souls to be pitied, they're not anymore. They have been hunting and killing us for centuries."

"Darron, get over yourself. We need to try to understand them," Leora said.

"We've had two of them with us for years, and we still don't understand them." Darron stole a glance at Rachel and sat back in his chair.

She almost smiled. Perhaps Darron paid more attention than she thought.

"Sorry." Darron shrugged. "The Council is different from us."

"Yes, that's true, but your father and I are different too. We were both Learners. We never knew what life was like outside of the cavern except for what our mentors taught us from the books they brought with them."

"You were both members of the Council for thousands of years!" Darron cried.

Leora scoffed. "Seriously, Darron, are you dense? She said that she and Chad are different from the other members of the Council. They knew what they had lost when they went to the cavern. She and Chad didn't."

"None of that explains why the Council hates Chad," Darron said.

"When the Creator made Chad for Stephen, the Council became instantly jealous. Chad was the first Learner. I was the second, but I came along many, many years later. Few Council members have been gifted with a Learner since."

"Well, if that doesn't suck, I don't know what does," Tabitha said as she strolled into the room wearing a long T-shirt and a grim expression, her blue-and-black hair pulled into a ponytail. "So, am I not invited to the party?"

With a pouting bottom lip, Tabitha cozied herself up on Darron's lap and kissed his cheek, then his neck. He wrapped his arms around her waist as dark mist drifted around her protectively.

"Sorry, baby. You're just a dead sleeper, is all."

"Oh. Well, please continue. I'll catch up quickly enough." Tabitha's eyes were bright with curiosity.

Rachel smiled as Tabitha's mood affected everyone else in the room. Having just unlocked her ability as an influencer, Tabitha didn't always have control over it. She studied Tabitha for a long moment. How would she handle the news that Shamus was alive? When would be a good time to tell her with all of this chaos around them? Given the vision she just had, Rachel didn't think she could wait very long.

"It isn't really fair of the Council to be angry with Chad," Leora continued.

"I'm sure there's more to it from the Council's point of view, but that's all the information I've gathered over the years from my time with Serena and other Council members."

Leora let out an exasperated sigh and looked at Darron. "What do we do? I can't go after Chad like this." She pointed to her belly. "I'm getting huge, and it wouldn't be safe for the baby."

Tabitha suddenly looked a bit green as she glanced at Leora. Their betrayal weighed on all of them.

Darron smirked. "And you say, I'm dense. Tabitha and I will go after Chad."

"We can't split up again!" Leora said.

Rachel sighed, knowing Leora wouldn't like what she was about to say. "I'm going as well."

"What? You can't go. You . . . you have to stay here

with me," Leora whispered.

"Darron and Tabitha don't know the cavern as well as I do. They'll be discovered easily, and the Council will be worried about Darron's presence. Who knows what they'd do to them?"

"She's right," Darron said.

Gavin's deep voice reverberated throughout the small room even as he shifted uneasily. "What about working with Marcus to stabilize his power?"

Rachel had never seen him so afraid. "We won't be gone for more than a week or two."

"What about the baby? What if she comes early and you're all gone?" Leora's tears slid down her cheeks.

Rachel climbed out of bed and pulled Leora into a hug. "Everything will be fine. I promise. We will get your father before it is too late and be back in time for the baby's arrival."

Leora hugged her back tightly. Rachel's heart twisted as she locked eyes with Gavin standing behind Leora, his own emotions hidden behind a stoic mask once more. Rachel and the others felt as if they had already betrayed Leora simply by knowing they had to send her baby away if they wanted her to live and to retain all of their memories. She hugged Leora closer as fear dug its thick claws into her back. She didn't want to believe that Marcus was the only logical choice for taking Sapphire; that they could easily claim he'd escaped back to the Council and Leora would not question his absence as she would Rachel's or Darron's.

Her vision of the baby's birth and how she would erase time was a cruel move by the Creator, and one that Rachel did not understand.

She kissed Leora's cheek, then brushed it softly with her thumb. "Rest, okay? Everything will be fine."

"I'll have a little chat with Marcus before I pack to

confirm the bloodbond is firmly in place and in no way at risk of being broken. We'll leave in a few hours." Darron took Tabitha's hand. "We have to hurry, though, if we're going to try and get there before the Council kills Chad."

Gavin grabbed Darron's arm. "What're you going to talk to my brother about? I can feel the bloodbond. It is intact."

Darron plucked Gavin's hand from his bicep and straightened his spine. "He and I made a deal. It's time for me to pay up."

"What kind of deal?" Gavin said, glaring as his mouth twitched and stretched his scar.

"That's on a need-to-know basis, and you don't need to know." Darron tapped Gavin's cheek. "You need to take care of my sister, or you'll have *death* to answer to."

Leora touched Darron's shoulder. "Please be careful with Marcus. I don't care what kind of deal you made with him."

Darron held Gavin's gaze. "Always."

Tabitha rested a hand on Leora's belly. "You be good to your momma while we're gone. Hear me, peanut?"

Leora smiled, and the corner of Gavin's lip pulled up. Tabitha had started calling the baby that before Rachel had seen that Leora would have a girl. The term of endearment stuck.

"You go get some rest," Rachel said, trying to usher Leora toward her room. "We will wake you before we go."

"No, I can help you pack."

How could Rachel refuse her with that deep line of worry etched on her face? "Fine."

Gavin left the room and Leora started buzzing around, opening drawers and pulling out clothes. "Do you think you can make it to Chad in time?"

Chad's beaten face flooded Rachel's mind. "I don't

know, but we have to try."

Chapter Five

Darron stood at the door to Marcus's room, staring at the handle. Rachel rested her hand on his shoulder. The house was quiet now that the packing was done, and they had all agreed to rest for a few hours, then leave at daybreak.

Darron had waited to go to Marcus once he thought everyone else was asleep, but Rachel wasn't going to let him anywhere near the Hound alone. He was too unpredictable, even after he was tethered once more to Gavin for balance. His gift was still erratic, and always kept him on the edge of insanity. Once again, Rachel wondered how they were supposed to give him Leora's child to raise. She prayed that by going to the Council to help Chad, there would be a way to stop her vision from coming true somehow.

"What did you promise him?" Rachel whispered.

He straightened and peered down at her, his pale-blue eyes dark with sins not yet committed. He pursed his lips, then said, "Immortality."

Rachel squeezed his shoulder. "What? A man like Marcus should never be given immortality—not for any reason."

He popped his neck to release some of the tension in his body. "It was the only way he would allow the bloodbond to be reset."

"Tabitha and Leora could have reset the bloodbond either way."

He took her hand from his shoulder, and then dark shades of night ran under his skin. Rachel took a step back. It had been lifetimes since she'd seen her son change into death.

"Are you certain they would have restored it without my deal?" He shook his head. "I couldn't risk the woman I love or my sister getting lost in the mind of a madman."

Black mist danced around them as cold licks of power tasted her skin, and Rachel fought back a shiver. "Are you sure about this? Are you sure you can even grant him immortality?"

"This is the first step in accepting my ability as death. I have never fully understood it because I was afraid. But, when I was in Afghanistan a few years ago and members of my team lay dying beside me, death was there. I gave myself over to the urge and simply lifted the souls from the bodies. The next thing I knew, I was in the cavern with Stephen. He didn't say a word to me, nor was he surprised to see me. He took the souls I brought, and then I was back, gunfire going off all around me."

Rachel touched Darron's cheek gently and nodded. She had known Darron's ability to sense souls that needed Leora's help would grow into something more one day, she just never thought he would collect souls for Stephen and the Creator.

"But how can you make him immortal if you collect souls?"

He shrugged. "It's a theory I have about my power. Marcus is a perfect test subject. I'll mark him with a thread of death's power, or essentially lay a piece of myself upon his skin, just like when he marked Leora and then knew where she was because he could sense that piece of himself on her. I'll be unable to take his soul because of the mark. It would be as if I was coming for my own soul."

Rachel rolled the idea around in her mind. "I think I understand. But, I am going with you."

Darron opened his mouth to protest, but then shut it when she raised a finger as if to scold him. He frowned and turned to open the door. His skin blackened completely and his eyes went white. He hovered off the floor, riding the consuming black mist. Rachel doubted he was even aware that his skin shifted in the same manner as the mist; that death was alive under his skin. It was a sight to behold, the carrier of death.

Marcus stood by the window with his back to them. He seemed stable, but Rachel was still leery of his fickle moods.

"I've come to cloak you from death, as agreed," Darron said, his voice an ear-splitting screech.

Marcus recoiled from the sound and peered at them over his shoulder, his face a mask of indifference even though his eyes were filled with malice as they raked over Darron's form. They were black orbs with a dot of red that never changed, his power ever-present. His large frame broke up the dim light streaming in through the window, emanating power and determination. Rachel lifted her chin and stepped closer to Darron. Gold light sparked at her fingertips, ready to hit him with a wave of her power if she needed to.

The mist surrounding Darron expanded until it blacked out the entire room. Rachel blinked on her night vision, but even then only saw shadows of light as Marcus and Darron moved.

"I've been waiting for what's owed," Marcus said.

Darron whispered to her, "Do you see the glow in the

center of Marcus's chest?"

"No, I only see the wisps of red and black twisting in his aura," she replied.

"It's a red orb with flames around it," he hissed. "An interesting soul."

Rachel watched Marcus's aura, still unable to see anything else but a dim glow as Darron drifted toward him. To his credit, Marcus stood unmoving as death hovered.

The moment Darron's fingers skimmed Marcus's chest, she caught a glimmer of what he had described: a blurry, red orb with shifting edges. Marcus seized his hand and shoved it away as if afraid of his touch.

Darron laughed coldly. "I smell your fear, and it is delicious."

Marcus took a step back. Rachel didn't blame him.

"Once you're marked, I'll always know where you are, just as you can sense where Leora is." Marcus pursed his lips as Darron went on with a grim smile. "Yes, I know you marked her so you could track her. I can smell the bitterness of your power on her skin, on the back of her skull. Don't think that Gavin cannot sense it as well."

Rachel held her breath to hold in the sob that formed in her chest. Leora could never escape him, not even in a future life. Rachel wanted to drop to her knees and cry. She stepped back and leaned against the door. Why hadn't Darron or Gavin told her about this sooner?

"It is only fair that I do the same to you. You will never be able to run from me. I may not be able to kill you, but there are far worse things than death."

"He can't be trusted!" Rachel called out.

Marcus's black eyes held her as he clenched his fists by his sides. "The same can be said for you, Seer. The thought of never again having to be reborn with the knowledge of a thousand lifetimes intact is worth the price of being marked." Marcus sighed, unexpectedly sounding vulnerable. "I'm ready for a new beginning, and to live without the heart sickness that has plagued me for far too long."

Darron reached behind Marcus and ran his fingers through his hair before getting a firm grip on it. Marcus's muscles clenched even as he made himself vulnerable, taking a chance that Darron would honor his word.

For a moment, they stared at one another. Rachel could tell that each was fighting his own demon. Suddenly, the mist engulfed Marcus's body so tightly that it visibly squeezed him. The temperature in the room plummeted and Rachel shivered. After a time, the mist vanished, and Marcus crumpled in Darron's strong arms.

"It's done. My debt is paid. Death cannot claim him."

Darron laid Marcus on the bed, his skin changing back to normal as he did so. Rachel watched, the power still swirling under her skin. A tendril of gold light left her fingers and pressed the base of Marcus's skull, testing to see if her power could enter his body at what should have been the easiest access point. When it couldn't, fear seized the essence of her soul and she walked out the door. Darron followed, locking it behind him. She sent a prayer to the Creator to protect them all.

Chapter Six

Three days passed before Rachel and the group found the eastern entrance to the Cavern of Souls blanketed in snow. It looked exactly as it did in her vision: the two large, gray boulders peeking out from beneath the snow with an ancient sequoia reaching for the heavens between them. It had been lifetimes since she'd been there, but this was her first time in this life ever seeing sequoia trees. Darron and Tabitha stared whenever she paused during their hike to walk around the base of different trees and run a hand around them, simply in awe of how small she felt in the presence of those giants.

Snowflakes fell silently, but the forest of giants carried an eerie hum of energy. Her skin tightened and began to crawl. She ran a hand up and down her arm, her breath puffing out in icy clouds. The last memory she had of this place floated to the forefront of her mind. Not used to the sensation of feelings associated with memories from other lifetimes, she shivered. They were cold and stained with sorrow—always sorrow. She didn't like it, but she closed her eyes and let the memory hold her anyway.

Rachel walked out of the cavern, the coupling bond with the Elapsed Seer newly cemented. Her hand was in his as he led her away from her life there. Tears ran down her cheeks. She knew there was so much more to learn and do than the Council could provide for them in the cavern, and she was ready for a chance to have children, but the thought of them not being Shamus's had nearly destroyed her.

Knowing he hadn't abandoned her, but was assigned to help raise Tabitha, had done little to mend her damaged heart. She wasn't sure how it would feel to see him again, but the same could be said for Chad. Her past emotions were exhausting and confusing. Rachel was still working on accessing her knowledge of the past while blocking the individual memories so she could be present in her current life and know what she was feeling then and there, not some thousand-year-old heartache. She never thought she was one to let wounds fester, but her past self was clearly a mess. She saw therapy in her future.

She pushed down the anxiety associated with the memory and focused on the bond, which drew her to the cavern's entrance. Being closer to where she thought he was made the ache in her body manageable. He was definitely there somewhere.

"Where should we start?" Tabitha asked, shifting her weight and rolling her knife in her palm nervously.

Rachel sensed she wanted to be there about as much as Darron did. She placed a hand on her shoulder. "It will be okay."

Tabitha looked away, but Darron pulled her into a tight embrace and kissed her forehead. "I haven't been back since Shamus's death. I don't know if I can go in there."

It was time to tell Tabitha what she'd seen in a vision a week ago. She knew how Tabitha had been confined to certain areas of the cavern and forced to fight and kill other Leechers as entertainment for the Council. Rachel knew the Council was corrupt, but she couldn't believe Stephen would allow such a life for his daughter; it didn't sound like the Stephen that Serena had loved.

Shamus had basically raised Tabitha and trained her to be the fighter she was. Tabitha told her Shamus died while they were in a match together, but that was not the case. He was alive, and waiting for her to return. Rachel didn't know why Shamus's recovery had been hidden from Tabitha, but she was sure Stephen had wanted it to be so for some reason. Only time would tell what that reason was.

Her recent vision of Shamus replayed in her mind. He stood at the eastern passage, waiting. Her heart thumped; he was still as beautiful as ever in black leather pants that stretched over his muscled legs and the armor framing a broad chest. With his sculpted shoulders and his arms crossed over his chest, he looked every inch the warrior she had loved. Time hadn't diminished her ache for him. Rachel shivered with desire for a man she had never known in this life. She struggled to merge the past with the present. She was not the Seer he knew, and she sure as hell was not the Seer she saw in her memories. That sinking feeling pulled her under a wave of anxiety. Did she really know what the hell she was doing?

Long ago, she believed Shamus had abandoned her. It broke her in a way she'd never thought possible. For a long time, she lived in a gray, melancholy world of cold, empty despair. Every muscle tensed as she remembered the pain of his supposed rejection, but now she knew the truth and couldn't help but wonder if he thought of her fondly.

Rachel shook her head. What was wrong with her? A man like Shamus wouldn't dwell on their time together, and the circumstances of their separation didn't lessen the hurt she still felt. He could have told her about Tabitha; she would have listened and understood.

Rachel sucked in a breath and let it out slowly. Shamus's beautiful green eyes faded from her mind.

"Tabitha . . . Shamus is alive. I saw him in a vision a few days ago."

Tabitha's eyes sparkled and her chin quivered. "Are you sure it wasn't a past memory?"

"He was there"—she pointed toward the boulders—"at the eastern passage. He was waiting for something."

Tabitha's hand wiped away a tear even as she smiled. "Me. He was waiting for me. Waiting for me to return with Marcus." She shook her head. "He knew I left."

"Your father must have told him."

Tabitha blew out a breath that sounded more like a sob. "Thank you for letting me know."

Darron let her go and kissed her on the forehead, then took her hand and tugged her forward. His boots crunched in the snow as they moved closer to the boulders that hid the narrow mouth of the cave, his back tensed and a dark mist floating around him. The Council had sent the Leechers to kill him the last time he was there. Chad had fought to the death to give Darron time to escape. Rachel didn't blame Darron for keeping death at the ready this time, but wondered if he could take a soul from an immortal body.

They all had their demons to overcome in this place. She wouldn't allow the weight of this mission to rest on Darron's shoulders, Navy SEAL or not. She would lead. After all, she was the Seer.

"We will search the outer tunnels, then work our way into the heart of the cavern where the Council members live."

Rachel waltzed through the cavern's opening; the biting fangs of the energy shield that held the Council members within did not take hold of her. This was where her life began, and where she learned about her gift while Serena taught her how to call forth visions, whom to stay away from, whom to trust, the rules of the Council, and the rules of the cavern. It was overwhelming for many, many years.

Rachel glanced back to make sure Tabitha and Darron were still following her into the darkness of the tunnels.

"These will lead us right outside the abandoned living chambers, which we'll see about two hundred and fifty yards to the left." She frowned. "At least, they used to."

"There are no abandoned living chambers," Tabitha interjected.

Darron looked at Tabitha. "She knows this place better than either of us. If she says there are abandoned living chambers, then there must be."

Tabitha scowled at him, but squeezed his hand.

Hundreds of years might have passed since Rachel stepped foot in the Cavern of Souls, but she remembered everything as if it had only been a day.

They traveled deeper, leaving the light of day behind. The tunnel was damp, dark, and muddy. With her heightened senses engaged, Rachel ran a hand down the dirt wall as she counted her steps, trying to get a sense of how far they'd traveled.

She knew that if anyone from the Council saw her or Darron, they would be taken to the meeting chamber and shackled. They looked different in this life, but their energy signatures were the same. She didn't know what would happen to Tabitha, though, so they had to be careful. There was no time to lose. Chad could die.

"Did Chad say why he was coming here?" she asked Darron.

"No, only that he had to leave."

It just didn't make sense that he would leave after Leora awakened and Darron went to retrieve her, and frankly, it pissed Rachel off.

"Did he act odd in any way?" she pressed, desperate

for some clue as to why he'd acted the way he did.

Darron said nothing for a few minutes. Then, almost reluctantly, he replied, "He seemed sad after we saved his life in the sacred circle. He tried to hide it, but I saw pain in his eyes."

"Why was he sad? Did you ever ask him about it?"

"No. I assumed it was because you were not with us yet and that he was worried about you."

Rachel stopped in her tracks, causing Tabitha to bump into her. Her heart warmed at the thought of Chad being so concerned about her, but it quickly cooled. Something still didn't feel right.

There were many unused tunnels that wrapped around the main common areas, and she had used most of them to slip away with Shamus. Her pulse kicked up with the memory of the first time Shamus had stood near her, lingering in her presence as Serena and Stephen took a private walk through the most beautiful spot in the whole of the Cavern of Souls. *Bioluminescent fungus dotted the cavern like stars in the night sky. Rachel had known Serena and Stephen loved one another, but had no understanding of what love was. Shamus had sparked a curiosity that grew into fondness during their many interludes that occurred because of Serena and Stephen.*

On this occasion, Shamus had stood a mere step behind her. The heat radiating from his body caused the taut muscles of her back to loosen. He inspired calmness that she'd never felt before. She'd peeked up at him from under her lashes as he watched Stephen and Serena walk hand in hand.

"Do you enjoy seeing them together?" she'd asked, curious as to what went on in a Leecher's mind. Since she was a Learner whose soul never left her body, no Leecher was assigned to her.

"Stephen deserves to be happy, just like any of the other Council members," he'd said.

Rachel had frowned. She was a Council member. Did she deserve to be happy and find someone to care about too? The question swept through her mind, leaving behind particles she couldn't pick up. Did she want someone to care about?

Gazing at Shamus's handsome face, she'd realized she wanted more; that she wanted to know love. She'd studied his strong chin, his prominent cheekbones, his straight nose, and his nicely shaped lips. A flutter took hold in her belly and a smile pulled at her lips. He must have felt her gaze on him because he looked down at her and a spark of something unknown to her at the time shone in those beautiful green eyes. They drank each other in for a long while, the rest of the world falling away. He'd placed a hand on her lower back, then stretched his fingers around her waist and stepped closer. His body pressed to her side, and the fluttery feeling spread to every part of her body before gathering between her legs. She'd gently rested her hand over his, wanting to feel his skin, then let out a breath and placed her head against his shoulder.

Movement at the edge of the cavern broke the spell: Chad. He had always stayed out of sight when Stephen and Serena were together, careful not to disturb them.

That walk in the cavern was the beginning of Rachel and Shamus finding love in one another. If Stephen and Serena had seen them that day, there was no doubt what would have soon followed.

Something that strong couldn't be forgotten. Rachel's love for Shamus had lingered long after the start of her relationship with the Elapsed Seer. She'd lost so much time with Chad because of it. She pursed her lips. She wouldn't let the past shape her present this time.

Skimming the wall with her palm, she continued counting her steps. The chamber was much too dark for normal eyesight, so she called forth her night vision and saw that the tunnel she'd been looking for was barely more than a rift in the wall. She tugged Darron's arm and guided him to the narrow opening. They were forced to shimmy sideways along the rocks to pass through.

The last time she'd used this tunnel was to visit Shamus's bedchamber and make plans for their year away from the cavern, a privilege the Creator granted all Council members and Leechers except Stephen. She'd rushed to Shamus's bedchamber after the announcement had been made, full of excitement and certain that Shamus would be waiting for her. But he wasn't there, so she waited . . . and waited . . . until the hours turned to days. He never came. Rachel had searched the entire cavern—or so she'd thought—and never found him. In fact, the cavern was empty except for Stephen. There had been no Serena. She, too, was gone without a word. She'd thought Shamus had left without her, and her heart crumbled to dust. That wound had never really mended.

They moved in silence, each lost in their own thoughts. The tunnel slowly widened, and it quickly became easier to move, but Darron and Tabitha still had to hold onto Rachel for guidance in the dark.

"I need to see Shamus with my own eyes," Tabitha whispered. "He may be able to help us find Chad. If anyone knows about a dungeon or a torture chamber, it would be him."

"You can't be seen by anyone," Darron said, tugging them all to a halt.

"If they see me, they'll think I've come back from working with Marcus, nothing more." Tabitha took her hand from Darron's as his body went stiff, signaling he was getting ready for a fight. "He'll help us, I know it."

"No. We don't have time to find him," Darron said.

Rachel placed a hand on his shoulder. "You don't have to like it, but we could use all the help we can get. Tabitha can move freely through the cavern, and no one will find anything odd about it. Time means little here. Some may not have even noticed she left with Marcus."

Tabitha's fingers skimmed over Darron's face and then tapped him on the cheek. "I'm a big girl. I'll be fine. But thanks for the concern."

Darron growled low and Rachel smiled. Yes, Tabitha was a nice addition to the family.

"Whatever you say, dear," Darron said sarcastically.

Rachel continued walking while the two of them finished their stare-down in the dark—if they even knew they were having one. A moment later, their footsteps crunched behind her once more.

After almost an hour, the tunnel narrowed once again and was lit only by a distant, dim glow. Rachel blinked away her night vision and focused on the light ahead. At the opening, she found a large passageway made of black, polished obsidian from floor to ceiling. Torchlight lazily flickered over the stone. She peeked around the corner before stepping into the hallway, in which oversize doors were equally spaced every five or six yards. The rich cherrywood of the doorframes sported carvings of ornate trees, moons, and characters from forgotten cultures. Tabitha stepped out next, while Darron stayed tucked in the narrow opening.

"Nice. I'll have to use that tunnel again sometime," said Tabitha. Her black leather pants crinkled as she pulled her knife from her hip holster, spun it in her palm, then put it back. "All this sneaking around is stinking cool."

Darron yanked her to his chest. "This isn't a game,

Tabitha. You have to be careful."

She pushed herself away from him, face scrunching up indignantly. "Actually, it's a game I've been playing since I was a teen. I'm Stephen's daughter, and he's the only person I have to fear."

She began to march down the hall, each stride radiating determination.

Rachel had seen Tabitha's mother display her vigor many times in a similar way. Serena had been a powerful Seer and a brave soul. The realization that both Serena and Stephen gave pieces of themselves to create Tabitha had moved Rachel beyond words. She still wondered why they'd gone against the Creator's edict that no Council member could have children because of their immortality. That particular act of rebellion was significant, especially for Stephen, with all of his roles and responsibilities. Did they know something the rest of them didn't?

Darron launched himself after her, grumbling as he went.

"Darron, get back here," Rachel whispered, failing to grab his black shirt as he passed.

She sighed and followed them. Why did he always have to be so willful? A very strong urge to spank him made her frown. She'd never spanked anyone in this life.

So weird.

"Stay away from your father," Darron commanded as he whipped Tabitha around to face him.

Tabitha's eyes widened, then narrowed. Rachel knew that look all too well. She'd seen it a thousand times from Leora. Tabitha wasn't a woman to be ordered around anymore. In the few weeks that Tabitha and Darron had been together, she'd come into her own. It was an honor to witness it.

Tabitha tenderly touched Darron's cheek. "Everything

will be fine. Remember, we're bonded. You'll be with me. You'll know if I need you. Have faith in me . . . please."

He closed his eyes, and Rachel had to look away. Sometimes it was painful to see such love, even if she couldn't be happier that Darron had found someone. Everyone deserved to find love at least once. When she looked back, the two of them were sharing a passionate kiss that spoke of a love that would last for all time.

Tabitha broke away first and marched down the hall, ready to resume the search for Shamus. Darron stood still for a long while, seemingly staring at nothing.

Rachel walked up to him. "She'll be fine. She's strong in ways we could never imagine."

Darron looked at her. "How's that?"

"She has no reason to doubt herself. In this life, she is as strong as she'll ever be because now is all she knows. There are no past lives to influence her. Innocence is a beautiful thing. See that you keep her that way."

She squeezed his shoulder, and Darron smirked.

"Innocent? My girl?"

He took a few more steps forward, as if his feet had a mind of their own and wanted him to go after her. Rachel held onto him and sent a silent prayer to the Creator to watch over Tabitha and bring her back safely.

"Come on, we should wait in the tunnel and try to rest," Rachel said.

They walked back to the tunnel, where Darron followed the rocky edge of the wall and sat down in a wider section just beyond the torchlight that reached them from the hallway. Rachel blinked on her night vision and saw concern for Tabitha etched on Darron's face. Rachel stared at him; he was with Tabitha through their bond, as surely as if he were walking beside her.

She sank to the ground feeling exhausted, her gaze

still fixed on Darron. Her bond to Chad had never been that strong. Even when it was open, they didn't hear and feel every thought or emotion from each other, only the overwhelming ones or when he wanted to share a thought with her. They were not a love match. The Creator had chosen them to be Leora and Darron's parents, and they did not dare refuse such a gift. Having a family was something she'd never thought possible, and Chad had always been kind and tried to make the situation as comfortable as possible for her.

She leaned her head against the wall. Things could have been so different if she'd never loved Shamus. After she thought he had abandoned her, her heart was broken, and a festering kind of sickness ate at the wound, destroying any hope of repair. Tears burned her eyes. It didn't matter that she later discovered that he'd left to care for Tabitha as a baby, or that Shamus had to hide her from the Council because her birth was not granted through the Creator. He never explained it to her himself, or even came to say goodbye, and she never allowed herself to love Chad—not the way he deserved.

Man, my past lives suck.

It was hard to understand why she felt so cold toward Chad when he was so gentle with her in every memory she had. She was really starting to think she was just a bitch. Sure, Shamus hurt her, but now it felt so distant, like a single brushstroke on a painting that was far bigger and more meaningful than that one application of color and texture.

She clenched her fists, opening and closing them over and over as she stared into the darkness. What was she going to do when she saw Shamus? How would she feel when she saw Chad? Did she care? Did she even *want* to care? She was in control of this life. She could make different choices. She could be like Tabitha and live for *now*. In this life, she was not looking back.

Her attention returned to the present when she heard Darron snore. She slowly rose to her feet. It would probably be awhile before Tabitha returned, so Rachel decided to look around and try to acquaint herself with the woman she used to be. That was certainly better than being stuck with her self-deprecating thoughts. Darron would be safe there.

She peeked out of the opening and listened carefully. Deeming the coast clear, she stepped out into the hauntingly familiar hallway, taking great care to remain undetected. She passed many chamber doors before she came to the end of the hall, where she turned to the right and hurried past a dozen more before coming to the last one. The large cherrywood door looked the same. It was strong and ancient, and in the center, two crescent moons framed a full one: the mark of a Seer. She turned the knob, but the door didn't open. She rammed her shoulder against it as quietly as she could, and it cracked a sliver. With all her strength, Rachel pushed it wide enough for her to slip through.

What had been her home for thousands of years remained just as she'd left it. Her red, silk comforter was still on her bed, as if waiting for her to rest her weary head at the end of a long day. She drank in the sight of all the personal items she had left behind: her love seat, her vanity, and the beautiful gowns she so loved to wear. She walked to the closet and pulled out a royal blue gown with an empire waistline and lace layered over the silk. Rachel wrinkled her nose. It was pretty, but not something she would be seen in now. She remembered how it felt the first time she wore it, but didn't think it would be quite the same if she were to try it on again. She let the dress fall from her fingers.

To pass the time, many of the Council members continued their chosen craft from their life before they were chosen to guide souls. There were many caverns dedicated to these pursuits: some for making clothes, others for making furniture, some even for farming, and much, much more. The cavern was a hidden city. The Creator brought what they needed when they needed it. It was the perfect balance. During their allotted year away from the cavern, many had brought back new items, or had learned new things they could teach others.

Memories flooded her heart and mind, and sorrow ripped through her. She remembered spending time with Serena in this very room as she learned to use her gift. Tears burned her eyes and blurred her vision. Why did she come here? To torture herself? Rachel's past was so at odds with her present; it was like being in a blender. Clearly, she hadn't compartmentalized each life as well as she thought she had. She sighed and wrinkled her nose.

Shit.

The last time she saw Serena, she was sitting on the edge of her bed with her hands gently placed in her lap. Her long, black hair was in a loose braid draped over her shoulder and reaching her waist. She wore an emerald-colored, velvet dress with gold beads lining the neck and bodice and running down the front of the dress to the hem, which brushed the floor when she stood. Rachel sat next to her, fidgeting with her own hands, her mind full of doubt.

"Take a breath as the fog fills your mind and let your body go still. Don't be afraid of it. Let it fill every corner and crack of your being," Serena had said in her soft, soothing tone.

"I . . . I don't want to see the future. It doesn't help anyone!" Rachel had cried as her head fell into her hands.

Serena's thin finger lifted Rachel's chin, and her bright gaze spoke of an understanding Rachel would never share with another. "To see things you do not yet understand is difficult. I know. I, too, have struggled with my gift. However, sometimes seeing is not meant to help you understand, but to know."

"To know what, Serena? That people are dying? That terrible things are going to happen to people I care about, but don't even know yet? I can't. I won't see."

Serena had sighed and wiped Rachel's tears away, then hugged her close for a long time. Neither said a word, both lost in the realities of their gift.

"There will be times when what you see feels like it will destroy you, but remember that the future is always changing. Thousands of choices affect one outcome that you may or may not see. That is why seeing is knowing: knowing a thing can be, but can also be changed." Serena had let her go then and taken Rachel's hands in hers. "Let's try again. Take a breath, let it out, and feel the fog creep out from the fountain of your power as you let the vision take hold of you."

Rachel's heart hitched in her chest. She missed her mentor and friend, but as Rachel peered around the room, she didn't feel connected to the things there anymore. So many lifetimes had passed since she was that girl in her memory.

She turned to leave, but paused when a faint pulse of energy called to her. She walked over to her nightstand and carefully pulled the drawer open. There it was: her tiger's eye. The stone was the length of her thumb, and its rich color was accented by golden streaks and deep, chocolate browns. A small smile pulled at the corner of her mouth. The stone was wrapped intricately with white gold wire and had a matching chain. It was warm to the touch; energy curled up her arm to her elbow. The stone, which was once her talisman of protection, was saying hello.

A knot formed in her throat as she ran a finger over

the smooth surface and then held the tiger's eye against her heart. It was a gift from Shamus that she'd left when the Creator bonded her to Chad. Shamus had told her he loved her the night he gave it to her. Wrapped in each other's arms, he'd placed gentle kisses all over her skin. He'd promised to go to Stephen and ask for permission to be together and no longer hide their relationship. She'd believed him and began to make plans for shared living quarters, but of course, that day never came.

She lovingly placed the necklace back in the drawer and closed it. Their time together was gone, and it should stay there no matter what happened with her and her family. Her fingers glided over the comforter one final time as she exited the room and didn't look back. She was no longer the girl she had been while in this place. The remnants of her innocence had long since been cut away by what Serena taught her. Time was relentless, and change was inevitable, but with it, she had found unconditional love and family.

Sticking to the shadows, she crept back down the hall to the tunnel. Ten feet from the jagged cut in the black stone wall, Rachel froze and sucked in a shaky breath. Her skin prickled with sudden heat and needles.

A vision? Why now?

The drumming of footsteps against stone echoed in the distance. Fear shot through her and she managed two steps forward into the middle of the hall. Anyone coming around the corner would see her in a matter of seconds. She tried to take another step, but thanks to the oncoming vision, her feet were rooted to the stone floor. A vision could not be held back. It would claim her, so she closed her eyes and surrendered to the unbearable heat roaring in her veins as the images seized her mind.

Leora gazed out a window as she rubbed the center of her chest, then glanced over her shoulder. Gavin was nowhere to be seen. The image flickered, then Leora went to the front porch. Zipping her fuzzy jacket all the way to her chin, she slipped on a pair of gloves and hurried down the road, her breath puffing out in a fog in front of her.

When she reached Main Street, her muscles tightened beneath her jacket and her jaw locked. Suddenly, she bent at the waist, and fear ripped through Rachel. Was Leora going to have the baby?

She stood, her expression tight with determination, and rubbed her chest again. It only took a moment before Rachel knew what was happening; Leora had felt the pull of a lost soul right there in town and was going to them without Gavin. She was the Awakener, after all.

Apparently reenergized, Leora jogged slowly, allowing her instincts to take over. She stopped at the hardware store and peered in through the display window before entering. A girl who could be no older than sixteen, with brunette hair and gray eyes, stood in front of her.

"Can I help you find something?" she asked.

Leora smiled. "Yes, I'm looking for some nails."

"Right this way."

Leora followed close behind her and carefully reached out toward the girl. Rachel saw a glow build around Leora, and when she touched the girl's arm, she unleashed her power from her fingertips. Gold light blanketed them both, and Leora closed her eyes. Frozen in that moment, Rachel felt Leora's power slip from her fingertips and into the young girl's veins, seeking the brilliant essence that every soul naturally possessed.

When Leora reached the innermost part of the girl, Rachel felt everything that she felt, saw everything that she saw. Leora's power wrapped around the girl and revitalized her. Leora's brow wrinkled in response to the pain of each of the girl's lives slipping further from her. Lifetimes of grief met her again and again; the images moved faster, playing like a movie in fast-forward in her mind until the girl's lost purpose became clear to Leora. She existed to guide young souls who had suffered from abuse.

Once her purpose anchored in Leora's chest, she pushed it into every vein of the girl's being. The moment the girl's purpose reached her essence, her aura brightened, and doubled in size around her. Leora pulled her power back and broke contact.

A knowing expression replaced the girl's blank stare for a fraction of a second ... and Leora knew the girl's higher self was smiling back at her and then was gone.

"These are all the nails we have."

"Thank you so much..." Leora peered at the girl's nametag. "Annie."

Annie smiled. "My pleasure." She walked away, standing a little taller.

Leora let out a deep, contented sigh as her eyes brimmed with tears. Rachel knew that Leora had been waiting for that moment for three hundred years: a chance to bring life back into a dying soul. She rushed toward the exit, and when Leora stepped outside, she ran straight into her husband's solid chest. Gavin wrapped his arms around her and held her tight.

"I did it. I saved a soul." Leora fisted her hands in his jacket, fighting back still more tears.

"I never doubted you, my love," said Gavin.

The vision faded as quickly as it had come. Rachel knew she saw what would happen in only a few moments because of the clarity of the vision. She smiled, and a tear rolled down her cheek. Leora was on her path. It had been blocked for so long by the Council that Rachel had feared she would never awaken another soul.

As Rachel blinked away the remaining fog of the

vision, the footsteps sounded closer than before. Suddenly, two large hands yanked her between stone and dirt, working around the protruding rocks to get away from the slim tunnel opening as quickly as possible. Scrapes along Rachel's back stung as she wedged herself deeper within the narrow passageway.

As she and Darron panted from their hasty retreat, a familiar, icy energy skimmed Rachel's cheek, causing her body to shake.

The footsteps marched one way and then the other before coming to rest in front of the tunnel's opening.

"What're so many members doing so far from their chambers?" said a booming, curious voice. "Has something happened?"

Rachel touched her cheek, having felt a brush of energy. *Do they know I'm here?*

An eerie tone crawled over the stone walls and down Rachel's spine in response. "Don't be ridiculous, Horas. We were checking on something, but it appears to have been nothing more than our imagination playing tricks on us."

Horas Shields was a round, little man full of laughter and fun. Rachel always enjoyed his company in the woodworking chamber, where he made almost anything one could think of.

"Imagination? Enlighten me," Horas said.

"We thought we felt the presence of someone here in the east wing. We were mistaken."

"Come, let's go have a drink. I need to discuss something interesting that I saw when I possessed the body acquired for me. I may have found Adam."

"Adam?" asked a cool voice Rachel did not recognize.

The men's voices grew fainter, and Rachel and Darron exhaled. Stupid, stupid: how could she be so irresponsible?

Darron's hand gripped her shoulder. "What were you doing?"

"I . . . I went to my old room to look around."

He growled. "Why didn't you take me with you?"

"You were asleep and . . . I wanted to go alone."

Darron tugged on her jacket sleeve. "You don't get to make decisions like that without talking to me first."

"I know. I'm sorry." Guilt knotted up in her throat as he released her roughly. "We have to go."

"I'm not leaving. I'm waiting for Tabitha."

"Those Council members know we're here."

"What?"

She braced herself for his ire. "One of them cast a thread of energy. It touched my cheek. They may know it was me, but it has been so long since I was here, it's just as likely that they are not sure what they sensed."

Darron hit the closest wall with his fist. "Where do we go?"

She ran a hand through her loose hair as she tried to think. There had to be somewhere they could go where the Council would never think of looking, but Tabitha and Shamus would. She swallowed hard as the answer came to her: Shamus's old room.

"I know a place."

Chapter Seven

"Stay here," Rachel said as she entered the hallway that led to Shamus's old sleeping chambers, as well as those of the other Leechers.

"The hell I am! I'm not going to let all the women do the work while I sit back in a corner," Darron complained.

She glared at him and commanded in her most motherly tone, "You'll stay because I'm telling you to. You would never make it past a Leecher. You don't know how to dampen your energy."

She wasn't going to tell him that the Leechers were more than likely with their respective Council members. Though the Council members were immortal, they still fought amongst themselves. Members' bodies had been cut apart while their soul traveled to guide those outside the Cavern of Souls, so the Creator had sent the Leechers to protect their bodies.

Darron instantly deflated. She would never admit it out loud, but she loved having the authority to make him submit, even if she hadn't earned that right in the traditional way in this life. He clenched his jaw and growled low. She chose to ignore his frustration in favor of protecting him.

Darron slipped out of sight, and then Rachel sent out the thinnest thread of power to sense some of the Leechers in their chambers. Closing her eyes, she reached for her power and placed a barrier around it. An emptiness took hold of her, and with her energy cut off, she walked right down the middle of the chilly hallway. When it came to Leechers, one had to move with determination. They could sense hesitation, so she had to keep going as if she belonged there.

When she reached the chamber door, her heart beat faster. She quietly stepped inside, unsure of what she would find. For all she knew, the chamber belonged to someone else, and this was all a terrible mistake.

As she looked around, though, sadness wrapped around her heart. It was exactly the way it was the last time she was there. For far too long, she had buried those memories away, afraid Chad would find them. It was one of the reasons she never fully opened to their coupling bond; she didn't want him to know she was in love with someone else before their bonding. In doing so, she never once shared her ability with him, nor he the gift of seeing the past with her. He never asked why.

Moving from the corner of the room, she skimmed a finger over the old dresser and a sword lying on top of it. She lifted it and wiped away the dust, but the writing on the handle made her drop it and back away. It was her sword, the sword he'd trained her with.

Only Leechers had the knowledge required to wield a sword; it was their gift from the Creator, and their curse from the Council. According to Tabitha, the Council had exploited it as a form of entertainment during the centuries she had been gone, forcing the Leechers to fight one another like the gladiators of long ago even though they were only ever meant to be protectors. Shamus did not trust many of the Council members and had wanted Rachel to be safe. He trained her to fight, as he had taught Tabitha years later.

The day she left the cavern with Chad was the last day she ever touched a sword.

She gripped the handle again, wondering if she still remembered how to use it. Its weight felt familiar, so she twisted her wrist and swung the sword around. A smile curled her lips. She swept the sword to the left before coming to a halt with her arms over her head. The sword pointed at a curtain hanging across the room. The corner flicked up as a large hand pushed it aside. The revolving door of her past lives stopped spinning, and then there was only him: the man she'd given all of herself to, and the one who had destroyed her.

She briefly wondered if he was the reason she never connected with the guys she dated in this current life. Had her subconscious mind been holding her back out of hope that she would see him again?

Bright-green eyes locked on hers and she took an involuntary step closer as the urge to throw herself into Shamus's strong arms engulfed her, but she stopped herself. He didn't know her like this, in this body, which was so very different from all her others. Her trademark blue eyes and the curvy body that followed her into most of her lives were gone. She no longer looked like the woman he had once loved. She squared her shoulders, lifted her chin, and lowered her sword.

Shamus hadn't aged a day. His strong cheekbones were covered in the same golden skin she remembered. His square jaw clenched as he stepped out from behind the wall hanging. Straight, black hair in the warrior's braid skimmed his shoulders as his wide chest rose and fell quickly. She listened to the deep pulls of his breath and realized he had been running. Even after all the time they spent together, she never knew there was a hidden passage that led to his room.

"I felt you . . . I had to be sure it was your energy I sensed," he said as he took another step toward her. His voice was still a deep rumble that caused her skin to tingle.

"Apparently, you're not the only one to sense me here," she said.

After all her lifetimes with the Elapsed Seer, this longing felt shameful. Besides, Darron was waiting for her. What would he think if he found them together? On the other hand, she might never have a moment alone with Shamus after this. Did she want this? The person she'd become said *hell to the no,* but she didn't know what to do because she also wanted to climb all over this guy. He was beautiful; at least she had good taste.

OMG.

She ran a hand down her face. All of this was too much. Leora was never going to believe all this crazy shit in her head. Or, maybe she would. Did this crazy shit happen to her in every life? She was so going to ask when she got back to town.

"How did you sense me? My power's closed off."

He marched around the large bed in which they had shared many nights together. She held still, even though the urge to be near him was so strong. He came to a halt a foot away, close enough that his breath caressed her skin. Yearning pulled at her core, but as much as her body wanted him, her heart ached from the pain he had caused her.

"I would know the scent of your essence anywhere."

She raised a brow. "The Shamus I used to know would never talk like that."

"That was before I knew what it felt like to lose you."

Aw, that is so sweet. OMG. Ugh, I am losing my shit.

It was like having an out-of-body experience. One minute she was her current self, and the next she was a thousand-year-old woman that she wasn't sure she even liked.

"You thought about me?" she asked, searching his beautiful eyes as her heart raced.

He cupped her cheek, brushing his thumb over her skin. She couldn't breathe, and his touch was electric. His full lips were a breath away. Her knees wobbled; no guy had ever made her wobble before.

"Every day."

"Shamus," Rachel whispered, reaching for him.

Darron entered the room slowly, dangerously; Rachel stepped back and dropped her hand before anything that would make his mood even worse could happen. A black storm raged beneath Darron's skin, and his eyes were white. He yanked her away and planted himself between her and Shamus. She pulled herself together as quickly as she could, drop-kicking all those crazy feelings and thoughts into their very own box in her mind.

"Who is he?" Darron screeched, his ghostly eyes fixed on Shamus.

Shamus grasped the handle of the sword at his right hip.

"This is the man Tabitha thought was dead. The man who raised her," Rachel said quickly. She sheathed her sword and then secured the belt around her hips. It couldn't hurt to take it with her. "He's the one she went to find for help."

Shamus's eyes shifted to hers, then back to Darron. "She knows I'm alive," he said quietly.

"Yes, I saw you in a vision with Chad, the Elapsed Seer." She swallowed nervously, unsure what to do next. "I told her about it to ease the pain that your death caused her."

He gave a nod of thanks.

"Shamus, this is my son, Darron. From my past life," she blurted out. Shamus raised a dark brow, and she tipped her head from side to side. "It's complicated."

His eyes darkened and his chin lifted as he pointed to Darron's skin, under which inky blotches twisted like cyclones. "He's the Thief of Souls."

Rachel frowned at that. That was a different way of looking at the situation, but it had a nice ring to it, she thought.

Darron hissed, "A thief? Want to find out just how good a thief I am?"

Black mist permeated the room, squeezing out what little light there was inside, and Shamus's body tensed for a fight.

Not wanting to see the confrontation turn violent, Rachel rested her hand on Darron's forearm. "Don't do something Tabitha will hate you for."

Darron glared at her over his shoulder, but his skin returned to normal and the mist vanished; his eyes were pale blue once again. He blew out a breath.

Shamus studied Darron intensely, and Rachel wondered if he saw faults in him.

"Where is Tabitha, and why is she looking for help?" Shamus asked, though his hand still rested on his sword.

"We're not sure where she is. She left a while ago to find you," Rachel said as she walked over to the wall hanging that obscured the passageway he had emerged from.

The curtain depicted a country scene with tall evergreens standing watch over imposing mountains. They reminded Rachel of those surrounding the sacred circle. The only thing missing was the cabin and the bloodstones that marked the circle. She yanked the curtain back, thinking about the baby growing in Leora's belly and how soon she would be taken there. The bloodstone circle was the only place Leora wouldn't be able to sense the life of her child, as it would be masked by the void the bloodstones created—the same void that had hidden Leora from the Council. The weight of the task at hand and what little time they had to work with settled on her shoulders.

"In a different vision, I saw Chad being tortured. We're here to find him."

The black, stone wall had no marks to indicate where she would find a door. Intrigued, she ran a hand over it to be sure there was no cut or seam. It took her a few moments before she felt a spot where the stone dipped. She pressed hard, and the wall pushed to the side to reveal a dark tunnel with a few torches lighting the way.

"Where does this lead?" she asked.

"To a crossing." Shamus said, though his gaze was still locked on Darron.

"A crossing?"

"If you follow the tunnel, it dumps you into a room with five other tunnels that all lead to other parts of the cavern."

"Where do you think Tabitha would've looked for you first?" Darron asked, his eyes sweeping from Shamus to Rachel.

"The Two Tunnels, where I watch over her father," Shamus said.

"I know about Serena and Stephen and what happened to her. I know what they did."

Shamus turned toward her, and something in his expression confirmed for Rachel that they had known they were going against the Creator when they created Tabitha.

"Tabitha knows about her mother and how Stephen partitioned her mind to stop her power from fully evolving," Rachel said, thinking it would be best if Shamus knew the truth.

"How do you know about that?" Shamus thundered.

"It's none of your business," Darron snapped.

Shamus glared at him. "Tabitha is always my business."

"Not anymore. She told me Stephen gave her to Marcus."

Shamus growled, "I did not wish that to be so."

"The short version of how we know all this is that Tabitha broke past the barrier in her mind and saw Serena's memories."

Shamus clenched his jaw and then ran a hand over his braid. Rachel's eyes were momentarily fixed on his flexing bicep.

"Where is Marcus?" Shamus took a step closer to her.

"Contained," Darron said. "Have you seen my father?"

"It has been nearly two weeks since I saw him last. He came to the cavern entrance and asked me to bring Stephen to him so they could talk. When I returned with Stephen, he was gone. There were tracks in the snow, so we assumed someone took him, but I felt him here. I've been searching for him ever since, but I have had no luck."

"How do you know someone took him?" Darron moved to once again face off with Shamus, who had a good six inches on him.

"There were two sets of tracks. Stephen thinks it was the Council."

"But how? Council members can't leave the cavern," Rachel said, not liking Shamus's unreadable expression.

"Stephen and I believe the members have joined together to possess the bodies of weak souls."

"Possession," Darron grumbled. "Chad called and said something about the Lost before you had the vision. We didn't know what it meant."

Shamus strode toward the tunnel. "Come, we must get to Tabitha and find the Seer."

Fear gripped Rachel as Darron touched her arm, then

gently pushed her aside to follow Shamus.

Rachel felt sick. The Council could still get to Leora if they sensed her. She prayed their powers were too weak to travel that far.

·●o～o●·

Chad's body convulsed in response to the sound of the many voices coming from the woman next to him. With every flick of the whip against his body, the shackles around his wrists ground deeper into his bones. Soon, his thumbs would be severed, which was a relief. Without his thumbs, his wrists would be free to slip from the shackles and his destroyed body could rest on the cold stone below.

"Why have you come to the cavern? We'll not ask again."

The glass shards at the end of the whip clattered to the floor, a stark preamble to the pain that would follow. Chad didn't feel the blood running from the wounds anymore. Pulling in his rage, his head fell back. This was what he deserved for betraying his family, and for his weakness.

"Tell me! Say it!" the woman yelled.

He thought he recognized a few of the voices even as they rang out as one: Council members who had once been his friends, had sat beside him and taught him the ways of the outside world as well as how best to use his gift as an Elapsed Seer of the past. The past was done and gone, but it tended to repeat itself, so if he paid attention, he could see the future, in a way.

None of his tormentor's efforts affected Chad by this point. His eardrum had burst during the last beating, every ounce of his strength left him days ago, and his heart beat weakly in his chest. He would die soon. There was nothing left to hold onto.

"I came here to die an eternal death."

"Why would the Elapsed Seer—Learner to the High Priest Stephen, father of the Awakener, and bonded to the Seer—wish for eternal death?" the voices demanded as they jumbled and buzzed together. "This is a trick."

"It is not a trick. I have claimed my death."

He didn't lift his head—didn't even try. He hung there, feeling nothing but shame and the burning in his right pec, even though his body was ice-cold. Very soon, the truth would be revealed to the Council.

The possessed woman circled him. Then there was a click and Chad hit the ground, broken. The cold floor felt like a good place to die. He tried to bring his arms down and wrap them around his middle, but both of his shoulders were dislocated.

The woman bent to address him. "How do you suppose you can claim death? Tell us!"

Chad didn't want to think about what he had done. He wanted this sick churning in his heart to stop. He didn't want to die and be reborn only to remember everything.

The woman gripped his right wrist and yanked his arm down to his side. The pain caused him to turn and retch onto the stone. Every inch of his body screamed.

"To claim eternal death is to throw away the Creator's wish that you be the Awakener's father." The woman's lips brushed his good ear. "Without you, the Awakener cannot be reborn after she dies in this life. Why would you want that?"

Chad pursed his chapped and cut lips as the backs of his eyes started burning. "Betrayal."

"Who?"

"My family."

The voices rumbled through the possessed woman as she stood, and the chuckling soon escalated to a mad cackle. "Betrayed the ones you were meant to love and protect. No eternal death for you on this day." The woman shoved Chad to his back and yanked the other arm down. "The Awakener has taken much of our power, and for that, she will die. We sense Marcus is contained for now, but he will kill her as always."

Chad flinched. How did they know about Marcus? How many bodies could they possess? Fear warmed his veins, giving him the strength to grab the woman's shirt.

"How do you know about Marcus?"

The woman pulled his hand away easily and smiled. "We have been watching for a long time. Always watching in the shadows . . . waiting, keeping tabs on you all."

"Waiting for what?" Chad ground out.

"For you." She turned and walked to the door.

Tears ran from his eyes and into his hair. He could hardly breathe. The world faded away, and he wished for death.

Chapter Eight

Rachel blinked on her night vision as she trailed behind Darron and Shamus, neither of whom said a word. Shamus did turn and look at her through the gloom in between torches, probably knowing only she would see him. The corners of her mouth turned down, yet her cheeks flushed. She forgot how easily he could make her feel . . . alive, in all the best ways. A few looks and she blushed; like, legit blushed. She didn't normally blush; she hung out of windows while Leora drove so she could yell at sexy guys. She wrinkled her nose.

Rachel remembered the last Council meeting she attended. Standing behind Serena's chair, she'd peered out at the many faces present. There were more than five hundred members, plus their Leechers. Chad had stood to the left of Stephen and never once glanced her way. Chad had always been reserved and diligent; he never said much, but his green eyes were always watching and taking things in. Rachel had been curious about his thoughts, but had also been so attuned to Shamus back then that she sensed and smelled him approach long before his actual arrival at the meeting. His unique scent of fresh soap and leather caused her core to burn with longing. As he stood beside her, his energy glided over hers. It was a game they played:

touching, but not touching, knowing the other wanted to, but wouldn't. After the meeting, Rachel had been burning with desire. She'd shoved him down an abandoned passage the first chance she got so they could make love.

She pursed her lips and bit the inside of her cheek. Desire made her skin overly sensitive, and her clothes grew irritating. She rubbed a hand over her face.

Oh, man! These memories just take over without warning.

They walked in silence for what felt like forever. The Two Tunnels was deep within the earth, but she'd never ventured out to find them. That was Stephen's domain, and where souls gathered to be reborn. Stephen didn't like to be disturbed, so few knew where they were.

The tunnel they were in widened, and light shone from distant torches. It opened to a large room where five tunnels branched off in different directions, just as Shamus had described. Before she entered the room, Shamus reached out and held her back. She turned off her night vision as he held a hand up to his ear. That's when she heard the quick footsteps and heavy breathing growing louder.

"Tabitha." Darron rushed into the room and took off down the second tunnel on the right.

Rachel tried to follow him, but Shamus wouldn't let her pass. Instead, he pulled her against him.

"How does he know that's Tabitha?" he whispered, his lips caressing her ear.

Heat rippled down her neck and pooled between her legs. Without consciously deciding to do so, she ran a hand up the tight planes of his chest. Her fingers glided up his neck and pulled his ear to her lips.

"They're bonded."

Shamus's body became as hard as the steel of his sword, but he said, "Thank the Creator it wasn't Marcus."

She was touched by the tenderness in his voice. "She means a lot to you, doesn't she?"

He stared deeply into her eyes, caressing her soul. He lowered his head and lightly brushed his lips against hers. "She's the daughter I could never have . . . with you. I'm glad you have the family you so desperately craved."

She tried to step back, overwhelmed by an intense wave of emotion, but he didn't let her. Why did he say that? It both wounded her and began to heal her broken heart.

"Shamus . . . why didn't you tell me about Tabitha? Why didn't you come to me? I could've helped."

He cupped her cheek. "There was no time." His hand dropped to his side, and he finally released her. "I wanted to go to you, but I couldn't risk Tabitha's safety," he said before he turned away and walked into the crossing.

He hadn't trusted her. Hurt jolted her back to the present.

Rachel walked to the opening of the second tunnel to the right and watched Shamus as Tabitha approached. She'd never seen him act this way. The anticipation of Tabitha's approach had him visibly vibrating, and his aura emanated a golden glow. Once Tabitha spotted him, he threw open his arms and Tabitha ran into them. He spun her around in circles as tears ran down her face.

"You were dead. I killed you!"

"No, you wounded and *almost* killed me," Shamus said with a chuckle before setting her down on her feet.

He held her out and inspected her. He touched the blue stripes in her hair and smiled. Satisfied, he hugged her once more.

"Rachel saw you in a vision and told me you weren't dead, but I didn't believe it. I didn't want to hope it was true. But here you are!"

He tenderly wiped the tears from her cheeks when he

let her go. "I've been waiting for you to return since the day I found out Stephen sent you with Marcus."

Darron stood with his arms crossed and wore a scowl of dissatisfaction.

"You've been waiting for me?" Tabitha asked. "But I didn't know if I would ever return again."

"I believed you would. And here you are." He touched a strand of her blue hair again. "I missed you."

Rachel was glad Shamus and Tabitha had had each other over the centuries. He had found a love he would do anything to keep; that much was obvious. Rachel understood what it meant to love another unconditionally, to give all of oneself over to the happiness of one's child. Despite all the chaos that tore through her past lives, that one thing had remained steadfast: the love she had for her family.

Tabitha glanced at Rachel with a look of concern, but it vanished before Darron could notice. Tabitha knew she and Shamus had been lovers, but also that Darron and Leora had never figured that out. Rachel hoped they never did.

Tabitha took Darron's hand and rested her head against his shoulder. He quickly wrapped his arms around her waist and kissed her forehead. "This is my Darron. We've bonded."

Shamus's eyes sparkled at her obvious affection for her partner. "We met earlier. A Soul Hunter and Death makes for a dangerous combination. Be wise, and don't share your abilities through the bond."

"Why? It's the coolest thing ever when he changes into Death. I love it. All that black skin, and those white eyes? Hot." She kissed Darron reassuringly.

Yes, Tabitha was Darron's perfect match; she knew how to calm all his insecurities. Rachel looked forward to watching their love grow, but there was a warning in Shamus's tone that Rachel knew not to ignore. Did he know something she didn't about her son? About Death?

"Why were you running, and how did you find this place?" Shamus asked, serious.

"I heard someone tailing me while I was looking for you," Tabitha said. "I knew it wasn't you because you would've revealed yourself without hesitation. So, I ran along the wall until it turned and I had to climb. Then, I felt Darron was close, so I followed the bond."

"Who do you think was following you?" Shamus questioned.

"I don't know. When I cast a web with my power, I didn't feel anything." Tabitha sighed. "I can't really cast that far, though."

Rachel locked eyes with Shamus, then Tabitha. "It could have been one of the Council members that almost caught me while I was having a vision not far from my old room."

"When whoever it was came within fifty feet of me, my skin itched as if bugs were crawling all over it. No Council member has ever caused that kind of feeling, and I have been near all of them." Tabitha wrinkled her nose. "I think someone else is in the cavern, and they don't want to be found."

Shamus frowned at her. "You're in the Cavern of Souls with Council members who have a variety of abilities. Don't you think they would have detected someone who should not be here?"

"Yeah, like us. We must find my father. What do we do now?" Darron asked urgently.

Shamus looked at Tabitha and said, "You take Darron and search all of the outer caves where we used to train. Look for narrow openings in the walls and see if they lead you anywhere new. If you run into anyone, project an image of your father. The Seer and I will search for the hidden tunnels, where few dare to go. We will meet back at my bedroom chamber."

"Sounds like a plan," Tabitha said.

"What should we do if one of us finds Chad?" Darron asked, releasing Tabitha.

"One of you get him out while the other goes to the chamber and waits for us."

Rachel's stomach rolled as she remembered the image of Chad's mutilated body in the vision. "If something goes wrong, head to the Two Tunnels. Stephen will keep you safe."

"Fuck no! The Council has been trying to kill me for lifetimes. Why would I go to their leader for help?" Darron growled.

"You're bonded to Tabitha. He won't let anything happen to you because it would hurt her."

"Says the man who let Stephen whip her."

Shamus slammed his fist into Darron's jaw. He crashed into the wall, sending chunks of dirt flying out around him.

"There will come a time in your life when sacrifices must be made so your loved ones can survive—even at the cost of their love. Remember that."

Darron dusted himself off, anger vivid in his blue eyes. "How do you know I haven't already made those choices a thousand times over? You don't know the lives I've lived. You don't know the choices I've made to save myself and my family. You don't know me."

The pain in Darron's voice sliced through Rachel's tattered heart but as Shamus moved closer to her, his eyes glowed with a savage inner fire. She couldn't hide the truth from her own expression, though, and he regarded her quizzically for a moment. He didn't know the things the Advisors had suffered throughout their countless lives while he was safely tucked away and protecting Tabitha.

The distance between them seemed to grow, and in that space, something clicked into place. Shamus would never be able to empathize. He hadn't been there. He hadn't lived it with her like Chad had. Theirs was an understanding that came with time.

Shamus moved toward the second tunnel to the left while Rachel grappled with acceptance. Was passion enough to forsake time? On countless nights, she'd dreamed of Shamus while she lay alongside her husband. Every time they had sex, she thought of Shamus. It was the silly dream of a selfish, wounded girl. She gave her body to Chad, but not her heart. She'd left that with a man she no longer knew. Rachel needed to be alone to work out her thoughts, but that would have to wait.

"Be wise in the choices you make," Shamus said.

She followed him, but not before glancing back at Darron and Tabitha.

Please, Creator, keep them safe.

"Have fun," Tabitha said with a wicked smile on her face.

Rachel's cheeks flushed again as she turned away.

•●○∼○●•

Footsteps rushed forward, and glass hit the stone floor. Knees dropped beside Chad. Hands gripped his matted hair and yanked his head back. A shallow moan escaped him just before his forehead was slammed into the floor. His sight grew darker around the edges, and he could feel himself inch closer to death as he was rolled onto his stomach and held down by strong hands. The burning in his chest was the only thing anchoring him to the world.

"I will ask one last time. Why are you here?"

Chad blinked swollen, crusted eyelids. The voices

rattled in his head. He wondered if the members were all in one room together, their bodies protected by Leechers, or if they were all alone, joined only by their power to possess this body. He didn't answer the question. He couldn't move his lips—or any part of his body, for that matter. He just waited for death to claim him.

A red glow rose from the woman's palms and crept over his wounds. Energy leeched into the ruined skin, but then her fingers yanked the power back and the wounds erupted in flames. He couldn't even scream as the woman twisted and turned her power, forcing the flames to burn so hot that the reds and yellows turned to blues and purples. A red ball of energy formed and expanded in her palm until it was the size of a grapefruit. Then she slammed it into his back. The second it touched the burning spot on his chest, she was flung back against the wall of the cell. Chad stopped breathing and his heart stopped several times, but found a way to beat once more.

She staggered to her feet, then rolled him to his back; Chad saw utter amazement on her face before the voices sounded as one in a laugh. Red mist danced around her. She pointed at the black stain of the destiny mark that had been pushing its way to the surface of his skin for weeks.

"You've been a very naughty boy to have received that. Betrayal you said. Family you said. We couldn't ask for better luck. We always knew you were the weakest of them all."

Still laughing hysterically, the woman walked out and locked the door behind her.

Chad squeezed his eyes shut.

Chapter Nine

Rachel trailed behind Shamus through the tunnels in an awkward silence until her stomach growled loudly. He glanced at her over his shoulder, the torch in his hand illuminating his raised eyebrow.

"Sorry, I can't remember the last time I ate."

"I have food in my chamber. We can eat and rest."

"Why do you keep food in your room when the great hall has food all the time?"

He stopped. "When Stephen forbids me from seeing Tabitha, he locks me in my room. I never know for how long." He shrugged. "So, I hide things."

"Stephen locks you away? Why?" Her heart beat faster; she knew unspeakable things had happened, but Stephen punishing Shamus was unreal.

"In the past, I taught Tabitha things he didn't want her to know, so I was punished."

"That's ridiculous. What could you have taught her that would warrant punishment?"

"I wanted Tabitha to know as much of the world's history as she could so she could survive among the men and women of the Council. The members all come from different decades and centuries; their cultural norms and behaviors vary greatly. I wanted her to be prepared for when Stephen presented her to the Council when she was grown."

Rachel reached for his shoulder. "Have things changed so much that the daughter of the High Priest should fear other Council members?"

He turned toward her. Heat rolled off him like the sun, and Rachel melted a little.

"Restlessness grows among the members. I fear many can't be trusted." He glanced past her. "The Council does not know that Tabitha was created from Stephen and Serena. They believe she was sent to him from the Creator as a gift. That is why he hid her until she was grown, though it took many years longer than it should have because of the cavern's hold over time."

She stared into his green eyes as he filled in many of the gaps Rachel hadn't understood about Tabitha's life before she came to them. "They haven't been trustworthy since they sent the Hound to kill my family lifetimes ago."

His nostrils flared as he looked down at her. "Stephen did not order that. The Council took things into their own hands when the Awakener took more and more of their power—and when Serena died and Stephen started spending too much time in the Two Tunnels."

Shamus cast his gaze to the floor, jaw flexing. When he glanced up, his eyes were glass. Hurt shone brightly there. A pang struck her heart at hearing Serena's name. She had never given Stephen's emotional state after Serena's supposed disappearance much consideration. She had been caught up in her own pain from Shamus's disappearing. She hadn't known what Stephen was going through at the time, but now she did. Stephen loved Serena, and losing a loved one could cripple a person in ways they couldn't recover from. She pushed out a breath and straightened her spine. To know love and loss was to live.

· • o ◦ ‿ o • ·

Shamus and Rachel skirted down tunnels she didn't recognize, then the tunnel they were in began to climb upward. She was swimming through a haze of conflicting emotions, trying to work through worry, heartache, and fear for her family, all while following Shamus even though she just wanted to be alone.

As soon as she reached flat terrain, a burning sickness overtook her. Something was terribly wrong. She bent over and managed a few more steps when heartache struck. It was so chilling, it froze her from the inside out. She staggered forward and smacked into a wall, bounced off it like a rubber ball, and landed on her backside. Blinking her night vision on, Rachel noticed the torchlight Shamus had held was gone. She was in complete darkness, with no recollection of when she lost sight of him, and she was staring at a dirt wall.

Where the heck did that come from? Where am I?

She rubbed her butt and then her chest. She couldn't sense anything, even after heightening her hearing and her sense of smell. She placed her hand on the ground to try and detect any vibrations that would indicate where Shamus was, but got nothing except the pain in her chest.

Oh, no—the bond.

Were they too late? Was Chad dead? Rachel shuffled through her mental boxes until she found a memory of Chad dying and the bond being closed. That had felt like a mortal blow to the heart, an explosion of shrapnel. This didn't feel like that. Every cell of her body felt sick and cried out to purge something she didn't even know she had within her.

Fighting down the bile rising in her throat, Rachel stood. There, in the center of her chest, was a pull no stronger than a spider's silk. She blocked out the sick feeling and focused on the faint pull. Sending a tendril of golden light down it, a warmth as familiar as early morning sunshine greeted her. Rachel smirked. The coupling bond was still intact. She infused that pull with power to strengthen and hold it tight. It wasn't as smooth as it should have been; the bond felt as if something had hacked away at it. Chunks were gone and barely held together. What could cause this kind of damage?

She stumbled forward and then turned right down a damp tunnel. The air was stagnant, and the chill caused her to shiver. The bond took her left, and she found that she didn't care where she was going, only that the bond was as thick as a piece of fabric and growing thicker with every step she took. Hope drove her forward.

Through the darkness, she heard a moan. Drawing her sword, she followed the sound with bated breath. The soft earth beneath her boots hardened to stone. The smell of rot forced her to cover her mouth and nose. Peering around, she saw a hall to her right; it was lined by large, wooden doors. She inched forward and spotted keys hanging next to an unlit torch. Without a sound, she took the keys and listened. Her entire body felt like maggots were crawling in her veins. Her skin was hot to the touch, and her stomach continued to roil. She heard metal scrape stone a few doors down. The scent of defecation grew more potent the closer she got to the door. She peered through a barred window on the door, but couldn't see much in the dim light of her single torch. Rachel flipped on her night vision once more and noticed something moving. She unlocked the door and pushed it open with a muffled grunt. Her gaze fell on the heap in the middle of the room.

"Back so soon?" said a raspy, tired male voice.

The man pulled himself away from her, but with her sword still drawn, she stepped closer. Her boots against the floor warned the man of her approach; his body trembled. Up close, she saw that his back resembled grilled flesh, and Rachel fought the urge to vomit.

He flopped to his back with a hiss, but she couldn't tell if it was Chad. This man had a beard, and his face was so swollen and bruised that he didn't resemble the man in her vision. His torso was . . . she looked away, not wanting to see what had been done to him. Ribs protruded and pieces of his dying flesh hung loosely. Every inch of him was coated in blood. How was he still alive?

He raised his face toward her, but she could tell he couldn't really see her. How could he with his eyes swollen like that?

She lowered the sword and slid it back to its scabbard, then sent a wave of energy over the coupling bond to see if this was Chad. As she increased the level of energy over the bond, the man stopped shaking and relaxed a fraction. Then, his jaw clenched. She couldn't tell by that reaction if it was Chad or not.

"No," he hissed. "No."

Confused, Rachel said, "My name's Rachel. I'm the Seer."

The man turned his head away from her. "Let me die in peace."

She bent down beside him and tried not to gag. If this was Chad, his wounds were far worse than what she'd seen in the vision.

"Are you the Elapsed Seer?" she asked. "Is your name Chad Harper?"

"Leave me," he said, rolling onto his stomach in order to crawl toward the corner of the room. "Leave this place before they return."

"You need help."

"There is no help for the evil of this world. Just go."

He pushed himself up against the wall, shaking with the effort that took.

What the hell was he talking about, the evil of this world? She didn't have time for this. She had to find Chad and get back to Leora.

She took off her jacket and knelt beside him, then carefully placed the jacket over his battered body. Brushing his hair from his face, she tried to see the man beneath the swelling. She touched the bond again with golden light. He did not move away from her touch, but lifted his chin, as if he were ready for whatever came next.

"You waste time on me." He turned away from her as a ragged breath passed his lips.

"You're hurt. Don't you want help?"

A tear trickled down his dirty cheek, and then the sharpest pain struck her chest, knocking her back. She clutched at her shirt and gasped through the pain. What little pull she had sensed through the closed bond vanished completely.

That asshole really is Chad.

He wasn't breathing. Heart racing, she tapped his swollen cheek. He didn't move. She tapped his cheek harder.

"Chad. I know it's you. Don't die. Leora will kill me if you die. Shit!" She leaned closer to his split, bruised lips and listened, then pulled him down to the floor and started CPR, trying not to cry as she compressed his already ruined body. "One one thousand, two one thousand, three one thousand . . ."

She placed her lips over his and blew air into his lungs. Nothing. She compressed his chest again. Strange energy stung her fingers, but she didn't stop. When she pushed air into his lungs a second time, she felt his chest expand with more air than she had given. She leaned back and waited until he choked and coughed, gasping. She took his hand in hers and pushed her power into his blood, his muscles, and his bones, praying that it would help him. She met resistance, as if the cells in his body were not open to her help. Then his eyes shot open, their green irises bright and full of agony.

"Chad," she gasped.

She was struck again in the chest, causing every muscle to seize. Dragging in a choked breath, she leaned over him and noticed that the faint bond was there again. She sent up a silent prayer as she breathed through the pain. She tried again to send him a healing wave of energy. When that didn't work, she sucked in a breath and ran her hand through her hair.

Then, she saw it. How had she missed the smeared, black mark resting over his heart?

Oh, no. A destiny mark!

What had he done? Fear like she had never known stole her breath. Slowly, she tried to run a finger over the mark, but it shifted and moved beneath his skin like a frantic animal, and its energy bit at her fingers. Those green eyes, once so bright with hope, were lifeless as Chad turned his head.

"We have to get you out of here and find Darron," Rachel ground out as she tried to think of a way to move him in his current state. He coughed, clutching his stomach. Tears streamed down his cheeks, and his face pulled tight in pure agony. "I'll help you up."

He tried to sit up, and Rachel wrapped her arms around him to help. As she rose with him, a chunk of skin came off in her hand. She couldn't hold it back; she scurried away and vomited in the corner.

Chad slumped down to the floor. "Leave me."

As she wiped her mouth, she realized she couldn't

move him alone. "I'll find Darron and bring him back."

•○⌒○•·

The scent of warm honey lingered in the cold air where Rachel had sat just a moment ago. All Chad wanted to do was touch her soft skin. The yearning for her had been unbearable since her awakening. The bond wasn't open, so he could not hear her speak to him over it, but he could feel her and knew she was okay. He had dreamed of her for months before his awakening: the flicker of a smile, the sound of a joyful laugh. It drove him mad until he awakened, and then the memories flooded his mind and nearly broke him: too much pain, too much loss.

Chad clenched his jaw as the emptiness within him expanded and darkness began to fill it. He struggled to his feet, only to fall back down to the stone floor. He tried once more, and the skin at his waist tore open, but he didn't stop. He couldn't be there when Rachel returned. He couldn't face his family—not after what he had done.

Working his battered legs, he rose to his knees and started crawling. He had to escape her scent or he would lose what little sanity he had left. The thought of Rachel in the cavern with Shamus caused him more pain than anything he felt in his body. He knew she still loved Shamus, always had, but he had seen glimmers of love toward him and had hoped—until he accepted that she hadn't.

Every movement took more strength than he actually had. Finally, after what could have been minutes or hours, the cell was behind him. But he couldn't escape her; Rachel's scent lingered in the tunnel as well. It was useless.

Exhausted, he sat back on his haunches and then dropped to his back with a thud. A small moan escaped his ruined lips. He stared into the darkness without seeing anything.

"Shit! You're a fucking mess."

Torchlight shone on his face and he turned away. The voice triggered a long-forgotten memory. Then, he felt a liquid sort of heat enter his body.

"Awesome. He's going to die before we get out of here," someone else said.

He looked up and saw two faces peering down at him. Darron placed his hand on Chad's arm, and he felt a jolt of energy. With all the strength he could muster, Chad shoved Darron's hand away. Nobody would be healing him.

"It's me, it's Darron. Take it easy."

"Don't."

"I don't have time for this shit."

Darron placed a hand on Chad's leg, but again, Chad shoved it away. Darron shared a look with the blue-haired woman next to him, then the woman punched Chad in the face.

· • o �～ o • ·

"Damn . . . it isn't working!" Darron cried, feeling like a bomb had been dropped on him.

Tabitha hovered over Chad's motionless body. "I don't think he's breathing."

Darron slammed a fist into the tunnel wall. "Why the hell can't I heal him?" The way his energy was moving through Chad didn't feel right. It felt dark, heavy, and sick. He pulled Tabitha down next to him and pointed to the center of Chad's breastbone. "Hold the light there. What's that?"

Tabitha squinted and ran her fingers over a black spot. It moved when her fingers came too close. "Holy shit. It won't let me touch it."

"I can see that. What do you think it is?" he asked, hoping she'd know more about this kind of stuff than he did.

She sat back on her heels, then scooched closer to Chad. "I think he's been marked."

"What do you mean?" His heart rate accelerated.

"I read about it in one of my father's books. There was a mark that could stop others from using their power on you. That might be why you can't heal him." Tabitha's face suddenly turned ashen. "Shit. Do you think the Council knew we would come to help? What if we walked into some kind of trap?"

Apprehension coiled around Darron's throat like a snake. He rubbed his neck and noticed his hands were turning black, so he held them out in front of them for a better look.

What's this? I'm not even pissed!

Tabitha glanced at him and wrinkled her nose. "What're you doing?"

"I'm not doing anything. I . . . feel . . . "

He cracked his neck and closed his eyes, aroused by the lifelessness around him. When he opened them, he saw a ball of dim, red light resting in his father's chest. He blinked hard; it was just like when he marked Marcus. When he reached for it, he felt the same grating sensation as he had then. Resistance: the light would not be easily taken, but it hypnotized him. He needed to touch it.

Tabitha shoved him back, and a sharp pain struck the back of his mind. "What're you doing? Stay away from him when you're like that."

Darron's head tilted from side to side. The urge to seize the light forced him to his feet. Tabitha stepped in front of Chad with a knife in her hand.

"Fight it, babe. You don't want to do whatever it is you

are about to do."

Darron blinked at Tabitha. What was she saying? He needed the light. He pushed her aside, and without hesitation, she raked the blade across his forearm. He barely noticed the blood on his black skin, but the smell was mouthwatering.

"Babe, I mean it. Get it together. I don't think you want to get in a fight over this."

Anger scorched Darron's veins. He pushed Tabitha into the wall. He needed the light.

Mine.

Before he took another step, Tabitha sprang at him. She turned her body and wrapped her arm around his neck, bending him backward so she could clamp his throat between her forearm and her bicep.

"He's dying. You have to control yourself."

Just as he was about to flip her over his head, a sliver of understanding pierced through his hunger for the light.

Shit. I want his soul.

Panicked, he tried to bury his power deep inside himself, but it didn't yield to his demand. His voice sounded like fingernails raking across a chalkboard when he pleaded with her.

"Help me."

Tabitha released his throat, and he felt his blood burn. Her hands pressed against his temples and a tearing pain worked its way into the center of his mind. All the air was expelled from his lungs and he dropped to the floor. He immediately felt like himself again.

"What did you do to me?"

"I told your subconscious that you didn't want to do whatever it is you were about to do to your father." She stared at him, wiping her blade on her leather pants. "What the hell was that?"

"I'm not sure, but I think I was going to take his soul like I have once before."

"Hmm, well . . . that sounds like a shit show ready to happen. I'm going to try my power on Chad since I'm all amped up. Maybe I can persuade the mark to hit the road."

Darron stood to the side, staring at the tunnel's ceiling. He'd almost taken his father's soul.

Fuck. What the hell would I have done with it? Would I have taken it to Stephen like the others that died in gunfire?

The bizarre thought occupied his mind as he pondered the possibilities. It wasn't until Tabitha sprang to her feet, slapped her hands together, and did a little jig that he dared look down.

"Man, I'm so good. I love myself. This influencer ability rocks. I like it so much, I'll keep it and make it stronger and stronger." She flexed her muscles as if she were a WWE wrestler.

Darron smiled. He loved her spirit, but she had to work on her timing. He turned his attention back to Chad, searching his chest. The mark was gone.

"Come on. Heal him before he dies," she said.

Her words drove him to pour his power into Chad and this time, there was no resistance. The wounds on his ribs, stomach, and back began to fill in with new skin and heal. Darron visualized his father's heart beating the entire time. Tabitha rested her hand on his back, and a silky heat filled him as she lent him her energy. She couldn't give the same kind of boost Gavin could as an Amplifier, but through their bond, she could strengthen and assist him like any other Advisor. Even with her help, it would take a few hours to heal his father. He needed Rachel. He wondered where she and Shamus were.

Darron's anxiety grew with every second that passed while Chad was still not breathing. Finally, his father's lungs filled with air and he took his first breath. It was choppy, but Darron was elated to hear it nonetheless.

When he watched the last of Chad's wounds close, he removed his hands. His entire body was covered in sweat and he was shaking, near exhaustion. He closed his eyes, wanting nothing more than to take a nap right there in the middle of the dimly lit tunnel. In any case, it would take some time before his father's mind could reboot.

Tabitha touched Chad's right temple, amping up his energy. A second later, his eyes popped open.

"There is no time for naps. Not with Council members wandering around," she said.

Chad stared at Darron now, but there wasn't anything behind those eyes to indicate that Chad was aware of what was going on.

"Can you get up? We need to go," Darron said, hoping to give his survival instincts a jolt.

Chad reached out a hand and Darron grabbed it. As he tugged Chad to his feet, his shaky legs buckled, and Chad's face smashed into Darron's chest before he fell to the floor.

"Let's try that again, but slower this time," Darron said softly.

"That was all you," Chad said in a small voice.

Seemingly more aware, he peered down at his stomach and ran a hand over the rough, purple scars that blanketed his skin. Darron grimaced; Tabitha had similar scars on her back. If he'd had more time, he could have healed the skin better, but given the damage Chad had sustained, he was surprised it even looked as good as it did. He wished he could go back and make it look nicer after the fact, but his gift didn't allow him to do that. He would have to develop his skills over the next few lifetimes in order to get to that point.

Darron helped Chad to his feet again. A weak smile pulled at the corners of Chad's lips, although the smile did not reach his eyes. Chad squeezed Darron's shoulder as they took a step forward together. Tabitha and Darron each wrapped an arm around Chad's waist, and they all slowly walked down the tunnel.

Chapter Ten

A Leecher paced ten feet in front of Rachel. She'd reached the meeting hall in her search for Darron and Tabitha or Shamus. Her wide eyes bounced from one lifeless body to the next. Fear, swift and sharp, pierced her gut. Leechers stood beside the bodies of their charges. The members rested on an assortment of lounge chairs. Small, wooden tables sat between bodies with checkered squares set into their surfaces of the tables for playing chess. The collection of Council members and their powers caused the air to crackle and pop with energy.

Why were there so many members in such a state, and in the open? There had to be at least seventy bodies. Rachel studied the Leechers more closely; they were tense, worried. Moreover, how were the Council members able to leave their bodies with Leora awakened and their power stripped? Something was very wrong.

A knot formed in her throat, and the world spun. Had something happened to Leora? No, this had to do with the possessions of souls. This had to do with the Lost.

Pulling her world back into focus, she thought of Chad. The Council wasn't her concern right now. She had to figure out how to keep moving and get help to Chad.

There were too many Leechers. If they saw her, they

would attack. One never dared approach a Leecher while they were guarding a member's body. It was a law set down by the Creator, and a law she didn't dare break.

She looked over her shoulder. She couldn't go back the way she came, having found the meeting hall by pure luck as it was. A door in the opposite corner of the space caught her eye; it led to the kitchen. She eased up on her power and prayed she could make it to the kitchen unseen. She pulled her hair back into a bun; its blonde color would stand out against the black walls.

For the first time in all her years of living in the cavern, she realized it resembled a dark, fairy-tale castle buried underground. She used to think of it as magnificent and grand. Now she recalled the members who thought of it as a cage. Why hadn't she seen that before? Maybe Leora was right to feel sorry for the Council members, who once led wonderful lives filled with purpose. How many would have refused the Creator knowing that they would be bound to the cavern and could never leave? She thought of the year when the Creator had lifted the bloodstones hold on the members and how happy they had been. Stephen could have never known what that year would lead to. The members changed after they were reminded of what they had given up and asked over and over for another year away. The Creator never answered them.

Rachel pressed back against the wall and silently inched toward the other side of the meeting hall. With her energy suppressed, her senses were almost that of a corpse. The cold stone caused goose bumps to form on her skin; she'd left her jacket behind with Chad.

The Leecher closest to her stopped pacing; his hands were clasped behind his back, and he was facing away from Rachel. She was thankful her outfit was as black as the stone she crept along. She pressed forward, never taking her eyes off the Leecher's wide back, but when she was three feet from the door, every Leecher snapped to attention and glanced at each other nervously. Booted heels clicked along the floor in the hall. They all straightened to their full height of nearly seven feet and faced the hall, their right fists raised and resting over the center of their chests.

Stephen and Shamus came into view. Rachel reached for the door handle and turned it a fraction. Her heart pounded so hard she thought it would give her away. She froze in place for several seconds. She hadn't laid eyes on Stephen since leaving the cavern centuries ago. He looked the same: exuding strength as he walked, his pleated kilt ruffling with each step, a wide strip of plaid tossed over his bare left shoulder, shaggy, ebony hair brushing his shoulders. Serena said that Stephen's last life was that of a Scottish laird, so he had brought his plaid with him.

She recalled the day he had come to her room and told her of the Creator's wishes for her to bond with the Elapsed Seer. The sharp planes of his face that day had made him look aged and sad. Had he known how hard things were going to be for her and Chad?

She stepped behind the door. Shamus's green eyes locked on hers and he frowned, but stayed beside Stephen. A moment later, she was in the kitchen with the door safely closed behind her.

She shook uncontrollably as she looked around the empty, massive kitchen for a safe place to vomit. Thoughts spun and spun until she was dizzy, but one ultimately prevailed. She shouldn't have left him; Chad's mangled body and the destiny mark pushed her stomach over the edge. She dashed for a corner, then heaved and heaved, emptying her stomach. A tear ran down her cheek and she angrily wiped it away. If Chad died, he wouldn't be reborn. A person received the mark from the Creator for a horrible betrayal. What had he done? Was he the reason the Council members could still leave their bodies? She bent over and dry heaved.

A moment later, she cursed and collected herself. There wasn't time for this.

In front of her was a table filled with fruit. She grabbed an apple, a banana, and two oranges before taking off in the direction of Shamus's old bedchamber, praying Chad still had time.

·●○᷼○●·

Chad lifted an arm and made a fist. Strength returned slowly as he sat in Shamus's new bedchamber, which did not look any different from his previous arrangement. He wondered why he'd moved only to have it all remain the same. Maybe to be closer to Stephen?

He leaned back in an old oak chair next to a table filled with books. Every part of his body ached after Darron's healing power pumped through him. It felt different, stronger, more violent.

Tabitha was stretched out on her belly on the bed, her legs bent and kicking back and forth as she picked her nails with her knife. Darron sat beside her, watching. Energy pulsed between them as strongly as Leora and Gavin's bond, which meant they had bonded for love. They would never know how powerful that was. He had wanted that for himself and Rachel, but love never solidified their bond. There was respect and affection at times, but not love. He scowled and waited for the pain that knowledge usually brought, but it didn't come. He was grateful for the emptiness; the cost of his betrayal had taken every emotion from him.

Chad flicked at the flecks of dried blood on his arm.

If Darron knew why he'd received the destiny mark, he wouldn't have healed him. A destiny mark meant an eternal death. Darron and Leora would not be reborn until the Creator chose another soul to be their father. His time was over.

Having no regrets for the past and no hope for the future was a new feeling for him. He was always the rock, never shaken by what the Creator had in store for his family. But poison finds a way into the hearts of all men. He couldn't be what his family needed anymore.

The chamber door opened and Tabitha jumped off the bed, sending her knife flying. Shamus sidestepped it before it sank into the door. He peered at her, then Chad.

"You really need to learn to knock. I could have killed you," Tabitha said.

"It would look odd if I knocked on my own door," Shamus scoffed.

"He's got you there, babe," Darron said, rising off of the bed.

Shamus ignored Darron and walked to Chad, dropping to a knee. "When I came with Stephen, you were gone."

Chad managed a weak smile and placed a reassuring hand on his shoulder. "Don't worry, old friend. I got what I deserved." Chad stared hard at Shamus and squeezed his shoulder. "It was a Lost soul . . . possessed."

Shamus clenched his square jaw. "With Leora awakened, they should not have the power to do such a thing." He pushed to his feet. "But they do. We had only begun to suspect when you arrived."

"It is not a singular possession. A woman appeared at the eastern entrance and spoke with the voice of at least a dozen members."

Shamus hissed, "I told Stephen something was happening with so many members leaving their bodies at the same time after the Awakener stripped their power. It should not be."

Shamus's eyes raked over Chad's bare chest. Dried blood covered every inch of him, as well as his boxers. He had no other clothes, and he smelled like rotting death.

"You need to go to the Recovery Spring. Your aura is stained, and energy is not moving around you."

"Stained?" Tabitha asked.

"The Council has corrupted his energy." Shamus pointed around his head. "There's a darkness in his aura."

Chad looked away, not wanting to talk about his aura, his energy, or anything to do with his gift.

"You're right. I see it!" Tabitha exclaimed.

She and Darron exchanged a worried glance before Darron leaned over and fixed his eyes on where Shamus had pointed. "How the hell can you see that?"

Shamus stared at Darron, bottom eyelid twitching. "I'm a Leecher. I can see everyone's energy moving around them."

"Right, Gavin can do that too," Darron said. "Sorry."

"The Recovery Spring can clean that?" Tabitha scrunched up her face as she pointed at his aura.

"Yes, but he'll have to stay in the water for a few hours."

Darron locked his fingers behind his head and tapped his boots against the floor, causing Chad's head to ache.

He rubbed his temple. "You were never good at hiding your feelings."

"You're in good shape, so let's go. You don't need the Recovery Spring; we can make it back to the truck in a day or two and you can rest on the way home."

Tabitha punched Darron in the ribs. "That's your dad. Tell Shamus what happened."

Darron exhaled loudly. "I'm not even sure what happened." He looked around. "Where's Rachel? Why isn't she with you?"

"We were separated. I saw her last in the meeting hall, sneaking into the kitchen."

"She doesn't know how to get here, asshole." Darron poked Shamus in the chest, at which, Shamus raised a brow.

"Darron, that's enough. Rachel knows her way around this place well enough. She'll be fine," Chad said in an authoritative voice. "She found me earlier before you and left me to find you. She knew I needed to be healed, and you did. Let's move on."

Tabitha smirked. "I wish I could shut him up like that!"

Darron glared at her, then seized her by the waist. "All you have to do is ask me nicely—and naked—and I will do anything you want."

She slapped him playfully, kissed him, and shimmied away. "Let's get serious for a minute, okay? When we found you in the tunnel, you were dying. Darron tried to heal you, but it wasn't working."

Chad leaned back in the chair and folded his arms. He knew where this conversation was headed, and while he would prefer not to have it with Shamus, it appeared he would have little say in the matter. So, he prepared himself to speak the truth.

"There was a black mark in the center of your chest. I thought the Council did something to him to stop others from using power on him," Tabitha continued with a glance at Shamus, who looked grim.

Chad stared at the wall. He couldn't run, couldn't hide. Death would always follow the destiny mark. The Creator marked souls with it when they committed horrendous acts of cruelty, and would send out Death to take the soul for judgment. He didn't know when, but it would find him.

"I persuaded the mark to leave him, so to speak. After that, it was gone, and Darron could heal him. Now I'm not so sure it was permanently removed. I suspect it just moved to his aura."

"Persuaded? How does one persuade a mark to remove itself?" Shamus asked, brows rising.

Tabitha smiled and then jutted out her hip. "By being an Influencer *and* the last Advisor needed for Leora's High Council."

Shamus's eyes narrowed. "I should have pushed you harder. You could have learned of your gifts sooner."

"What's there to learn? Look at me. I can influence others, hunt souls, and project."

Chad scrubbed a weary hand down his face and noticed his beard for the first time. "Don't be too hard on yourself, Shamus. I tried to teach my son many things. He didn't care to waste his time with a book or to listen to me. We are a dying breed."

Shamus studied him for a long time with a disappointed frown. He knew what the mark meant, but didn't say a word to Darron or Tabitha.

"Okay, got it: we're ignorant fools. Moving on to more useful information," Darron said.

"I'll find Rachel faster since I can sense her energy," said Shamus.

Chad didn't argue or even look at him. He would find her faster because of their love. "Tabitha, could you please take me to the Recovery Spring? I've only been there a few times and can only vaguely recall how to get there."

"Afterward, we should go and see Stephen," said Shamus.

"I'm not going near that man, and neither is my father," Darron argued.

Shamus's green eyes locked on Chad. He nodded, rested his right hand over his heart, and bowed his head. Shamus would bring Stephen when the time was right, of that, Chad was sure. Stephen was the closest thing to a father he'd had before leaving the cavern. He was his friend, and Chad wanted to see him before death came for him.

Darron helped him up, shouldering his weight. He followed Tabitha and Shamus as they slipped out of the room undetected.

"Are you okay, Chad?" Darron asked.

"No," he replied.

A storm passed in his son's eyes, darkening them to a rich blue. "I hate this place. We should just leave."

"You will."

Chapter Eleven

Rachel huddled in the corner of the closet she was hiding in, doing her best to combat the icy chill that had frosted over her skin since she'd lowered her energy level so as not to be detected. She'd forgotten how cold the cavern was, but didn't dare don one of Shamus's old garments and torture herself with his scent. She scrubbed her hand over her face, irritated with herself for wasting so much time wandering the halls of the cavern, trying to remember her way around.

The closet door opened, and Shamus's wide shoulders cast a shadow over her face as he gazed down at her, frowning. "Do you know how dangerous it was for you to enter the meeting hall?"

She fisted her hands in her shirt and glared at him. He didn't have the right to scold her or show any kind of concern for her well-being.

"Don't pretend you care about me. You stomped off and left me behind when you knew I hadn't been here in forever. And why? Because you allowed a boy to upset you?"

She rose to her knees and shoved shirts away from her face.

"Your son is far from a boy."

"And you're the protector of the High Priest. Since when have you allowed a soul like Darron's to get under your skin?" She stepped out of the closet and poked his chest, feeling more like her current self than before.

He straightened his spine. "Anger is a natural response when he questioned my affection for Tabitha. I raised her the best I could."

"That may be so, but you were wrong to judge him."

His chest deflated as he brushed her finger aside. "Stephen told me of the suffering your family has endured since the Creator bonded you to the Elapsed Seer."

Her heart beat erratically. "Did he tell you how the Council sent the Hound after us over and over? Did he tell you how I watched the Hound kill Darron and Leora—my children—countless times?" She clutched her chest and turned away from him. "There were lifetimes in which my daughter or Darron only made it a few years before the Hound found us. Chad and I fought hard to keep them safe, always, and sometimes, we even died together."

Her heart was heavy with the grief of the past. Tears ran down her cheeks. "I thought being chosen to have a family was a gift. At times, it was the most beautiful thing I ever experienced, filled with love and hope for a future of watching them grow up and have families of their own." She turned back to him and lifted her quivering chin. "Do you know what it is like to see your daughter, pregnant and dying, with her dead lover in her arms?"

These were some of many memories she'd placed in boxes and secured with mental chains. She didn't ever want to see or feel those memories again.

Shamus shook his head. "I'm sorry, my love."

"Don't call me that—never again." She wiped her cheeks. "Do you know what the worst part of being the Awakener's mother is?"

Shamus caved in on himself, and she remembered Tabitha's back and all the times she must have been whipped because she wouldn't take a Leecher's life. Some of the anger and hurt drained out of her. It was unfair of her to think Shamus couldn't understand her pain, but she answered her own question anyway.

"When she dies, I have to conceive her all over again to give her a chance to appease the Creator's will, all while knowing that with the Hound out there, she could die all over again. It breaks my heart."

They both stood in silence for a long while, neither knowing what to say.

"Stephen said you would suffer if you believed you were not worthy of love."

"What the hell does that mean?"

A wave of golden light shot from Rachel's hands and slammed into Shamus's chest. He stumbled to the floor, electric charges shooting from his chest and down to his arms. He held up a hand in surrender as he climbed back to his feet, but his words echoed in the deepest part of herself and cleared away a thick fog that had clouded her mind for a very long time.

She dropped to her knees and whispered, "My family has suffered because of me."

A gamut of perplexing emotions caused the room to grow small around her, and she felt as if she couldn't breathe. Memories of the past morphed into something she didn't want to see. Chad's outstretched hand, him waiting for her to take it, only for her to turn away to tend to Darron. Countless moments like that flashed through her mind. She ran a hand through her hair as her words to Tabitha came to mind.

"A bond without love isn't as strong, and is easily broken."

Tears fell. Was her unhappiness her own doing? Had she sabotaged what could have been amazing because of what happened with Shamus? Had she put her family at risk because her bond to Chad wasn't as strong as it could have been? Could she have protected her family better? She shook her head. "No, no . . . you didn't love me or trust me enough to know about Tabitha."

Shamus placed a finger under her chin, tilting her face up toward his. "I'm sorry I caused you pain. I never meant to. When Stephen told me what Serena had done, I knew Tabitha needed to be hidden until Stephen decided what to do with her. I wanted to come to you and say goodbye, but there was no time. Stephen was so devastated by the loss of Serena and afraid for Tabitha's safety, and then he told me that the Creator had chosen you to couple with the Elapsed Seer to bring about the coming of the Soul Hunter and the Awakener. I was thankful you could have children and the life you'd talked about: a life both of us knew would never happen for us here."

She stared into Shamus's beautiful green eyes, and the truth and sincerity of his words caused her heart to flip-flop even as sorrow flowed from her and frosted over the room. "I should've seen what I was given: a man who chose me every day, for hundreds of years, even when he had no reason to. I never gave him one."

Shamus and Rachel were silent for a while. Then Shamus said, "Darron and Tabitha have Chad."

"What? Why didn't you say that sooner?" She jumped to her feet. "Did Darron heal him?" She pushed past him to the wall hanging. "Take me to him," she commanded, sounding very much like the Seer she used to be.

He brushed past her and kept his eyes trained forward. As he touched the stone wall, he took a step. "You know what the destiny mark means. It stopped Darron from healing Chad."

"What? No," she cried.

"Tabitha tried to remove it."

"How?"

"She said she 'persuaded' it to leave his body."

"That is impossible." Rachel ran a hand over her hair, then bit her bottom lip.

"Yes, however, it did allow Darron to heal Chad. I believe the mark now hovers in his aura. There's no telling what's to come for him now."

·●○～○●·

The Recovery Spring looked as beautiful as it had the last time Rachel was here. Multiple springs sprang from a single source, steam rose from the water, and the spattering of neon blue light overhead reminded her of the night sky. The blue, glowing water was otherworldly; it was all so wondrous when she first discovered it.

Rachel came to a screeching halt when she saw Chad and the others. She leaned against a boulder as her recent revelation swung her emotions back and forth like the pendulum of an old clock.

Shamus prowled toward Darron and Tabitha, who were standing over Chad as he sat in the water. She saw the back of his head and shoulders resting against the side of a natural pool, his arms thrown over the edge. Purple scars smattered his upper back.

"You two come with me to Stephen's library so we can find out what to do about the mark."

"Will Stephen be there?" Darron asked.

"I am not sure."

Darron crossed his arms over his chest and raised a challenging brow at Shamus. "Does he know we're here?"

"Yes, members reported your appearance in the cavern when you were looking for me, and I gave him an update when he began to suspect the Lost were being used. We went to the meeting hall to confirm his suspicions."

Tabitha bit her upper lip. "Great. He's going to be pissed I haven't reported on Marcus."

"Do you really care if he's mad at you?" Darron snapped before turning to Shamus. "Does he know why we're here?"

"Yes, he's aware of the situation. Stephen sensed Chad's presence, but could not find him—just like me. He believes the Council cloaked his energy. But, there were more pressing matters than your arrival for him to attend to."

"Like what?" Tabitha's beautiful features scrunched into an ugly ball of disapproval.

"It's not for me to discuss. Talk to your father; he's worried."

Tabitha looked over her shoulder at Rachel pressed against the wall and pointed to Chad. "Stay with him. If anything happens, go to Chad's old chamber."

All three of them left, making no more sound than a mouse.

The image of Chad's flesh ripping free in her hand was still fresh in her mind and caused Rachel's stomach to turn. That had to be the second-grossest thing she'd ever seen. Well, in this life, anyway. The top item on that list occurred five lifetimes ago, when she held Leora and watched her die with her belly sliced open and her baby hanging out of the wound. She sent a silent prayer of thanks to the Creator that Chad was okay for now, and that she had the strength and clarity to begin again as herself in this life. She waltzed toward Chad, wanting to get a better look at him now that he was healed and had cleaned up a bit.

Her gaze traveled over his newly shaven face. The

swelling was gone, and she could see the sharp angles in it that spoke of power and ageless strength—a strength she'd chosen to ignore. Not anymore. She was more than happy to learn all there was to know about this man.

Tight cords of muscle stretched over his torso and rippled over his shoulders and down his arms. A tingling in the pit of her stomach forced her to pause her perusal. A bubbly kind of excitement tugged the corner of her mouth into a smile. For the briefest moment, her current reality dissolved. She was a happy girl spying on a boy who could change her world. She rose to her toes and bounced a few steps closer, wanting to see more of him. Her jaw dropped, and a small giggle escaped her. She wouldn't lie; he was gorgeous in this new life with all those scars. Was this how Leora felt when she looked at Gavin? She would ask her when she got back.

His relaxed expression changed when he caught her ogling him, practically drooling. Her cheeks heated as his brows drew together over an affronted frown, and then he sat up in the blue glowing water.

Her heart beat so fast she didn't think she could move. It was as if she was a new soul seeing her bonded for the first time. She didn't understand. How could Chad cause her to feel this way? She tried to think of the last time she flirted with anyone in this life, but nothing came to mind; hell, she didn't even know the last time she went on a date. Work at the hospital had been so consuming; plus, she was still writing her thesis when all the past memories came rushing in and forced her to admit herself. There was no time for a guy—not that any had really interested her. Until now.

His exhaustion was palpable. She tried to tear her eyes away, but was unable to and completely okay with it. Sinking to the cold, stone floor, her desire sparked. Wanting

Chad the way the Creator had intended was a new feeling. Shamus had always lingered in the back of her mind, but now she was free, having gotten the closure she needed. The longer she sat watching Chad, though, the more natural it felt to desire him. She was moving forward. That was all any of them could do: move forward. Her father would be proud of her.

She ran a hand through the water and studied it in her palm, then let it run between her fingers. Her dad would have loved this place. He and her mother loved adventures and seeing new places. She missed them. Rachel wondered what they would think of her if they knew the truth. Would they like the woman she used to be, or the woman she was today?

She shook off that thought by reminding herself that she was the optimist: Smiley, as Leora liked to call her. A silky heat churned inside her; it was hope that she could right her wrongs with Chad by being who she was now, not who she was in the past.

·●○↜○●·

The scent of honey drifted over Chad, and he felt the raking heat of her gaze. His muscles tensed and he sat up with a scowl.

They didn't owe each other any loyalty in this life. Leora and Darron were grown, awakened to their power, and didn't need them to open the coupling bond. He would ignore Rachel and the annoying pull in his chest. Leaning his head back against the edge of the pool, Chad closed his eyes and let the healing water restore some of his energy. His time was at an end. Darron would be compelled to take his soul to the Creator for judgment. This would be his last life.

He thought about his parents and his brother in this life, and wished he could see them one last time. He wished he could have been the son they believed him to be, but he just couldn't keep enduring the pain that stained every life he'd lived. That was why he struck the bargain with Marcus.

He ran a hand over his bristly hair and down his face. What was done, was done.

A small splash caused his eyelids to pop open. Rachel sat by the water's edge, her delicate feet and toenails painted red dipped in the water. He'd dreamed of what she would look like in this life, and he wasn't disappointed. Her signature red curls had been replaced by long, straight, golden locks. Her baby-blue eyes were a dark chocolate color. He lifted his head so he could see her better. Her heart-shaped face wasn't plain, yet she didn't radiate power like she had in past lives. She looked . . . innocent and untouched by the disappointments of the world.

A wide smile split her face and a spark of hunger flickered in her eyes. It caught him by surprise, and his body hardened unexpectedly. He clenched his jaw. She seemed pleased with his reaction.

"What do you think?" she asked boldly. She leaned back and lifted a foot from the water and pointed her toes in the air, her rolled-up black jeans hugging her slim curves. A sword at her hip tapped against the stone edge of the spring. A black, long-sleeved, thermal shirt covered her lean body, but he caught a glimpse of her small breasts between the buttons of her shirt. She slapped her foot against the water, splashing him playfully. "I'm waiting."

"For what?"

She let out an exasperated sigh. His brows stitched together as he tried to suss out her behavior. Then she beamed and asked, "How do I look in this life?"

Unaccustomed to her attention and enthusiasm, Chad squirmed a bit. "Oh . . . you look nice."

She squinted at him and her smile turned to a scowl. "That good, huh?"

"You don't like how you look in this life?" he asked curiously.

Intrigued, he swam from the shallow side of the spring to get closer to her. His body yearned for her because of the coupling bond. It pulsed in his chest, wanting to be reopened. Her dark eyes remained locked on him as he traveled the short distance that separated them and then rested his arms on the edge of the pool next to her.

My bonded.

"Chad Harper," he said, holding out a hand for her to shake.

She blinked at him, a bit confused, then smiled. It was contagious, as if it held a promise of good things to come. The corners of his mouth twitched, but he didn't give in to the urge to return it.

"Rachel Perry," she said, taking his hand.

Silken heat shot through his veins in a seductive dance, caressing all that it touched. He wanted to let go, to push her away, but he didn't.

"Where are you from?" he asked, wanting to put some distance between the past and the present for just a little while and get to know this version of the Seer.

Her dark eyes widened as her grip eased, though she held onto him, placed her other hand on top and set them all in her lap. Did she feel the heat between them too?

"You know where I'm from—"

"No, I don't. Not in this life." He didn't know why, but that mattered more so now than ever before.

She looked down at their hands and caressed his knuckles. Not quite sure how to react to her touch, he gently pulled his hands back.

Her chin quivered. "You really want to know about me…in this life?"

"Yes. Why wouldn't I?"

"Is this really what you want to talk about? I mean, after everything you've been through the past few weeks."

"Yes. I want to forget about all that for now."

"Well, okay. Let me see . . . I was born in San Diego. My mother died from breast cancer, and my dad is . . . was . . . my best friend until I met Leora. We worked together at the Mental Health Center of San Diego. I worked with her for about three years." She hit him with that blinding smile again. "Can you believe it? Three years together before awakening."

This wasn't the Seer he knew; she was always so serious and quiet.

"I'm working on my master's degree. I . . . I was supposed to complete my thesis this December." She looked past him, as if she'd gotten lost in distant dreams cloaked by a fog of uncertainty. Her eyes glistened with unshed tears. The small bit of happiness she'd shown was snuffed out. Then she shook her head. "But that doesn't matter anymore. I love coffee, the color pink, and I sometimes like people—when I don't want to slap them. How about you?"

"I was born in Chicago, but I grew up everywhere. My father was in the military, so we moved a lot."

She reached over and ran her fingers through the curls on the top of his head. Sides cut short. "Doesn't look like high and tight. But if I had to guess. You're a Marine."

Apprehension forced him to remove her hand from his hair. How was it that in this life, in a span of only five minutes, she'd touched him more times than she ever had before?

"Good guess."

"Nailed it."

She did a little jig, and Chad could not hold back his amusement. He smiled as she mimicked pulling out an imaginary nail and hammering it in midair. Then his smile fell away as he realized something.

She's different, and so am I.

"What do you do with the Marines?" She leaned forward to dangle her feet in the water and make little circles with them.

"I'm a sniper."

"Really? Way cool."

He smiled again at the sight of her so impressed. Pride swelled in his chest; he'd never impressed her before. Then again, they'd never spoken like this either. It really was as if they were meeting for the first time.

"Have you killed anyone?" she asked, then snapped her jaw closed. Too late—she knew the answer to that. Chad stayed silent. "I'm sorry. I don't know why I said that. It just came out. I forgot . . . I got caught up in the moment."

"It's okay."

He pushed away from the edge and swam to the center of the pool. Her eyes remained on him until her cheeks colored and she looked away, trailing her fingers in the water. She played with it for some time, seemingly lost in thought.

All of a sudden, she stood and tugged her shirt over her head, revealing beautiful breasts cradled in a red, silk bra. He swam in the other direction. The polite thing would be to look away, but he couldn't resist. He glanced back over his shoulder; she was shimmying her pants down over her hips, revealing matching underwear. Was this a test? His eyes skimmed every line of her beautiful body, and every fiber of his body came alive with desire.

Shit.

He turned his back. All of this was so confusing.

The water rippled around him. He turned and found her just a foot away, her eyes golden and glowing. He paused. That was new. They were dark brown only seconds ago.

"You can't get away that easily," she said as she moved closer, her golden eyes searching his.

He didn't retreat, but he couldn't help going over every reason for his betrayal in his mind and thinking that all of this had to be a sick joke.

She circled him twice and pointed to his chest. "Do they hurt?"

He ran a finger over some of the purple scars. "I might have Gavin beat with all these."

His arms started to feel heavy as he tried to stay afloat. The excitement was depleting what energy he had left. He returned to the shallow side of the pool, where he could sit and rest.

She trailed after him. "Are you okay? Is there anything I can do?"

He closed his eyes, hating his body and hating himself for wanting to pull Rachel closer. "No. I need to rest."

Rachel quietly sat beside him. Under the water, she touched his fingers. It didn't seem like a good time to be touchy-feely, but he didn't move. Slowly, she laced her fingers with his and relaxed so she could soak up some of the recharging energy from the spring along with him.

He focused on the water, and the destiny mark that smeared his aura.

Chapter Twelve

"Chad," Rachel whispered.

A wet hand rested against his chest; his eyes flicked open at the heat of her touch. His arm dropped from the edge of the spring with a splash. She still held the other hand under the water. Her grip tightened as her eyes went white so she could stare into a future he could not see. She trembled against him.

"Damn. Not here!" he cursed.

Visions never seemed to have good timing. He brushed her wet hair off her face. Lines of fear creased her features. It was a look he had seen countless times. Pulling their laced fingers to his lips, he kissed them and rubbed her cheek with his knuckle, yet despised himself for wanting to comfort her, to touch her in this small way while he could.

"It's okay. I'm here. What do you see?" he asked softly.

In a distant, hollow tone, she said, "Leora lies in a pool of blood."

"How clear is the vision? How long do we have?"

"It is a reflection, like a mirror . . . " She tilted her head. "The image ripples. It is not set. It could change."

Before he could process what she was saying, hurried footsteps crunched against stone in the hall leading to the spring. Chad pushed out of the water as fast as he could, taking Rachel with him even though she was locked in her vision. There was a dark crevice across from the pool and he backed her into it, then braced himself against her to keep her in place and hide them from view.

He waited for the new arrivals to reveal themselves, but cursed when he caught a glimpse of Rachel's clothes and sword in plain sight. He dashed over and collected her belongings, then shoved them next to her and covered her body with his once more.

The footsteps slowed as the woman that captured and tortured him stepped into the cavern. Her black eyes swept the area; power emitting from the healing spring disrupted energy frequencies within a fifty-foot radius, and the steam from the springs helped hide them. Chad prayed that would give them a chance to escape her notice entirely.

The woman's black eyes flitted in their direction. Chad's power began to pulse, but in his current state, he knew he could not win in a fight. She approached the pool they had been resting in, bent down, and dipped her hand in the water. She jerked upright and peered in their direction again.

Hot, protective energy unlike anything Chad had ever felt ripped through him. Blinding green orbs formed in his palms and he cursed under his breath. He didn't have control.

The orbs intensified, and without warning, they shot toward the woman. One hit her square in the chest, but she seemed to absorb it. She threw up a hand and redirected the second orb toward the tunnel she'd come from. Bolts of red lightning erupted from her palms, hitting Chad's shoulder and right thigh. He screamed in pain, but then the woman dropped to one knee, apparently frozen in place.

Agony dragged thick claws through his muscle and he dropped to all fours. Blood pooled on the ground and he gritted his teeth, but managed to reach for Rachel's shirt, tear a piece off, and tie it around his leg in a crude tourniquet. Struggling to his feet, he clasped an arm around Rachel's shoulders and stared into her white eyes.

"Rachel, we must go. Find your way back to the present."

He lifted her off her feet, then tossed both her and her clothes over his shoulder, trying to minimize their skin-to-skin contact. His gift pushed and pushed as memories of her past probed at him, but he managed to hold them back by studying the possessed woman.

She did not move. Her eyes were no longer black, but a lifeless gray. She was dead.

He staggered past her, but weakness set in before he made it very far down the tunnel. He sank to his knees, unable to carry Rachel any further. He gently laid her on the ground and placed her clothes beside her. He hoped they were far enough away that the Council members wouldn't sense them. His arms fell to his sides, exhausted. His ability gripped him hard and fast, yanking a buried memory to the surface of his conscious mind.

An outstretched hand beckoned the Seer closer to the western opening to the Cavern of Souls. Rose petals created a path that was symbolic of the coupling bond they had learned about from their mentors. Her pale-blue gaze landed heavily on him. She didn't take his hand; hers were fisted in her royal-blue, ankle-length skirt that flowed out and around her in the air flowing from the cavern opening. Her loose, white blouse was cut low to reveal the tops of her round, perfect breasts. She didn't look at him as they walked side by side to a dark-green bloodstone with red flakes that hummed, much like the bloodstones from the sacred circle. Her scent of sweet warm honey was intoxicating. Her red curls were down except for strands in the front that she'd pinned back and to the side.

He had wanted her to take his hand and show him that she was willing to take what the Creator had given them—a chance to leave the cavern and create a family—and trust him to care for her heart should she choose to give it to him.

Once they reached the stone, Chad nervously ran a hand over his white tunic and his black leather pants. When Stephen told him they would be joined, he'd hesitated to accept the arrangement because of Shamus. They had trained together, learned together, and had become friends, brothers by virtue of the fact that they were both bound to Stephen. Shamus was missing, Stephen hadn't told him why; he knew better than to push for answers. But he knew Rachel must be missing him.

Standing in front of the large stone, the Seer placed her hand on it, and Chad rested his over hers. She didn't pull away, but her entire body stiffened, and it pricked at his pride. Their gazes locked. Hers contained a sadness that he understood. She was lost without Shamus.

She pulled her hand free of his and said in a flat tone, "Let's begin."

He nodded, and she closed her eyes. Golden energy snaked out of her palms, and sparkles shimmered within her aura. Her energy wrapped around his leather boots and then danced higher. When it touched the exposed skin on his arms, he stopped breathing. It was ice-cold and cutting. Though they had occupied the cavern for many years, there had never been a time or a need for their energies to interact. He was caught off guard by the promise of such brittleness in their future and the energy it inspired within her. The golden energy gathered at his chest to become a ball of brilliant light.

It was his turn. He opened his energy, and it lazily wafted from him all at once to blanket the Seer in a soft,

*green glow. Her eyes popped open and her lips parted with
a soft moan. His energy was consuming and seductive. His
energy was fueled by the past, so its touch felt like all of the
best things a person could remember. The energy gathered
into a green ball and slammed into their chests; it ripped
him apart, remaking him. His body burned, making breathing impossible as every muscle tensed until they lifted from
his bones. The Seer grimaced, but didn't look away. Second
by second, their emotions collided—panic, sadness, fear,
overwhelming dread—as the ball of light sank into his skin.
He swallowed, unsure of what she was sensing from her
side of the bond.*

*Suddenly, a lightning bolt struck both of them in their
hearts, locking them together for all time. It was an anchor,
heavy and cold. It wasn't what he expected, and from the
look on her face, she hadn't either. As soon as they could
breathe again, brokenness rolled through their bond. He
reached for her; she turned and ran, leaving him at the
bloodstone altar.*

The memory vanished to become another reminder
of why he was there. He would still die in this hellish pit,
bleeding and broken, just as he'd planned. And yet, it
felt wrong while the Seer was vulnerable in the grips of
a vision. He didn't want her to die there because of him.
That wasn't the plan.

He slammed his fists into the ground. Why was this
happening? Why, after all those past lives, would she show
interest in him now? He wanted to rage, to scream into the
emptiness of the tunnel. There was no starting over with a
destiny mark. Complete and utter defeat seized him. He'd
destroyed everything the Creator gave him because he was
tired of things being so difficult; he had stopped fighting for
her, for his family.

When he made the deal with Marcus to get him past

the bloodstones and into the sacred circle, he hadn't been captured like the others assumed he had when Leora awakened. He had willingly hiked to the circle and waited for Marcus. When he appeared and told him it was time, he'd stabbed himself so Marcus could bathe in his blood and pass the bloodstones. He had offered up his family, knowing the destiny mark would be the punishment for his betrayal. Unable to face them, he left to go and see Stephen one last time before judgment for his misdeeds would fall upon him.

Gentle hands cupped his cheeks and soft lips pressed against his forehead. He froze, but was unable to deny how desperately he wanted those lips on his skin. He gathered Rachel closer with his good arm and breathed deep her sweet scent of honey. He pressed his lips to hers, drinking her in. She returned his kiss, and his pent-up desire broke free. It occurred to him that this could be his only moment with her, his last chance to taste heaven. She met the demands of his lips and tongue with her own desire and wrapped her arm around his neck. He could almost believe she wanted him as much as he wanted her. He forgot his pain, but slowed the kiss to a mere whisper of need.

He rested his forehead against hers as their breathing slowed. He didn't want to think about how different things could have been, if, had he gone to find her after his awakening, they could have had a chance. It didn't matter now. He pulled away.

"Everything will be okay," Rachel whispered as she brushed her lips against his again.

He didn't have the strength to stop her from caressing him. When she touched the gash on his shoulder, she paused, then jerked away.

"You're hurt," she said with a gasp. "What happened?"

He remembered she could see in the dark, although

he could not. "The woman the Council possessed found us . . . and I killed her."

He heard her rummaging around; it sounded like she was tugging on her clothes. The next thing he knew, she was pulling him to his feet by his good arm.

"We have to clean those wounds up. Let's go to your room and wait for Darron."

·●○⌒○●·

Rachel sat him down carefully on his old bed, then started fumbling through his old dresser drawers, which were mostly empty. Upon discovering this, she decided to take the sheet from the bed and tear it into strips. Pulling the fabric off of his leg, she studied the wound for a minute, then turned her attention to his bleeding shoulder. She was methodical and precise, and when she was done, he inspected her handiwork.

"Where did you learn to do that? You could've been a medic in my platoon."

"Oh, it's nothing. I thought I wanted to be a doctor before I chose psychology."

"Why did you change your mind?" he asked, rolling his shoulder and flexing his bicep to be sure he could still move it.

"The mind fascinates me far more than the body—but yours is not bad."

He blinked at her. She was teasing him—flirting with him, even. He frowned and looked down at his bare chest and black boxer briefs, suddenly uncomfortable with his lack of clothes. She knelt and fussed with his leg next, but he grabbed her arm, forcing her to stop.

"That's enough, Rachel."

She pulled her arm free as a scowl settled on her features. "I'm just trying to help."

She swiveled away while he adjusted the bandage she'd started on his leg, then he slid off the bed to limp over to his old closet, eager to get dressed so he would feel less exposed.

He shuffled through a few shirts, then snatched a pair of loose pants and clean boxers from a shelf. He yanked off his dirty boxers after stepping behind a chair in the corner and tugged on the clean ones; the pain in his leg and shoulder flared, but he met her cold look with what he hoped was a blank stare. He pulled on his pants—they sagged low on his hips—and then rummaged around for some shoes.

A warm hand rested on his shoulder blade, then trailed down his side, leaving a devastating heat in his wake. He went as stiff as the stone walls surrounding them. She came around in front of him, and there was tenderness in her gaze that made her eyes glow with golden light once more. He liked seeing that so much that his irritation evaporated, leaving him confused.

He pushed past her to grab a black, long-sleeved shirt from a hanger, but she blocked his path, her foot tapping furiously. He glared down at her, willing his body not to respond.

Still, Rachel persisted. She caressed his cheek and whispered, "Don't push me away."

His heart turned over in his chest as he removed her hand. "I'm marked, Rachel. You know what it means. You need to stay away from me. I am not the man you remember."

"I know, but I'm not the person you think I am either. We don't know each other. I don't think we ever have. Not really."

She wrapped her arms around herself as her face grew pale. He wanted to hold her, to tell her he was sorry, but he didn't. He couldn't.

"Ask me what I did to get the destiny mark."

She shook her head, causing her hair to fall around her face. "I don't want to know. I don't care!" she yelled as she threw her hands above her head. "Everything is so awful: so many lives, so many terrible memories. I don't want to do this anymore, Chad."

He grabbed her shoulders and gave her a gentle shake. Tears filled her eyes.

"I just want to be Rachel Perry from San Diego. I want to visit my parents' graves and bring them flowers. I want to finish grad school and see my best friend have her baby."

He swallowed hard and then wrapped her up in his embrace. He rested his chin on top of her head. Her body fit perfectly against his, and her heat seeped into his bones to chase away the chill of the cavern. The Seer he knew would never confess what difficulties she was facing. Her arms tightened around his waist and she buried her face in his chest. He rubbed his cheek against her hair, breathing in her scent once again. He understood her frustration, but didn't know what to do with that knowledge, or even what it meant.

"When you're ready, I'll tell you why I received the mark."

He felt her nod, and they stood there for a long while, simply holding each other.

"What did you see in the vision at the spring? What is going to happen to Leora?" Chad finally asked as he ran a hand down her back. "If you don't want to tell me, I can look now that the vision is in the past and see it myself."

He didn't know why he said that. Rachel never let him use his gift to review her visions before.

And yet, she sucked in a deep breath and peered up at him before saying, "Are you sure you want to see?"

He couldn't believe she was willing to trust him so easily, especially with a destiny mark. He brushed her hair back from her face. "If it will help you, I will look."

She nodded and closed her eyes. He placed his hands on both sides of her neck, cradling her jaw. His gaze lingered on her lips; he wanted to kiss her in that moment. Instead, he reached for the fountain of his power and allowed it to flow to the tips of his fingers and seep into Rachel. She leaned heavily against him and moaned as her energy coiled around his, pulling toward her heart and the coupling bond. Hesitantly, he moved the energy from her chest to her mind, searching for the vision. He found it alongside the memory of their kiss in the tunnel. He could easily reach for that memory and see how she felt about it—and him—but he didn't. The vision played like segmented clips because of the future's flexibility. The fear Rachel experienced during the vision filled him, causing his skin to break out in goose flesh.

He hadn't seen Leora in weeks; her belly was so round! He guessed that her pregnancy had come to term faster than normal because of her power. Her belly glowed blue, and then she dropped to the ground in a pool of blood as she screamed. The vision rippled, just as Rachel had said. The future could be changed, but how?

"The baby. It's stronger than Leora," he said.

"It may kill her before it is even born," Rachel said as she tightened her hold on him. "I'm not sure how long we have."

·●○⌣○●·

Rachel masked her inner turmoil with a deceptively calm facade. Foreboding thoughts crept in slowly, suffocating her with the heaviness of the vision. Her heartbeat was erratic, and a wave of hysteria threatened to drown her. They needed to find Darron and Tabitha, get out of the cavern, and go back to Leora.

She took a deep breath and stepped out of Chad's embrace. He nodded and went to the door. He knew what had to be done; dealing with the Lost and Chad's mark was a problem for tomorrow. Besides, she didn't believe Darron and Tabitha would find anything about the destiny mark in some book in a library. If her instincts were correct, Shamus didn't want to tell them what it really meant and had used the assignment to give her and Chad time alone.

Chad opened the door to leave, and she was at his side in an instant. They looked into the hall; the coast was clear. Rachel pulled in a breath, then blew it out and clenched her jaw as she considered the challenges that lay ahead. The most pressing one was getting Darron to Leora so that, no matter what the future held, Darron would be there to heal her. Then they could deal with the other crap.

"Follow me. I know a shortcut to Stephen's library."

He grabbed her hand and yanked her into a dark, shadowy corner. Chad then snapped his fingers and torchlight ignited around them, illuminating their path. He was still holding her hand, but she doubted he was even aware of it.

Chapter Thirteen

Chad gripped Rachel's hand and slowed his strides as they neared the library. His energy surged, and his gift washed over him like a cool river with a rigorous undercurrent. The past came alive, and because it could not be changed, he simply watched. He thought it would be a memory of Rachel's since he was holding her hand, but images of Gavin and Marcus consumed his mind. He stiffened and glanced at Rachel's hand in his, wondering how he was seeing an event from Gavin's perspective in this moment.

"Is everything all right?" Rachel rested a hand on his shoulder.

"The past grips me."

She squeezed. "I'm right here."

Chad nodded as he continued walking. The past didn't immobilize him as the future did Rachel; he got to keep one foot in the present while one was in the past. Gavin's world fell in around Chad, and he did his best to interpret it. It felt as if he was about to walk over a landmine, but there was nothing for it, so he would get through it however it was meant to be.

Gavin shoved Marcus off the front porch of his cottage, his brow furrowed. "We need to talk away from Leora."

Marcus shot him a death glare, black eyes dotted with red. He turned his back and stalked up the road, his large feet sinking into the accumulated snow as he snarled, "What is it, brother?"

Gavin pursed his lips, and his nostrils flared as he followed him. "I need your help."

Marcus stopped and turned to Gavin. "What can I do to help when my power is sealed?"

Gavin's amber eyes darkened, and the vein in his forehead pulsed. Marcus scoffed, then turned and stomped into the woods behind Gavin's home.

Gavin caught up to him and blurted out, "I am sorry."

Chad paused in the tunnel, surprised by what he was experiencing, but only for a moment. The stagnant scent of the tunnel eased, and he could feel the movement of fresh air. They were close to a corridor.

Marcus stopped. "What are you sorry for?"

"I am sorry that Leora had to lock away your power. It was the only way to reform our bloodbond and be brothers once more. I know we've caged you like an animal."

The concern in Gavin's tone made Marcus visibly shift uncomfortably.

Chad was intrigued; he'd never seen Marcus so vulnerable and normal. He paused at an opening in the passage where the dirt became black stone again so he could focus on Gavin's memory and try to understand why Gavin was having this conversation with Marcus.

"Leora has the right to see me suffer, and you know why." Marcus smirked.

Fire erupted from Gavin's hands. He stormed toward Marcus and subdued the fire. He snarled, "Yes, she does. And unless you wish to die, you should never bring those reasons to my attention again."

"Would you really do that, big brother? After all your

efforts to get me back in your life? To be bonded once more through blood? I think not."

Gavin stood toe-to-toe with Marcus, his dark eyes turning black with a single blink. "If you try to hurt Leora or my daughter, yes, I would."

Marcus laughed in Gavin's face. "What do you want, then…brother?"

"The baby will be born with her ability—like you. She will be able to erase time, or, in a way, hit the reset button. And not just for this life: for all times, and for every soul. No one will remember anything from any life."

Marcus's face reflected indifference, and that was when Chad realized that he wasn't surprised by that information. Did he know something they didn't? For the first time, Chad cursed the fact that the coupling bond was closed. Otherwise, he could share this memory with Rachel and she could try and help him figure out what he was missing.

"When Sapphire is born, I need you to take her to the sacred circle so Leora won't be able to sense her. I can't take her and leave Leora. She will be devastated enough as it is."

"Why?" Marcus asked, arching a single brow before sniffing the air. "Do I detect the scent of betrayal?" Gavin looked away. "I do. You would have me take your only child from the woman you love. But for what reason?" Marcus clicked his tongue as he thought. "To save her life and numb her soul. Interesting. You know if she finds out, she'll never forgive you."

Marcus smiled, and Chad felt like he would be sick. This couldn't be their plan: sending his granddaughter off with a madman.

"Why me? Can't you have one of the others take the child?"

Marcus led Gavin to a small copse of pine trees and

stared at the heavy, gray clouds.

"She would be suspicious of anyone else. We will tell her Sapphire died and that you escaped while she gave birth. In her grief, she will not care about finding you." Gavin stepped closer to Marcus and placed a hand on his shoulder. Marcus peered at him, then at the hand on his shoulder. "You're the only one that can help Sapphire understand and control her gift." Gavin took hold of both of his brother's shoulders.

For a split-second, Chad saw compassion in Marcus that he hadn't seen since he was a boy. Maybe there was hope. Maybe Marcus still loved his brother.

"You have always been stronger than any of us will ever know. If anyone can help my daughter—your niece— it's you. I need your help, brother."

Marcus brushed off Gavin's hands and kept walking, his own hands stuffed in his pockets. "Why would I take her to the sacred circle? There are better places to hide her."

"I would like to be able to see her from time to time. I am sure the others would like to as well. But Leora can't know until you think Sapphire can control her gift. I had a guy from town do me a favor and drop off some supplies to rebuild the cabin."

"I think you are making a terrible mistake," Marcus said drily.

Gavin's expression hardened. "Why?"

Marcus stopped beneath a tall evergreen. "I learned to blink."

Gavin frowned. "Blink?"

"I can travel anywhere I want to go with just a thought. I only have to think of the person or the place I want to see, blink, and then I am there. It is something I have been developing over the last few lifetimes."

"You can teleport?" Gavin stared past him, deep in

thought.

Marcus looked back at the house with an expression Chad couldn't read, then jogged up to the small ridge in the distance. Gavin stayed close beside him. Before they reached the ridge, a scream tore through the air. Marcus froze and tilted his head as if contemplating something.

"Leora." Gavin took off, forgetting all about Marcus.

After another scream, Marcus cringed as if he felt the physical pain that inspired the cry for help.

Chad started to run down the tunnel, tugging Rachel along with him. They needed to get Darron and get the hell out of there. The memory shifted, and Chad stopped.

Leora wandering down the stairs, then stumbling into the wall.

She gripped her belly and looked down. "What's wrong, little one?"

Leora's skin began to glow as she wrapped herself in energy, trying to calm the baby. She dropped to one knee, still leaning against the wall. She scanned the room, desperately looking for help even as she amped up her power.

"Be still, Sapphire. You're going to hurt yourself. Please be still," Leora said as she panted. She moved to rest on both knees and sank back on her haunches, slowly rocking back and forth for her unborn daughter. "Good girl. Thank you."

Tears fell as she gazed at her belly, but she wiped them away. After a short while, Leora rose to her feet and shuffled to the kitchen. With shaking hands, she took a mug from the cabinet and placed it on the counter. Suddenly, her stomach glowed blue, and then red spots dotted Leora's T-shirt. She touched the fabric and raised her hand to inspect it closer. Blood.

A scream of horror ripped from her throat as she held her side and sank to the floor. She screamed and screamed as her stomach glowed brighter. By then, her shirt was soaked in blood, and it had begun to pool around her.

"Please, Creator, let my baby live. Give her a chance." Her head dropped to the floor. "Darron, I need you! Come back, before it is too late!"

"Leora!" Gavin shouted.

He ran down the hall toward the stairs, but stopped in the doorway when he found Leora crumpled in a heap on the floor. His gaze landed on the soft, blue glow surrounding her belly. He sank to his knees and reached out a hand as if to touch her stomach, but pulled his hand back and stared at it.

"You're killing her. You're killing your mother, Sapphire. If she dies, you die. I'm going to drain your power. Don't resist."

A few moments later, Gavin pulled his hand back, his brow furrowed with confusion. He glanced at Leora's round belly, gasped, and jumped to his feet. He bumped into the wall as he rushed down the hall, found the phone, and dialed 911.

"There's a woman in my home. She's bleeding. Please hurry."

He hung up and raced back to the kitchen, then gently gathered Leora in his arms.

"Shit." Chad started running once more. "We have to go—now."

"What is it?" Rachel asked.

"It's Leora."

"Did you see something?" She tugged at his arm. "Chad?"

He tugged her along, fear forcing him to sprint. After a few minutes, they entered the library.

"This is bullshit. I can't find anything," Darron said as he shoved a book back onto a shelf.

"Oh, get over it. Did you think this was going to be easy?"

Tabitha wrinkled her nose and ran her finger over the spines of each book in front of her, then walked over to a large, oak desk to consult an open book on top of a pile of others.

"Death shall descend upon the soul marked for eternal death. The soul shall be carried to the heavens, where the Creator will pass judgment. The destiny mark can only be placed upon a soul that has been stained by the darkest evil . . . " Her voice trailed off. "This is about the destiny mark. Why is it at the top of the pile?"

"Death shall descend . . . " Darron pointed to himself. "I'm death. Stained by the darkest evil . . . " He looked up and rushed toward Chad. "What did you do?"

"We'll talk about it later. Right now, we have to go," Chad said.

Tabitha continued reading. "A destiny mark can only be removed by the purest heart at judgment. Then, fate will be rewritten." Tabitha shook her head. "I don't understand. If the Creator passes judgment, what is this garbage about the purest heart?"

Tabitha glanced at Shamus, who was expressionless, but peering closely at Chad.

Before anyone could explain anything, black mist poured around Darron as he lifted off the ground. Black ink twisted under his skin, and the color drained from his eyes.

"What is happening? What did you do, Chad?"

"There's no time to explain. Leora needs us."

Darron grabbed Chad's arm and the mist instantly consumed both of them. Rachel reached out for them, but they vanished.

Chapter Fourteen

"No, no, no." Panic gripped Rachel as soon as Darron and Chad disappeared. Chad had seen something, something that scared him. "No . . . what if it's already too late? That's why he didn't want to tell me. He saw it. It already happened." She shook her head. "No, if Leora is dead, the Council members would have their power back." She looked at Shamus. "Do you feel a shift? Do they have their power?"

Shamus breathed and faced the door. "No. There is no change."

Tabitha was at her side. "What the fuck just happened?"

Shamus pulled Tabitha away from Rachel. "Darron is Death; he has taken Chad to be judged."

She thought they would have more time. She ran shaking hands through her hair and tried to focus. If Chad was facing judgment, then their time together was over. There was nothing she could do—nothing at all. She stole a glance at Shamus; his expression was grim. She didn't know how long Darron would be gone, or if he would return at all. Leora was going to die if she didn't do something. But what could she do? Even if she managed to get to her in a day or two, she couldn't heal her without Darron. Who else had the power to heal?

Shakily, she grabbed Tabitha. "We have to go to Stephen."

"Why? What's going on?" Tabitha yelled.

"We can't do anything for Chad and Darron, but we have to help Leora. I saw her in a vision, and I believe Chad saw something as well. She's going to die if we don't get to her. Stephen will know what to do."

"Fuck . . . but what about Chad and Darron? We can't leave them," Tabitha said, locking her fingers behind her head.

Two large hands gently wrapped around Rachel's waist and turned her around. Shamus's beautiful eyes held understanding and compassion. "I'm sorry about Chad."

"What the hell are you two babbling about? What am I missing?" Tabitha said.

Rachel was grateful for his concern, but there was no time to dwell on it. "I need to see Stephen. *Now.*"

Shamus touched a small spot on the wall next to her and a hidden door opened. "This is the fastest way to get to him. Follow me."

He took her hand and pulled her into the darkness with Tabitha following close behind them.

·•○～○•·

Darkness captured every cell in Chad's body and pulled him apart. He felt nothing; he simply existed in space. Millions of pieces of himself drifted into the ether. Death was with him, protecting him, taking him home. It had been far too long since he'd been with the Creator. Guilt for his sins pushed the pieces of him further apart in a futile effort to escape.

Suddenly, death was no longer with him. The darkness vanished. He was light, strength, and power. His cells came together, and he was whole.

He stood in the center of the sacred circle. The blood-stones that created the space were white beacons of light. They hummed, alive with power far beyond his comprehension. The cabin was no longer there. The dead carcasses of trees that once grew beyond the circle were alive again with lush, thick leaves and pine needles that radiated golden light. Soft grass touched his bare feet. Glancing down, he realized he was naked.

His eyes drifted to the spot where he'd almost died, where Leora awakened and seized her birthright. After so much loss, pain, and suffering, she never gave up. A knot formed in his throat. He should have believed . . .

He dropped to his knees and lowered his head to the ground. Emotions tore through him like the strongest winds the earth had ever felt. There was no hiding from their devastation as the sorrow of a thousand lives lived in pain and fear broke free. Tears fell for every fear, every lost dream, and every hope shattered. He poured himself out until there was nothing left.

He simply was, and was not.

"I am ours. Always and forever."

He lifted his head. Nothing could have prepared him for what he saw before him.

Chapter Fifteen

One second Rachel rushed down a tunnel alongside Shamus and Tabitha, and in the next, she was blinded by the purest light. Throwing up a hand to shield her eyes, Rachel tried not to panic. Catching her breath, she blinked hard to try and get her eyes to adjust.

A familiar hum of energy caught her attention. She gasped when she caught sight of the bloodstones. The area was beautiful again, not scorched and dying as it was the last time she saw it. Her wide eyes drank in the grass, the trees, and the stones, all glowing with brilliant amber light. The sky was the palest blue with soft, wispy clouds stretching as far as she could see.

Is this heaven?

Wonderment pulled up the corner of her mouth. Wind wrapped around her and she giggled. The scent of grass and sunlight filled her lungs. She sucked it in, but a dark thought formed and seized her mind.

Am I dead?

Spinning around, she spotted a crumpled figure in the distance. Apprehensively, she approached the figure, then reached down and touched his shoulder. Green eyes shot up and held her gaze with an intensity she'd never seen before.

"Oh, Chad." She shook her head when she remembered what Tabitha and Darron read in the library. "Oh, Creator . . . I do not wish to judge. I cannot be the purest heart. I don't want to do this." Her tears fell freely, and Chad rose. The black mark was once again visible over his heart, but he cupped her face and wiped her cheek with his thumb. "How did we get here, Chad?"

She sniffled and studied those green eyes; they were the richest, brightest green she'd ever seen. A storm rolled in behind them.

"I'm not sure, but I am glad you're here. This is my chance to ask for your forgiveness," he said. She smiled weakly and took his hand in hers. "I was marked because I lost hope in us, in our purpose. I stopped believing that we could make it through anything as long as we were together."

He looked away, but she touched his face and gently brought him back to her. "It's okay . . . "

"I wanted more from this life. I wanted more from you." His green eyes darkened. "In this latest life, before I awakened, I knew unconditional love. I had parents and a brother who would die for me, and I for them."

"How could something so beautiful garner you the destiny mark?"

Her fingers trailed down his chest as she fought the overwhelming need to be closer to him. He took her hand and dropped it as he stepped back. Nervous, she ran a hand through her hair and tucked a strand behind her ear. She watched as tears collected in his eyes and he clenched his jaw.

"I knew love for the first time outside of Leora and Darron's love for me as their father. The thought of being with you in this life after all the pain we'd already been through suffocated me. The destiny mark was my way out. With it, I would never have to repeat this cycle of loss, loneliness, and suffering." He turned his back to her. "I made a deal with Marcus when he came for me after I awakened. I met him at the sacred circle, knowing Leora and Darron would come for her awakening." He peered at her over his shoulder. "Marcus did not stab me. I stabbed myself so he could pass the bloodstones."

Her heart beat faster, and her ears rang as she shook her head. The Elapsed Seer she knew would never do such a thing. "No . . . you love Leora and Darron. You would never put them in harm's way. You're their father."

"Not in this life. And never again," he said sharply. "My time here is over."

She shoved him as hard as she could. "You're an asshole!"

He turned to face her and she kicked him square in the gut. He bent forward, holding his stomach. As soon as he straightened back up, she started to slap him, but curled her fingers into a fist at the last second and slugged him in the jaw with everything she had. His head snapped to the side.

"How could you betray your family? Why didn't you just tell me how you felt?"

"Would you have listened? Every time I touched you so we could conceive Darron or Leora, I saw memories of Shamus. He was the one that lay with you, not me—never me."

She lifted her chin as fear and shame merged within her.

"You never wanted me. You wanted children, a family. I saw that, so I gave it to you."

Stifling the sob in her throat, she wanted to protest, but she couldn't. He was right; she wouldn't have listened. She was stuck in the past, and she had not wanted to move forward until very recently. This was her fault. She never gave him a chance. Why would anyone want to go through that again and again?

She blurted out, "I was in love with Shamus."

"I know. I knew even before we left the cavern. I knew before the bonding."

She put up a hand. "Let me finish. When we were allowed to leave the cavern for a single year, I waited for him, but he never came. I thought he didn't want me, and it broke my heart. The life the Creator offered was something that I would never have with Shamus, so I took it even though I felt broken." Tears ran freely down her cheeks. "I thought if *he* couldn't love me, why would you?" Chad reached for her, but she pushed his hand away. "Discovering that Shamus left to care for Tabitha changed how I saw the situation."

Chad's hand fell back to his side. "Do you still love him?"

Rachel was afraid to move, to breathe. So much of her heart rested on her next words, but she didn't know if she could form them on her tongue.

"I thought I did."

"I see." His voice was emotionless; it chilled her.

She touched his arm gently and decided to take a chance. "When I saw him again, my eyes were opened. I watched him interact with Darron and realized that he could never understand what I've been through…what we have been through." Slowly, she stepped closer to him and took his hand. She couldn't look at him because her heart hurt too much, but she continued. "I thought it was because of him that I couldn't show you love, but the truth is, I thought I wasn't worthy of being loved at all. I was broken, and you deserved someone who was whole."

She felt the tendons in his hand flex and forced herself to look at him. There was an invitation in the smoldering depths of his eyes.

"You can be with him now," Chad said.

"I don't want Shamus." Her lips brushed his as she spoke. He didn't push her away. Instead, he rested a hand on her hip. "I want you. I always have. I was afraid you wouldn't want me."

He tenderly cupped her face in his hands. "You're worthy of so much love."

"Of your love?" she asked, uncertain, but hopeful.

Claiming her lips, he crushed her to him. She locked him in her embrace and unleashed her passion. Her heart hammered against her ribs as a shiver of hot desire coursed through her. His mouth covered hers hungrily and his fingers gripped her. Every cell of her body was fully aware of his presence.

Lifting her off her feet, he spun her in a small circle and smiled against her lips. He brushed his fingers tenderly through her hair. He released her to stare into her eyes. She saw a myriad of emotions pass through his, and her body warmed.

"Thank you for setting me free."

"What? What do you mean?" She clung to his waist. "Chad?"

His lips barely touched hers, his tenderness heartbreaking and perfect. He stepped back with a tempting smile; he had never looked more handsome or so strong to her.

"You have always been the purest of heart." With every step he took, the constant pull from their coupling bond eased. "Just because you're broken doesn't mean you have to stay broken."

The black mark over his heart vanished, and then, so did he.

A blinding light struck Rachel through the heart. Every cell in her body felt as if it was being purged of its essence. A scream tore from her lips, her arms flung back, and she dropped to her knees. A golden orb emerged from her chest and as it left her, so did the pain. The coupling bond—the power that joined her and Chad—had been removed. And just like Chad, the orb faded away.

"No . . . no . . . it's not his fault. Please forgive him. Don't take him!" she sobbed. "No, please!"

Next, she was back in the tunnel right behind Tabitha and Darron as if she'd never left. She pulled in a shaking breath trying to process what had just happened. *Chad is gone.*

Chapter Sixteen

Rachel had never been to the Two Tunnels, but she'd always thought it would be a beautiful room with white marble walls spattered with amethyst, lepidolite, and rose quartz. In reality, the main room where the Two Tunnels flowed out was nothing more than crude clay and stone pulled from the ground. It was just another rough cavern, complete with dirt walls, gritty floors, and ancient air—not the dream she'd seen in her mind.

A soft glow came from the ceiling and as she looked up, she could see the souls gathering. Her jaw dropped, and she toddled to the center of the cavern. Hundreds of thousands of differently colored orbs shot like stars across the dark ceiling.

An orange orb and a pink one glided down and stopped in front of her, then circled her to touch her cheeks, chin, and forehead, then skim down her nose. Her father's handsome face flashed through her mind, and she gasped.

"Dad." The orb tinkled as it bobbed up and down, then zipped around her. Tears burned in her eyes as the pink orb hovering nearby sailed forward. Rachel reached up to touch it, and the orb came to rest in her palm as the image of her smiling mother anchored in her mind next. "Mom!"

The orb rose from her hand and glanced across her

cheek like a kiss. Then the two orbs danced together, glowing brighter than the rest. They each touched her cheeks softly, and she closed her eyes and smiled as love warmed every cell of her body from the inside out. It filled her, lifting her soul in her chest. Stillness took hold as the chaos of the past few months melted away. Her mind was cleared, and she knew everything would be fine if she led with love.

Rachel sat in that quite moment, waiting for something she didn't fully comprehend. When she opened her eyes, the two orbs slowly floated back to the larger group. She touched her cheeks, feeling very much like the girl she was before she lost her parents: innocent and unstained by time. Her parents were together; they were safe.

Holy crap. Mom and Dad: I can't believe it.

All the orbs in the cavern sailed around like a twisting cyclone. It was the most beautiful thing Rachel had ever seen. She only remembered Tabitha and Darron were there with her when she heard a laugh.

Shamus stepped forward and batted the orbs away. "Go and wait."

The orbs drifted back, and most of their lights dimmed noticeably. Her parents' lights stayed bright and close by, as if they wanted her to see them and know they were with her. Another tear ran down her face.

"I miss you. I love you," she whispered so softly the others couldn't hear her.

"Stephen!" Shamus called out.

A figure emerged from a nearby tunnel. Dark eyes greeted her; their owner's displeasure and impatience were evident by the red dotting their centers. Stephen looked the same as he did the last time she saw him; his plaid kilt swung around his knees, and his long, black hair was braided along the sides of his head. Plaid was draped across his otherwise bare chest, and his boots were laced up over his calves. Shamus bowed and placed a fist over his heart, keeping his eyes down.

Stephen waltzed past him and stood in front of Rachel. His large finger pointed at Rachel, and she withered.

"What have you done?" he roared.

Rachel cast her gaze to the ground, unable to face the implied meaning behind his rage. Stephen knew about Chad. How could he not? He was the Keeper of Souls, so he knew when the destiny mark had been placed. He might have been the one the Creator asked to place it. He could even know about her role in Chad's judgment.

"He is gone because of you," Stephen growled as he began to pace.

Darron stepped up beside her, black mist twisting and turning beneath his skin. "It wasn't her fault. The moment Chad entered the library"—he scrubbed a hand over his agonized face—"I was consumed. My power amplified so fast . . . I just took him. I didn't even know where I was taking him."

Stephen's eyes faded to reveal his normal gray ones, but otherwise he appeared unaffected by Darron's confession as he pointed at Rachel. "This is what you let them believe? How could you let this happen?"

He reached out and lifted her off the ground with one powerful hand. Shamus stiffened, but didn't go to her defense. Rachel gripped his forearm for support, but she didn't fight. She knew better than to try that with the High Priest.

"I didn't mean for it to happen. I didn't know how he felt."

Stephen shook her.

"Let her go," Darron hissed.

His skin was black, his eyes were white, and mist filled the room. The orbs of light huddled together, almost as if they were trembling. Tabitha had a knife pointed at Darron's throat in case she had to try and control him, but she looked worried when Darron's body went rigid.

"Silence, Soul Thief. It's not your place to speak."

Immediately, the black mist and the white eyes vanished. Tabitha lowered her blade, tipping her head to the side.

Stephen blew out a breath as if he were dealing with ignorant children. "Do you know what will happen now that Chad has been taken?"

Rachel nodded as best as she could with his hand under her chin. "Our time is over. The coupling bond has been cut. He will not be reborn."

Stephen tossed her to the ground and turned away from them all. "Nothing will stop the Council from coming for you all now."

Shamus knelt beside Rachel, tenderly brushing her hair away from her face and inspecting her neck. "That wasn't necessary, my lord."

Rachel pushed his hand away and got to her feet, using Darron and Tabitha for support. "I cannot change what's happened, but I can try and change what will be. We have to go. We have to get to Leora. She needs Darron."

Suddenly, her body was squeezed, making it difficult to breathe.

"I didn't say you could go. We're not done here," Stephen said. "The destiny mark may have been lifted, but I am the Keeper of Souls. If you wish to pass through the Two Tunnels for your next life, you will listen."

Rachel met Shamus's and Darron's panicked expressions with one of her own. Tabitha just looked pissed off as she glared at her father. It seemed that they, too, were being held by Stephen's power.

"The Creator's coupling bond has been lifted, but at

what cost?" Stephen said in a placid tone as he circled her. "What about your family? Your soul?"

"Please, Chad is gone, but I need to get back to Leora. I had a vision." Her throat felt tight as she tried to plead her case. "She's going to die if we don't get to her."

A heartless laugh rumbled from Stephen's chest. "And you think you can save her? Haven't you figured it out yet? She always dies; that's the way it is meant to be."

"No, it isn't," Rachel said.

"Oh, but it is. And it's because of you." Stephen opened his hand and a ball of green light began to grow. "Because you couldn't let go of the past to love the Elapsed Seer—a man chosen for you by the Creator for his courage, his ability to love, and his belief in others—you are unworthy to live another life."

Rachel's blood pumped so fast she was afraid it would shoot from every orifice.

"Stephen, please. Don't," Shamus said.

"The Elapsed Seer will not be the only one who pays for this sin today."

The green light rippled and swirled like the surface of the sun. Green flames traveled down his forearm.

Rachel's body trembled. "I didn't know! I didn't know I was making Chad suffer, or that I would push him to such extremes. Keep me here if you must, but please let Darron go and give Leora and her baby a chance at this life."

The ball of green light was so bright she had to turn away. Stephen's arm rose and then swiftly dropped. The ball of light slammed into her chest, and her very veins screamed as Stephen's power coursed through her cells. The taste of toxic gas coated her tongue.

"You, too, shall receive a destiny mark and be judged."

He held his arms straight out in front of him with his hands pointed at her chest. He twisted and turned his palms as his power tore hers apart and screams ripped from Rachel's lungs. Her vision blurred, and suddenly, her head felt very heavy—too heavy to even hold up.

"Let her go," Tabitha commanded, her face pinched by the depth of her concentration.

Suddenly, Stephen's power dimmed and a look of satisfaction settled over him. "Stay out of this, Tabitha. Your power to influence is nothing compared to mine. You're wasting your energy on me."

"Father, please don't do this. I don't want to use my power on you at all. We must get to Leora."

"You will not go anywhere with them." Rachel gasped as Stephen's hold on them tightened. "You will stay here with me."

It happened so quickly, Rachel thought she was seeing things. Tabitha's skin turned black and her eyes went white; she'd tapped into Darron's ability through the coupling bond.

"Let us go," Tabitha commanded with a voice that sounded like a banshee.

"Tabitha, you don't know what you are doing with his power!" Shamus yelled.

"He called my bonded a Soul Thief. Sounds intriguing. I would like to try and steal a soul."

"No," ordered Shamus.

Stephen held up his free hand to silence him, almost as if he wanted to see what she would do. In a puff of black mist, Tabitha stepped through the hold her father had on her and right through his body as if he were made of dust. When she emerged on the other side, she held a small, green orb in her hand.

"Interesting," she purred as she studied the orb.

The hold on their bodies disappeared and Rachel collapsed to the floor. Shamus and Darron looked at each other, neither knowing what to do. Tabitha hissed as if she were trying and failing to laugh. She stared at the orb and then looked back at her father's body.

"I don't think I will be staying, Father. I did want to talk with you about the barrier you placed in my mind to hold my other gifts at bay, and about my mother, but now you've pissed me off. You can't keep me here." She sighed. "How does it feel to truly have no soul? Or does it feel like every other day of your existence?"

Stephen's body sank to its knees, its mouth agape and the light in his eyes missing. Tabitha squeezed the green orb and her body shook.

"Am I everything you could've asked for in a daughter, Father? You tried so hard to make me an obedient little girl." She squeezed the orb harder, and Stephen's body teetered before it dropped to the ground on its side. "You've nearly killed me several times in an attempt to see if I would submit to you and the Council members." She knelt in front of the body, and her tone took on a deadly edge. "How's that working out for you?"

"Tabitha, stop this game you're playing." An authoritative female voice vibrated throughout the room, seemingly coming from everywhere at once. Rachel didn't know where to look. When it came again, it was softer and sounded closer to the group. "There are more important things to do than right your father's wrongs. He is what he is: lonely and tired."

A tall, dreamy woman stepped out of one of the glowing orbs. Her black hair fell to her waist, and her eyes were as gray as Tabitha's. The woman wore black leather pants and a matching chest piece; it was the feminine equivalent of Shamus's armor. She reached out to touch Tabitha's cheek, but never reached it.

Tabitha lifted her chin in defiance but her body shook

violently as she clutched her father's soul. "He deserves this for what he has done to me, to Shamus, and to my bonded's family. He is supposed to be the best of all the souls, but he is the worst. Who allows these kinds of tragedies? I'm ashamed to call him my father."

"You're right, my daughter. He does deserve to die . . . and he will. Just not today."

The black skin of death faded, and Tabitha stared into those eyes that matched hers. "I saw you in one of the memories behind the barrier of my mind."

"I'm Serena, but *Mother* would suit me better, my girl."

A tear ran down Tabitha's cheek as she released her father's soul and went to embrace her mother, but passed through her. Tabitha let out a cry.

The green orb glided back to Stephen and anchored itself in his chest. Taking a deep breath, he stood tall and powerful once again. "You're not the only one who can project. I can project outside of myself and make you see anything I want."

The image of Serena disappeared. Tabitha spun around and drew her knife to strike at her father. Her blade caught her father in the back and sank deep. He grunted but didn't fall.

Shamus unsheathed his sword and stood between him. "If you are wise, you would leave this place before I am forced to kill you all."

"Oh, don't be such an old-school warrior, Shamus," Tabitha spat as she put her knife away. "I only wounded him, and he deserved it. How awful must he be to project my mother just to get his way?"

Darron took Tabitha's hand and kissed it. Rachel could see tears pooling in her eyes. Her father had wounded her as well, so it did seem like an even trade, but they had to get out of this place. It was toxic.

Shamus's green eyes cut across each of their faces, one at a time. He set his jaw and pressed his lips, but his gaze drifted to the floor as he pulled in a breath. Then glanced back up. He was willing to protect them from Stephen, but his loyalty would always be with Stephen. That was his purpose.

"Go to Leora. And good luck."

"You don't have to tell me twice. I'm out of this damn place. Assholes are everywhere here, and being one myself, that is saying something," Darron said.

He took Tabitha's hand and marched them out of the Two Tunnels. Rachel moved to leave as well, but paused. She locked eyes with Shamus and gave him a small nod of thanks. She would never see him again—not in this life, and not in her dreams.

The orange and pink orbs zipped down and spun around her so fast that they disturbed her hair, then touched her cheeks. A memory of them locked in an embrace came to her.

"Love you," she whispered. The memory morphed so that it was her, Chad, Darron, Tabitha, Leora, Gavin, Marcus, and Sapphire all together, all laughing. It was beautiful. "Thank you."

They danced around once more and then floated off. Rachel left and didn't look back.

Chapter Seventeen

Rachel rushed down the mountainside, slipping numerous times over the icy snow. Exhausted and pushed well beyond her physical limits, she still moved faster. The burning in her right breast had begun the second Stephen touched the ball of green light to her skin.

She could see Darron's Explorer in the distance as twilight fell. Their descent had been much faster than the journey up, and she thanked the Creator for this small favor.

Tabitha and Darron hadn't spoken a word since they left the cavern, though she was certain they were communicating through the coupling bond. Both wore expressions of indifference, so they were probably hiding something, but she didn't care. Leora was the only thing that mattered to her in that moment, the only thing she could think about. If she thought about Chad and what happened to him and how that would one day happen to her as well, she would fall apart. That wasn't an option.

An hour later, the sun was setting and they'd reached the vehicle. Darron unlocked it, and Tabitha and Rachel climbed in. Darron stood by the driver's door, his skin inky black and the veins in his neck bulging as he started to shake. Rachel's chest burned hotter; his eyes locked with hers. His gaze was intense, and one she'd never seen directed at her before. She instinctively scooted back in her seat. Tabitha drew her blade and blocked Darron's view.

Rachel had taken note of Tabitha's protectiveness after her awakening; she'd been her protector when no one else was. She would always have a place in her heart for Tabitha.

"He's struggling to control his power now that you are marked," Tabitha said, watching him strain to hold himself together.

Rachel closed her eyes and blew out a breath, wondering what the Creator's plan was. "It's okay, Darron. I understand if you need to take me for judgment."

A minute passed, and then Darron growled, climbed into the truck, and started the vehicle. Still, Tabitha's blade never left her hand, nor did she shrink away from Darron.

They pulled onto the highway, and Rachel kept her eyes fixed on the chilling white world being steadily swallowed by darkness. As beautiful as it was, there was a sense of loneliness and danger about it.

Snow began to fall as fractured thoughts rampaged in Rachel's mind, making it difficult to focus on anything specific. She'd come here to save Chad, despite her doubts about their coupling bond and to see Shamus, to try to understand what all these lifetimes of pain meant. She bit the inside of her cheek until blood coated her tongue. The taste reminded her of how vulnerable they all were now that Chad was gone, and how easily life could be taken from them. The guilt she felt for not loving Chad pushed her deeper into her seat as she closed her eyes to focus her thoughts on Leora. She had to see something that could help, something she'd missed earlier.

The chill of her power moved through her and called her deeper into herself. She gave herself over to it completely. Her mind drifted with the ebb and flow of her power, but the future refused to reveal itself.

Without warning, Rachel was ripped from the chill of her power as her body slammed into the roof of the truck, then back down to the seat. Glass exploded all around her, and then she was flying through the air and landing in the middle of an intersection, where her body folded in on itself. Her ears rang and she tried to breathe, but her lungs would not expand.

She blinked blurry eyes and saw that the truck had landed upside down. Arms dangled from the front passenger seat, and blood coated her mouth as she called, "Tabitha? Darron?"

The sound of a vehicle door opening drew her attention. A small female figure came into focus against the glow of the headlights. Every part of Rachel's body rebelled as she tried to sit up.

"Thought you could get away so easily, my lovelies?" the woman said, her voice reverberating as if more than one person was trying to speak through her.

The woman came close enough that Rachel could tell she was dirty and covered in blood. Four others emerged from the only other vehicle around and circled them like a pack of wolves. Rachel didn't recognize any of them.

Forcing her arms and legs to move, she started to crawl across the ground. Pebbles and glass dug into her hands. Every muscle in her back and shoulders pulled her toward the Explorer, where Tabitha hung out of the cab, unconscious. She clenched her jaw to combat the sharp pain shooting down her back to her legs. Where was Darron? Was he thrown out of the truck like her?

"With the Elapsed Seer out of the picture, the time has finally come to kill all of you." The woman bent down and studied Rachel with her black eyes. "Come."

She grabbed her hair and dragged her closer to Tabitha with far more strength than someone of her size should have at their disposal. Glass tore into Rachel's back as she struggled to rip her hair free. Who was this woman?

The glimmer of a blade flashed in the glow of the headlights before she was yanked to her feet and felt the knife brush against her throat. The men closed in on her, but the woman ordered them back with her many voices.

Voices. Shit—she's one of the Lost being possessed by the Council.

The spot on Rachel's chest burned hotter than before and she screamed into the night as she struggled against the woman, whose breath smelled like a rotting corpse. The cold blade sank into Rachel's throat. As a trail of warm blood trickled down her neck, a black cloud emerged behind one of the men.

"The only one who's getting killed is you."

Darron moved so fast that Rachel could barely see him. He swiftly stole a gun from one of the men and shot him in the head, then turned to the others.

"Come, Soul Hunter, you can do better than that," the woman said.

His white eyes glowed red, and fear seized Rachel. Was Darron coming for her, or for the weak soul of this woman who was possessed by Council members?

He shrieked, and the black cloud expanded around him until she couldn't see anything. The blade at her throat dropped. She blinked on her night vision to find that Darron had heaved the woman up and over his shoulder. She landed on her neck with a bone-crunching thud. He hunched over with his hands on his knees, breathing heavily.

Rachel took a step toward Darron and his head snapped up, his red eyes locking on her just before he rushed at her.

··●○∾○●··

Mr. Cross, the old man who once took Gavin in and watched over Leora when she came to Anne's inn months ago, shuffled into the hospital. His glasses were slipping off his nose, and his heart raced faster than two dogs fighting. The smell of death was so strong he was nauseated within seconds. He shot out a web of energy and sensed her stillness in the thread that bonded her to the Creator. He had felt her distress, as well as Gavin's. Something was terribly wrong. Leora's energy signature was as chaotic as a palm tree in a tropical storm, and Mr. Cross didn't sense Gavin anywhere near her; but that didn't make sense. Gavin was never far from his bonded.

A nurse bumped into him and nearly knocked him off balance. She gripped his elbow to help keep him upright. "I'm sorry."

"I'm fine." He winked and pushed his glasses up on the bridge of his nose. "Thanks for saving me from a fall."

The nurse smiled. "Can I help you with something?"

"Yes, a young woman came in here a few hours ago. She's in her twenties and has red hair and blue eyes. Her name is Lily McMaster. I'm a friend."

"Let me check for you. It has been busy today."

Mr. Cross scrambled after the nurse to a desk down the hall. The dread he felt that the world could lose the Awakener even after everything she'd accomplished in this life made it difficult to remain in this form or to be objective when it came to the Council. Even as the thought crossed his mind, his back stretched and he stood a little taller. Mr. Cross cursed under his breath; now was not the time to lose control of his power. With the web of energy still cast throughout the hospital, Mr. Cross felt a soft vibration that brought forth images of a heavenly garden of life: vibrant greens and countless species of plants covered in flowers.

"There's a woman here who doesn't have a name on her chart. What did you say her name was?" said the nurse as she frowned at the computer screen.

It took a moment for what the nurse said to sink in. Mr. Cross shook his head and said, "Lily McMaster."

"Let me take you to her to confirm her identity."

"Yes, let me see her. Who brought her in?"

"She came by ambulance."

Mr. Cross hurried behind the nurse, more worried than ever. When they approached a small room on the third floor, a warm, tingling sensation urged him forward, and in his eagerness, he bumped into the nurse.

"Sorry about an old man's clumsiness, love."

"You're fine. Here she is."

When the door opened, Mr. Cross's arms fell to his side. It was her. Leora's face was screwed up with pain. Blankets were piled on top of her, making it difficult to see what was wrong; if it wasn't for her low energy signature, he wouldn't have believed she was even still breathing.

"Yes," he said as he nodded and rushed to her side. He pushed a red curl from her sweaty forehead and then tenderly took her hand in his. "This is Lily McMaster."

"Well, it's a relief to put a name to the face."

"What's wrong with her?" he asked, noticing that her energy was twisting and turning around as if seeking help.

"They're running some tests, but there's not a lot to go on. They're both stable for now."

"They?" he asked, his brow furrowing.

The nurse shot him a questioning glance. "She's about nine months pregnant."

His jaw dropped. His hold on his power wavered, and he felt his hands grow larger.

Pregnant. Why didn't Gavin tell me?

But Mr. Cross knew why. Gavin hadn't visited much

or called since Leora, Darron, and Tabitha came to town. However, Gavin was the closet thing to a son Mr. Cross had had in a millennia. He sure as hell was keeping tabs on Gavin and the others, though he became confused when the Hound's energy signature arrived. He was not a man to trust, even though Mr. Cross knew the Hound was once Gavin's brother.

He'd observed them for quite some time eight hundred years ago, give or take a decade. Gavin's arrival was a tipping point because he was important to the Creator. He'd been curious enough to travel just to see this new soul. Then the Hound arrived a few years later, although he was not the Hound then—just a boy with more power than he could control. Mr. Cross watched Gavin drain the Hound's energy and stabilize him. The poor boy did not understand the images running through his mind.

Mr. Cross blew out a shaky breath, thinking about what was to come. He'd seen Leora pregnant before in past lives, but he'd never felt or sensed the child. It was as though the Creator didn't want him to know about it.

"I'm sorry. You didn't know?" the nurse said, a trace of suspicion in her voice.

He struggled to come up with a lie to cover for his lack of knowledge. "No. I saw her a few months ago, but I guess she wasn't showing yet. We have spoken over the phone many times since then, but she didn't say anything. Probably wanted it to be a surprise and give an old man a heart attack."

Mr. Cross gave the woman his most nonthreatening, puppy dog look, and she immediately softened.

"Could I come back and get some information from you after I make my rounds?"

Relieved that she bought his lie so easily, he winked again. "You know where to find me."

As soon as the nurse left, he pushed his energy into Leora's body. His power rebounded with a jolt, and a razor-sharp pain zipped up his arm. He carefully pulled back the blankets to reveal her round belly. He stared at it for a long while, then gently rested his hand on it. A blue glow radiated from the life inside her.

It can't be . . .

He rested his other hand on Leora's belly and tried to fill her body, as well as the child's, with his energy once more. This time, there was no resistance. One heartbeat at a time, he shifted into his true form; the wrinkles on his face smoothed out, and he grew tall enough that he had to bend down to remain close. His hands became larger and his shoulders wider; golden-blond hair emerged from his bald head to hang over rich, blue eyes. Leora's body was weak, as was the child's, but the energy signature he'd been searching the world over for since the beginning of time was right in front of him.

Adam was an Observer, and the first soul to travel to this world; it was possible he'd be the last soul to remain. He was also the strongest, but he didn't dabble in the affairs of man. Revealing himself would mean that he was no longer an Observer, but a participant in the world he'd helped create.

The child reached out to him with her power. It circled him tenderly, just as his enveloped her in a cautious dance of forgotten love. Abruptly, he was locked in a tight embrace. Her energy seeped into his pores, and his body surrendered to the euphoria of her love. His knees buckled and he dropped to the ground, but carefully rested his forehead against Leora's belly.

"I've missed you," he whispered. The blue glow became a radiant gold, and he smiled with his entire being. "I've been waiting for you for so long."

•●○⌣○●•

The bloodstones glowed so brightly that Rachel couldn't look directly at them. Her shoulders sagged. Was this really happening? The bloodstones hummed so loudly they filled the air with energy, the likes of which she hadn't felt when she was summoned for Chad's judgment. The surrounding trees were lush and bright, with no hint of the destruction her last life had marked them with. Fresh air danced around her, lifting her matted hair, and the salty, metallic scent of blood reached her nose. She looked down at her bloody shirt and grimaced at the stinging reminder of being dragged across the pavement by her hair. She touched her throat, where the possessed woman had held a dagger. What was the Council doing? As far as she knew, Tabitha had been left behind in the Explorer.

Please be okay.

A chill crept up her spine as she turned to see Darron's red eyes staring at her. There was no cloud of black mist, no black skin—not here. Slowly, the red faded from his eyes, and then he blinked and peered around. She knew then that Darron would be her judge and jury, just as she had been for Chad.

"Why do you have that?" Darron pointed at her chest. "Why did Stephen give you that destiny mark?"

She swallowed. "It's my fault Chad's gone and that everything will change."

"What're you talking about?"

She studied Darron's concerned expression. He deserved the truth. "I never loved Chad . . . not in the way a wife loves a husband." She bit her quivering bottom lip. Her eyes darted anywhere but to Darron. "The thought of sharing another life without love was more than he could handle, so he made a deal with Marcus so he could pass the bloodstones and kill Leora and you."

"He would never do that."

"But he did . . . because of me. In every life, he tried to show me his love, and I turned away. I left him alone. If it weren't for you and Leora, I think he would have done something like this sooner."

"I don't believe you."

Suddenly, Darron was only an inch away from her. His eyes were tinged with black, giving away how his emotions were overwhelming him.

"I didn't believe it at first myself, but I understood why he would feel that way."

"My father would never sell Leora and me out. Not to Marcus, and not after everything he did to us." He pointed to her. "Maybe you, but not us. He loves us."

She stepped closer, and he moved back. "He does love you. He always has. *I* always have. This is not about your love, or his love for you." She pulled her collar down so Darron could see the destiny mark. "This is about him, me, the Creator, and our inability to love or trust ourselves or each other."

Darron ran a hand through his short, bristly hair. "Why didn't you love him? I mean, didn't the Creator pick you two because you were the best fit and because you could love each other?"

Rachel's gaze fell. It was true. She had thrown away the chance the Creator had given them. She wrapped her arms around herself and walked over to where their family home once stood. She could see Chad on the front porch with Leora on his lap as he whittled a piece of wood, and Darron was at his feet doing the same. She peered at the bloodstones near them. Gavin was there too, also whittling.

"Why didn't you love him?" Darron spun her around and squeezed her shoulder.

"I was in love with Shamus."

Darron let go of her. "That prick at the cavern? The one that let Tabitha be whipped?"

She nodded. "I loved him before your father and I were selected for the coupling bond."

She watched Darron's eyes flash with hate, confusion, and then finally, understanding. "He knew you loved someone else all this time, didn't he?"

She nodded again. "I've since realized that me not loving your father wasn't because of Shamus—not the way you're probably thinking. When Tabitha was born, Shamus vanished. I was broken. I didn't know why he left until I helped break the barrier in Tabitha's mind. All these years, I thought he didn't want me, and that pain prevented me from believing I was worthy of love. So, I never let your father in."

"Fuck me!" Darron said as he ran both hands down his face, looking very much like the boy he once was. "What a shit show. I knew we were all screwed up. I mean, how could we not be? But I didn't think it started off that way." He sighed heavily. "Mom, what am I supposed to do? I heard what Tabitha said in the library. I can't be the purest heart and remove the mark."

Rachel touched his cheek. "But you are. No one else could understand what not having love feels like, especially after finding Tabitha, bonding out of convenience, and then breaking that bond to reestablish it with true love."

Darron's eyes pooled with tears as the humming from the bloodstones grew louder. The air lifted her off the ground, and a brilliant white light wrapped around her.

Darron began to fade in a puff of black smoke, but before he disappeared completely, he touched her cheek and said, "I forgive you."

"Darron!" she whispered, reaching out to where he'd

been standing.

She would never see him again, or Leora. She dropped to the ground and saw Leora learning to walk as Darron held her hand. Chad smiled with pride as Darron healed a hurt bunny. Darron brought her flowers. A kaleidoscope of beautiful memories unfurled in her mind, and every feeling she'd shared with them merged together. She didn't let the thought of Leora dying, never to be reborn, steal the beauty of the moment. The Awakener's role would be forever changed.

She stared at the nothingness that would soon be her eternity . . . and surrendered.

"Thank you for the lives you've given me, for the chance to be a mother to amazing souls. Thank you for the chance to live outside the cavern. I understand it was never just about Darron and Leora; it was also about Chad and me loving each other. Together, we were stronger."

The humming from the stones quieted down and the air around her became lighter and colder. She shivered, hugging herself. A snowflake touched her lips. She shot up, rushed to the bloodstones, and tried to leave the sacred circle. When she stepped forward, she passed beyond the perfect realm. Once more, the trees were burnt reminders of the woods that once surrounded her home. She glanced back and saw the half-burned cabin in the center of the circle.

Thank you, Creator.

The relief and gratitude she felt made her sob, humbled as she was by the second chance she'd been given. Leora was only a two-day hike if she stopped to rest, but if she used her energy and pulled energy from the earth, she could make it back in a day.

She started running as fast as she could, the cold air burning her lungs as her booted feet pounded the snow and rocks. She couldn't heal Leora, but she could be with her.

Chapter Eighteen

Bodies littered the ground. Darron was back at the scene of the accident and feeling disoriented. He grabbed his head to try and make it stop spinning. The last thing he remembered was driving the Explorer, when a strange buzzing filled his head like a million cicadas during summer. A high-pitched ringing soon blended with the buzzing, and his energy just exploded out of him. He peered over at that woman whose neck he'd broken. Her body was bent unnaturally, and she was unmoving. He searched in vain for the gun he used to kill the other men. Rubbing his aching temple, images of the sacred circle emerged.

"Rachel," he whispered. "Fuck."

She was gone. Was he ever going to see her again? A knot formed in his throat, but he swallowed it down. Now wasn't the time to wallow; he had to act.

He rushed to the passenger door of the Explorer and was surprised to find the seat empty. He amped his power up and cast a web out into the night. He listened, sensitive to any movement within his web of power, and tapped into the coupling bond to try and sense where Tabitha was. He could feel her nearby, but where? Someone was obscuring her energy signature.

Then he felt someone moving slowly through his web.

It came from behind him, so he ran around the truck and saw a man dragging Tabitha toward a ditch on the side of the road, where a car was parked behind a billboard.

He started to run for her when he was knocked to the ground.

"Not today," not one, but many voices said behind him.

When he turned to see who had spoken, a tall man with black eyes greeted him. Cuts and scrapes marred the sharp planes of his face, and long, brown hair skimmed his shoulder. Darron was instantly taken back to a mission in Afghanistan, when a woman with eyes as black as death stared through him. He didn't know where these men had come from—he killed all the others he'd seen before—but then it hit him. The Council.

Those sons of bitches are possessing the Lost and trying to make off with my girlfriend!

A quiet storm rolled through Darron as the first man shoved Tabitha into the car. His father and mother were gone...and maybe Leora too. He couldn't lose Tabitha. If he died, he wouldn't be reborn until the Creator chose another soul to birth him and Leora, and who knew how long that could be. This could be his and Tabitha's only life together, and no one was taking that away from him, not after he'd waited so long to find her.

He opened to his power completely. No longer was it flowing up from within him in a fountain calm and controlled. It roared and saturated the fountain and shot out in all directions and went off like a bomb that destroyed any control, tore him apart, only to rebuild him as something more, something stronger. There had always been a part of him that was closed off, which never fully allowed his ability to come forth and let death rule him. Now he had nothing to lose but this moment. Without Tabitha, he would never be the same.

Black mist formed around him, pulling at his body until there was nothing to pull. He was nowhere and every-where at once. He was darkness: an end and a beginning.

Darron didn't have to hear the man pursuing him stumble, or see the other man drop Tabitha to know it happened; he sensed it through the mist. He drifted toward the closest possessed man undetected. Together, the Council members were stronger, but they were also arrogant, thinking they were untouchable. Their bodies may have been safe in their little cavern, but what of their souls?

Darron wrapped the black mist around both men, locking them in place. If he was a Soul Thief, then that was what he would do: steal the souls of the Council members. All he had to do was reach into the bodies they possessed and take them. He wondered how many were needed to possess a body with their power stripped, but that was a question he could easily find an answer to. The mist thickened, excited by the prospect of stealing the souls.

Faster than forming a thought, Darron's misty form dove into the men, slamming them to the ground. He reached into where the souls would rest. There was not one light, but at least twenty or thirty. They dimmed, shrinking away from Darron, then abruptly scattered in all directions, abandoning the bodies to travel to the spiritual plane.

Fueled by the rage of a thousand lives, Darron followed them. There was no beginning, and no end. Colors twirled, danced, bobbed, and wove in all directions at once. Every thought he'd ever had was there, was part of him. He knew he was traveling, but was unsure of exactly how. Thoughts of the souls were all he needed to hold onto. No soul could hide from death.

Suddenly, Darron was in what his mother had called the meeting hall. Bodies were draped over the arms of chairs, or sagged in the seats, their heads lolling to the side, motionless. Leechers paced, their boots tapping the floor. When his mist settled into the room, they froze, sensing his energy, but not understanding it. Death had never been to the cavern—not like this. Darron hovered between the physical and the spiritual worlds. He didn't see the glow of the Council members' souls, but he could feel them coming. Frantic, scared.

Good.

It would only be a matter of time before the souls looked for their bodies. Darron stretched himself out over them, settling his mist like the thinnest layer of skin, and waited.

A faint light in the corner of the room and on the spiritual plane grew brighter. Orbs of light hovered over the bodies. They turned red and tried to drop into the chests of their respective bodies, but death seized hold of them all and wrapped darkness around them like a snake choking its prey. His hate and anger was all-consuming. He lost control of his power for a second, but then Darron became whole again and found himself holding four dozen orbs in the palms of his hands. The Leechers drew their swords when he suddenly appeared out of thin air. He wanted to smash the souls and get it over with, but he couldn't. Something was stopping him, urging him to return them. But to where?

Before the Leechers could jump him, Darran was once again everywhere and nowhere. He traveled, pulled by some unseen force. It was gentle, loving; it was all of the colors at once, the light for all things. It was everywhere and in everything. He could feel a connection to the light, as if it was in him and forming him. He held the souls within himself, and lost all sense of time. Time meant nothing on this plane.

Darron was dropped into the center of the sacred circle, whole and himself, although his skin remained black. He still held the many souls in his palms. The golden glow and hum of the bloodstones were familiar, and the trees reached into the sky as the breeze kissed his skin, but he wasn't sure why he was there.

A glowing white form appeared before him. The souls lifted from Darron's grasp, and the black ink under his skin no longer moved. Serenity took hold of him, and Darron wasn't afraid.

The form drifted back and forth as if it were pacing. Darron watched as the grass within the circle was pressed down in the shape of a foot, just like it would be if a physical being had stepped on it. He didn't know what to do or say, but something told him all he had to do was wait because this being knew everything about him…was part of him.

The differently colored orbs of light came to rest in what Darron thought was a hand as another form drifted forward. The two beings seemed to be having a conversation of sorts. He stared, puzzled. The first form disappeared, taking with it the souls of the Council members. Darron wanted to follow, but something kept him in place. The second form drifted closer before coming into focus.

Chad's green eyes twinkled before he pulled Darron into an embrace. "It's good to see you."

All Darron could do was hang on. His father looked different, and yet the same.

"I'm so proud. You've fully accepted your gift." Chad pulled back and gave Darron a little shake. "You were always holding back, always scared of what you could do."

"What're you talking about? I never hold back," Darron smirked half-heartedly.

Chad gripped Darron's shoulders more firmly. "You couldn't have traveled here unless you'd fully accepted your ability as death. When you collect souls, you'll bring them here now."

"What about the Two Tunnels in the cavern? Doesn't Stephen collect the souls there?"

"Yes, the ones that will be reborn. Others you bring will not."

The bloodstones of the sacred circle softened to clouds, as did the grass beneath his bare, black feet. Other golden beings drifted toward them, surrounding them. Light was everywhere.

"Where did the Council members go?"

Chad's arms dropped to his sides. "They're going to be cleansed and review their purpose."

"What does that mean?"

"The Creator will decide whether they will remain in the heavens or be reborn. Their time as Council members is over either way."

"What? They get to stay in heaven after everything they've done? That's bullshit! They can't be *happy*." Black mist worked up and around Darron's legs.

"The Creator knows what he is doing."

"Are you sure about that? You're here, Mother's here, Leora is going to die . . . none of it makes sense."

Chad's smile vanished. "Why do you say Rachel is here?"

"Stephen placed a destiny mark on her because she was the reason you received yours. I brought her here, just like I did with you. She told me about the true nature of your relationship."

Chad's expression was thoughtful as he glanced over his shoulder at the clouds. "She's not here."

Darron wondered what he was thinking, but didn't ask. If Rachel wasn't here, maybe she was on her way to Leora. Hope flared inside him.

"I have to get back."

"Yes, you do," Chad said as he closed off any hint of

emotion.

•●○﹏○●•

Back on the physical plane, the body of the man who'd tried to shove Tabitha into the car lay on the ground. Darron nudged it with the toe of his boot. The man's soul, which was too weak to survive without the Council member's possession, dimmed and went out completely, lost for all time. A wave of energy leeched the black ink from Darron's skin, and he exhaled. Tabitha was still unconscious, half in and half out of the car. He gathered her up and stroked her hair.

"I'm here, baby, waiting for you to wake up." He kissed her tenderly as he sent a wave of love over their bond. She moaned, and he quickly healed the cuts on her forehead before nuzzling her neck. "Come on, baby. Please wake up."

She wrapped an arm around his neck and kissed him sleepily, then rested her head on his shoulder and sighed. "What a weird dream. Someone was trying to steal me. Can you believe that? I couldn't stop him; my body wouldn't listen to me. I kept trying to get my arms and legs to move, but nothing. I was so pissed."

"It wasn't a dream." He kissed her nose. "But there's nothing to worry about now. I'm here."

Slowly, she lifted her head. She, Leora, and Gavin were all he had left. They were on their own. His chest felt hollow; he couldn't really believe his parents were gone.

Except . . . Chad said Rachel wasn't there with him. Was she somewhere else? Did the Creator let her stay? He didn't let false hope take hold of him. It was too dangerous.

"Are you okay?" She ran a hand over his cheek and up into his hair as her beautiful gray eyes searched his.

He wanted to hold her close and never let go. "As long as I have you, I'll survive anything."

"Why do you sound so sad?" She lifted his chin with a finger.

He took her in, loving everything about her. "Rachel's gone."

"Oh, baby . . . I'm sorry."

He laced his fingers with hers and looked away, but she grabbed his chin and forced him to face her. She pressed her lips to his as love reverberated through the bond. "We can do this. We can get to Leora."

He smiled. God, he loved this woman. Standing, he gently placed her in the front seat of the car the possessed souls left behind and drove off toward Kaloosh.

•●o⌀o●•

Rachel hiked all night, stopping to rest for no more than fifteen minutes at a time. She was on the brink of collapse, but thoughts of Leora drove her on. Half frozen, she finally stumbled onto a road and reached Kaloosh.

Relief lifted her heart and gave her a boost of energy. She bent over to catch her breath, shivering so hard that every muscle ached.

In the distance, headlights approached. Pain shot through her, and she blinked before her mind was suddenly transported elsewhere.

Marcus appeared and stomped into Gavin's house, holding his head. Rachel gasped.

How did he get out of his room? Did he just teleport? How can he use his power at all when Leora bound him? Oh, no—Leora.

Inside, Gavin sat in the recliner, staring into a dying fire, eyes empty and distant.

"Where's Leora?" Marcus bellowed. "The recording of time in my mind is chaos. I can barely think!"

Gavin peered up at him, obviously confused, then sprang up from the chair. "Who are you, and what're you doing in my house? Get out before I call the cops!"

"Cops? What the hell is wrong with you?" Marcus shoved past Gavin. "What've you done with Leora? I need her."

Gavin stood inches from his face. "I don't know what you're talking about. Get out of my house!"

Gavin shoved him back, but Marcus hooked his arm and swung him around. Fear presented itself in Gavin's dark eyes, and there was no sign he recognized his own brother. Marcus turned him loose and grabbed his head.

"What's wrong with you?" he asked, even as he struggled to make sense of the events he'd recorded. He frowned and his nostrils flared. "Why can't I see what happened here when you left the woods? I can always see what has happened in relation to the High Council."

The air around Marcus crackled and popped.

Rachel could feel him playing out the events as if they were happening to her and gasped again. *I'm in Marcus's mind.*

He lay in a pool of blood, his power slowly draining. Pain wrapped around his stomach, squeezing the life out of him. The world began to fade.

Rachel stopped breathing. This was Leora's point of view through Marcus's ability to recall time. She never knew he could play events back through another's point of view. No wonder he could kill them so easily. He understood them.

Marcus's view shifted as he watched the scene unfold from Gavin's perspective next.

His heart hammered, and fear drove him through

the woods. He arrived at the house and saw Leora on the floor, her blood pooling around her. He searched her body for some kind of wound, but saw nothing. That's when his daughter's power reached out; he placed a hand over Leora's belly to drain his daughter's power, hoping to calm Sapphire and stop her from killing Leora.

Marucs's jaw tightened.

Then, Rachel saw the world through Sapphire's developing perspective.

She was angry and scared, searching for Marcus. She wanted him—no, needed him, although Rachel couldn't figure out why; before the perspective jumped back to Gavin's. *Holy shit, I'm going to be sick. Is this what it's like all the time in his head?*

Gavin drained Sapphire's power, and then his mind was blank. Marcus shifted his point of view to Leora, but there was only darkness. Shoving it all back, he turned his attention to Gavin, who was still trying to get Marcus, who he thought was some stranger, to leave.

"Out of my house!" Gavin yelled again.

Marcus shook his head as fear gripped him. He ran a hand through his long hair, then looked at Gavin's chest. His mind seemingly made up, Marcus went to the kitchen and grabbed a knife, but concealed it from Gavin as he made his way to the front door. Gavin hesitated, but followed him.

Marcus ran the blade down his forearm, then gripped Gavin's arm without warning and made the same cut. Gavin cried out and instinctively locked his arm over his brother's. Their blood mixed. Rachel waited, praying the vision would continue. She heard a horn blaring in real time, but couldn't move.

Gavin's eyes went black as he straightened his posture. He broke free from Marcus and stumbled to the floor, his body trembling. "Leora! Where is she?"

Marcus stepped over him and walked down the hall to sit in front of what was left of the fire. He trembled and cradled his head. "I don't know. Stop blubbering, get up, and figure it out."

"Last time I saw her, she was dying on the kitchen floor." Anguish was etched on Gavin's face. "I can't remember anything after picking her up and leeching the baby's power." He paused and touched his head. "She made me forget."

"Who?"

"The baby. I must've drained too much of her power." He looked around and then ran up the stairs. Marcus listened as he opened the door to every room on the second floor, calling for Leora.

"She's not here. Quit wasting time and call her through the bond," Marcus said.

Gavin's feet sounded heavy as he entered the room. "I don't feel her...anywhere."

"Someone came for her. Where would they take her in this town if she needed medical attention?" Marcus asked.

Gavin blinked. "The hospital is about a half an hour from here."

How long had he been sitting there? How long had Leora been gone? Question after question turned in Rachel's mind before a horn blared again. This time, Rachel opened her eyes in time to see a white F-150 swerve around her. She pulled in several panicked breaths and choked back the urge to vomit.

The vision was strong and clear. It was about to happen, or it was happening right then. She had to get to Leora.

A man stepped out of the truck. "Do you need help?"

"Yes, yes I do," Rachel replied, jumping at the opportunity to get to the hospital as soon as possible. "Can you take me to the hospital?"

"Sure, get in."

Chapter Nineteen

Rachel held her hands in front of the vent; feeling came back to them in throbbing heartbeats. If not for the power coursing through her veins, she would have more than frozen fingers and toes. As it was, by the time they reached the hospital, she was thawed out and ready.

"Thank you for the ride," she said, slamming the door and darting across the poorly lit parking lot.

She wondered what she should expect as she gazed at the large, red emergency sign on the building. Was she too late? Was the baby okay? Her heart backfired like an old truck.

She made her way to the glass double doors, but a large male appeared seemingly out of nowhere and blocked her path. She froze when she saw his black eyes locked on her. She jumped behind a green Ford Focus.

A hand closed over her shoulder and Rachel let out a yelp before she tore herself away, her palms crackling with gold light.

Gavin stared at her, his expression darkening. "How did you get here?"

Her gaze drifted from Gavin to Marcus behind him. "Where's Leora? Am I too late?"

"I just got here," Gavin said.

She pointed to Marcus, and he pursed his lips. "Is it safe for him to be here?"

Gavin took in his brother. "Yes."

She stared at him hard and thought about the vision. Marcus was connected to the baby somehow; she didn't understand it, but if it helped Leora, then so be it. She tried to muscle past the two large men before her and get into the hospital, but they didn't move.

Deep breath in, then out. Calm the fuck down. Don't fall apart.

Just as Gavin took Rachel's hand, another car slammed in to park right next to them. Two people jumped out and ran toward them. Rachel gaped when she recognized Darron and Tabitha. She couldn't believe they had made it back in time. Tears of relief formed in her eyes.

"What the fuck is this asshole doing out of his room?" Darron cried, stepping up to Marcus as he all but vibrated with hatred.

Gavin shoved him back. "We don't have time for this."

Rachel placed a hand on Darron's arm and squeezed.

Darron's jaw dropped before he pulled her into a tight embrace. "He said you weren't with him—Chad. I didn't want to hope, couldn't let myself think you could still be here."

"You forgave me and set me free. I walked out of the sacred circle and came here as fast as I could."

Darron released her with a nod. Rachel saw confusion in Gavin's expression, but not Marcus's. Since he recorded time for the High Council, he would've known that she had been marked, and probably when it happened. Come to think of it, he'd known about Chad before he left, but never said a word.

Gavin asked, "No Chad?"

"I'll explain later. For now, just know that he's gone,"

Darron said, looking up at the night sky.

Gavin didn't ask for an explanation, and Marcus turned around and squeezed his eyes shut. When he opened them again, his gaze fell on Rachel.

"Had an eventful week, have you?"

Rachel pulled herself away from Darron, ready to slap him, but Tabitha chimed in, "Isn't it always?"

She crossed her arms over her chest as if to silently remind them that there were other, more important things going on.

"Come," Gavin said.

He led them inside and walked up to the front desk. The hospital was small, but the waiting room was large and had high ceilings. Twinkle lights were wrapped around fake trees. Pictures of rivers, bears, and elk littered the walls along with pale-blue wallpaper that cut off halfway up. Not one of them sat on the soft chairs splitting the room in half while Gavin spoke to the dark-haired woman behind the front desk.

Images of Leora swam through the polluted thoughts swirling in Rachel's tired mind. Overwhelmed, hopelessness burrowed deep inside her. How was she going to get through the next few days? Even if Leora lived, it would only be a short time before her world unraveled, and Rachel would be the one pulling the string. The thought of taking Leora's baby and telling her it died was a horrible eventuality she didn't want to face, so Rachel closed her eyes and concentrated. She opened to her power and to the bloodbond with Leora, but she felt nothing. She blinked back tears as despair crept into her heart when she remembered that Gavin and Leora didn't share a bloodbond with Rachel from this body.

"Darron, can you sense Leora?" Rachel asked.

He closed his eyes. When they opened, he shook his

head. "I don't feel her."

Gavin walked back over. "She will be with us in a minute."

"What happened?" Darron asked. "Is Leora hurt?"

"I don't know why, but the baby is killing her," Gavin said. "I found her lying in a pool of blood, but she had no open wounds. When I tried to drain the baby's energy, I forgot everything."

Rachel hugged herself. Everything was a mess, and she couldn't see a way out of it. Darron's warm, strong arm draped over her hunched shoulders, pulling her into a tight embrace. How was it that the simplest act of kindness could shatter every wall she'd ever erected in a single moment?

Everything she'd been holding back since her confession to Chad welled up and tore past her trembling lips in a sob that physically rocked her. Darron's grip tightened as his deep breath blended with hers. So much loss…so much pain for a future that would never be more than what it was now: torn. She sobbed harder.

Please, Creator, help us. Get us through what lies ahead.

Darron swayed her like one might to comfort a child after a bad dream.

"I'm sorry." She clung to him. "For everything."

"There's nothing to be sorry for," he whispered.

"Things could've been different if I had seen what was right in front of me sooner."

"Don't do this, not now. It won't help." He rubbed her back. "Now is all we have."

He was right. All she had left was this moment, and her best friend needed her.

·•○～○•·

Leora's skin glowed a pale blue where she lay in the hospital bed. She cupped her belly and mumbled, "Sapphire, it's okay."

His Eve would be called Sapphire in this life. It was a new beginning.

Invisible, Adam studied the crease in her brow and the set of her jaw. She was different in this life: stronger, determined. He felt her coupling bond to Gavin, their energy twisted together like a rope. He smirked. Gavin had waited for Leora, had felt her power growing, and still he waited in Kaloosh for her to come to him. He gave her the time she needed to be ready for what they would face together. Adam admired his adopted son's self-control. Most souls didn't exercise restraint of that caliber, but Gavin's quiet strength was what had drawn Adam to him all those years ago in the first place. Soon, Gavin would be a father, and he was overjoyed for him. He just prayed the child came into the world safely.

Resting his back against the chair, Adam kicked out a leg, his boot heel thumping the linoleum floor. He pursed his lips. What would Gavin do if he knew about him and that he had watched all of them from the beginning, but never helped? That he had abandoned the world, his world, because he didn't know how to be without her? His Eve. He was hopeful and afraid of what it meant for Eve to be coming back into the world.

Adam sat up abruptly as Leora moaned and Eve's warm, smooth energy fell away from him. It reached out and skimmed the fractured shards of a madman's mind: Marcus. The moment her energy connected with Marcus's, an electrical storm surged around Leora's weak body. Adam growled and shot up from the chair. His tall, powerful body moved unseen down the sterile hospital hall. Cloaking his energy, Adam strolled into the waiting room. Rachel,

Gavin, Darron, Tabitha, and Marcus came into view; they stood, talking amongst themselves in the waiting room. The energy level was charged so much that a normal soul would likely walk by them and immediately feel uncomfortable, though they would not know why. It had been more than five hundred years since he'd seen the Awakener's High Council all together. The formerly aged, gray eyes of Mr. Cross glowed with contempt. Why was his Eve reaching for Marcus, and why did he link with her just then?

Marcus's narrowed eyes locked on the space where he stood, unnoticed by anyone else. Marcus knew he was there, but Adam didn't care. The time to reveal himself was coming.

A nurse gathered Gavin and Rachel, then ushered them down the hall. Tabitha and Darron took seats in the waiting room. Adam walked toward Marcus, who was still standing with a commanding air about him, as if he knew something no one else did.

"I'll be outside in the truck," Marcus said to Darron.

Darron scrubbed his face with his hands, exhausted. "I don't care where you go. I marked you. I always know where you are. Remember that."

Marcus's gaze narrowed, but he walked outside without any further comment. Sparks of light set off like fireworks around him. Marcus turned to put his back against a black truck and scanned the area.

Adam, too, peered around, but saw no one; it was an upside to living in a small town he loved. "Why is your energy linked to the child?"

Marcus leaned an elbow against the truck and cocked his head to the side, pretending to be confused. "To whom do you refer?"

Snowflakes drifted from the sky to coat the ground in a fresh, fluffy blanket of white.

"Don't play dumb, Keeper. It's not becoming."

Marcus scowled. "Since when do you care what happens to any of us?"

Adam had never intervened in any of the Council's shenanigans to dissolve the Awakener's High Council or to change the path of the Creator's workings, even when he could have. If he so chose, all he would have to do was reach for Marcus's energy, rip it from his soul, and keep it for himself. Then he would never have to deal with him again. Marcus had killed Leora and her child countless times, and now he knew that the child was his Eve trying to make her way into the world. He wanted to kill Marcus, but not before he learned why she was connected to him.

Adam balled his hands into fists, pulled in a deep breath, and then let it out. The Creator had many strings of fate knotted together. If he had learned anything from being an Observer, it was that one never knew how fates were intertwined. Adam would not risk losing Eve because he didn't see what the Creator was doing until it was too late.

Marcus smirked as he studied Adam. "Don't worry about Leora and her little family. I won't be hurting them. I have other plans."

"You will not touch the child."

Adam amplified his energy in a flash of blinding light. It hit Marcus swift and hard, slamming him into a small, green car next to the truck. Marcus unleashed his power to seize Adam's throat, but only for an instant before Adam flicked his power aside as if it was nothing more than a pesky fruit fly. Marcus righted himself and tried to wrap Adam in his power once again.

"Are you done?" Adam asked, shoving his hands into his coat pockets. "Your power has many more life cycles to go through before it could even begin to challenge mine, so save it."

Apprehension sparked in Marcus's eyes. Adam doubted it was a feeling he was familiar with. But then he asked, "Do you hear her screams? The child is killing her mother because she cannot reach me, but knows I'm here. I can continue to block her if you wish, but if you want to see her born into this world, you'd better back off. It is not *I* who reaches out to *her.*"

With that, Adam's suspicions were confirmed. But why would Sapphire reach for energy such as Marcus's? He was chaos, pieces of events, and perspectives that had all been ruined by time itself. He couldn't handle his gift, even after Gavin reestablished the bloodbond. Marcus was always on the edge of madness. Why would the Creator want that for Sapphire?

Adam took a step back and put his hands up in surrender just as Sapphire's power glided over Marcus's and stabbed into the base of his skull. He dropped to his knees, and his chaotic energy subsided noticeably. Even Adam, with his hypervigilant hearing, could hear no more screams as Marcus's face twisted with pain. Adam watched the link Sapphire had forged. There was always a reason and purpose for everything. This was no different. His brows stitched together as Marcus leaned against the truck's closest tire, visibly weakened.

"You are stained, marked by death and destruction. You have no power here. I have seen what you are, and you will die by my hand if you hurt that child. I may not know why Sapphire reaches for your energy, but it is clear that you don't have the upper hand you think you do." Adam turned and began to walk away. "Being the first soul, I'm the master of patience. I will learn why she needs you, and when I do, I will come for you."

Chapter Twenty

A scream ripped from Leora's throat. Rachel held her hand as tears ran down Leora's cheeks.

"Do something," Leora cried, gripping the collar of Darron's T-shirt.

"I've tried, Leora. The little brat won't let my energy touch you." Darron pried her fingers away and ran a hand through his hair. "She knows I'm trying to help you."

"Don't say that. She's a baby. Babies don't do that," Leora snapped, closing her eyes out of sheer exhaustion.

Rachel glanced at the others. They all knew this baby was dangerous to Leora. The vision Rachel had before her awakening resurfaced in her mind.

A child is born. She's beautiful. Love flows into her from many others. My blood is her blood. She's the strongest soul. She will erase time. The light will be extinguished. Only the Keeper can find redemption and save the light. To do this, the circle will betray the light.

Soon, Gavin would drain Leora's strength so she wouldn't witness the birth of her daughter. Rachel's chin quivered; she didn't like the idea of Marcus taking her granddaughter, but he was the only High Council advisor who could use his gift at birth. Marcus never slept like the others, and could recall every memory from every life since his inception. The others' abilities were dormant until they reached puberty, or sometimes even later on in life. Their power grew until their awakenings took place and they saw their past lives. Never had they had to control a gift at such a young age. Marcus was the only one who could help. She prayed he would not be a threat with the bloodbond in place and with Darron's mark. After seeing through Marcus's eyes, she knew Leora didn't have a hold on his power any longer, and yet he was still here.

Rachel's heart was sick with the weight of their impending betrayal. She wasn't so certain anymore that it was the only way to keep them safe. Rachel bit her lip, knowing Leora's entire world was about to change. She wished Chad was there. He was so good at calming Leora, who had always been a daddy's girl.

"Gavin, do something!" Leora sobbed.

"The last time I tried to stop her, I forgot you were my wife and that you were dying in my arms," he said, pale and shaking, even as he held her other hand. The scar at the corner of his mouth pulled tight. He was scared; they all were.

Rachel stared at the blue glow pulsating from Leora's stomach.

"Why is this happening?" Leora asked no one and everyone.

Rachel swallowed hard. Her best friend was going to die if the baby didn't come out soon. In no other life had this happened, and Rachel felt helpless. If Leora died, she would not be reborn and there would be no one to help guide the souls on this plane. Darkness would fall, and all the souls would be consumed by dark times. She pressed her forehead to Leora's, clasped her hands, and prayed. She surrendered all that she was to the Creator.

Please help us. Forgive me for not trusting in your will

*and for not breaking the chains of the past to see all that I
had been given. Please, give us one more chance. I can do
better for you, for myself. I can be a better woman, one who
believes in the power of your love, and the love of others.
Take me, not her. Let her live. Let them both live.*

With each heartbeat, Rachel felt lighter. A broken piece
of her healed, and she could breathe easily for the first time.
The burden of her guilt for not giving Chad a chance to love
her dissolved, and hope ignited.

"If that's what labor is like, I'll pass," Tabitha said
with eyes round as marbles. "I don't want to have kids.
Like, ever!"

"It's not labor. It's Sapphire. Something's upsetting
her," Gavin said. He'd barely uttered the words when Leora
screamed louder and blood dotted her gown around her
belly. "Not again. I have to drain her energy. This is what
happened at the house."

"No." Leora gripped his forearm. "No, you can't
forget. I need you." Sweat beaded on her brow and she
sank deeper into the bed. Her breathing was labored, and
her entire body trembled, but then she calmed. Gavin gently
touched Leora's cheek and she whispered, "See? I'm fine."

There was so much pain in his eyes that Rachel had to
look away. When she dared to look back, Gavin was staring
at the door, and his lips were pressed into thin lines.

Rachel brushed a strand of hair off Leora's brow. "It
will be okay."

Leora closed her eyes, exhaustion etched in every line
on her face. If Chad were there, he would have known what
to do.

Minutes passed, and while Leora remained still, her
grip on Gavin never eased. Rachel wished she could have
watched her daughter's love for Gavin over their lifetimes
together and seen what they shared. Perhaps then, things

could have been different between her and Chad.

Gavin climbed into bed with Leora and held her close as they both fell asleep. Darron and Tabitha pulled out the small sofa bed so they could rest as well. As much as Rachel wanted to do the same, her anxiety was vibrating too high for sleep. Her stomach grumbled, and Darron glanced at her from the corner of his eye. It was seven o'clock in the evening; the cafeteria closed soon. She decided to go grab something to eat and let everyone else rest. She snapped her fingers, and when Darron looked up, she made a gesture as if she were shoving food into her face. His hands flew up and signaled for her to bring some back. She smiled.

Quietly, she exited the room and followed the maze of signs to the cafeteria. There was one clerk at the register: a petite redhead with ivory skin and freckles. She chewed on her thumbnail and looked bored. She couldn't have been older than eighteen or nineteen.

Rachel picked up a plastic tray and meandered the perimeter of the cafeteria to see what was available. There was vegetable soup, clam chowder with bread, a tray of lasagna, and Caesar salad. Her mouth watered, and she continued perusing until she came to what looked like the tastiest cheeseburgers ever. She snatched one up and placed it on the tray. She felt as if the heavens had opened up when she came to the dessert station and grabbed two slices of chocolate mousse pie so she could properly eat her feelings. Next, she headed for the coffee stand. She would grab food for everyone else after she stuffed her face.

Balancing the large coffee and everything else on the tray, Rachel spotted yogurt and fruit, so she hurried over and snatched both from the standing glass fridge. Satisfied with her choices of sugary goodness, she turned toward the register. The Styrofoam box containing her burger slid from the tray and landed in the hands that shot out from behind her.

"Thanks," Rachel said, looking back to address her hero. What she saw caused her to gasp and drop the tray. It hit the floor, and scalding coffee drenched her jeans. She let out a cry and shoved her pants down to her ankles. "Holy crap!"

Red welts were already forming on her right thigh and shin. It took her a second to gather herself and process that she was half naked in a public cafeteria.

At least I have on cute red panties.

The clerk rushed around the counter with a handful of napkins that she promptly used to pat Rachel's leg, but Rachel didn't notice. Her attention was locked on Chad's unshaven face. Emerald eyes sparkled at her, pinching at the corners as if they were smiling. He wore faded jeans that hugged his muscled thighs, and a black T-shirt under a navy, zip-up sweatshirt. He picked up the tray with the pies that had somehow managed to remain in their clear, plastic containers. The yogurt and the fruit remained intact as well.

"Chad?" Rachel took the napkins from the panicked clerk and turned to calm her. "It's okay. I'm fine. Thank you for the help."

The coffee on Rachel's pants had cooled, and she shimmied them back up to button them.

"Are you sure? Your leg is pretty red. Can I get you some ice or something?" the clerk asked, wrinkling her nose at the two of them and disappearing before either could respond.

Chad placed the tray on the counter and dropped the burger back on it. "I think the pies are dead," he said, obviously entertained.

He placed another cheeseburger on the tray with hers, then threw a stack of napkins on the floor to mop up the coffee with his foot. Then picked them up and tossed them in the trash.

The clerk reappeared with an actual mop.

"I'm so sorry about the mess," Rachel said sincerely to the young woman.

"Happens more often than you'd think. I hope your leg will be okay."

"It will be fine, I promise," she reassured the clerk.

Chad walked over to the coffee stand and filled two new cups with regular coffee. He set one cup down in front of the condiments, opened four creamers and five sugar packets, poured them in, and stirred the coffee several times. He strolled back and paid the cashier for the items, then joined Rachel and handed her the cup with the cream and sugar. Her bottom lip quivered. She thought only Leora knew how she liked her coffee. Her stomach did a somersault as she took it and their fingers brushed. He felt real—like blood and bone.

He held out his elbow for her to tuck her arm into it. She did, and he smiled brilliantly, taking her breath away and warming her from head to toe. They walked to a corner booth, and Chad gestured for her to go first. She slid to the wall and he sat beside her. Their shoulders were touching, and heat rolled off him, helping her relax. For a moment, it was just him and her: no Leora in labor, no ultimate betrayal about to take place, no Council getting the upper hand, no endless desperation because Chad was gone. She was just a girl with a very cute boy that she wanted to kiss and rub her hands all over. She was drawn to him even without the coupling bond.

Oh, jeez, I really am hopeless.

She didn't know what to say, or if she should say anything at all. A shy, awkward kind of excitement filled her as he took the items from the tray and set them out in front of her. It was such a normal, couple thing to do, but this was anything but normal. She fidgeted with her fingers. Did he know Stephen had marked her as well? Did he know that Darron had been her judge?

"How are you here?" she asked.

He skimmed her lower back with his fingertips and pulled her into his side. His touch was almost unbearably tender, causing her eyes to flutter closed. She needed this, needed him.

"Leora needs me. The Creator allowed me to return."

Chad's touch left her back and found her hand, lacing their fingers together. Her gaze locked with his, and a myriad of emotions connected her to him like an anchor to a ship. A yearning for something they'd never shared settled between them.

"You need me too," he eventually said.

Chad's gaze dropped to her lips, then flitted back to her eyes. Her stomach became a tornado of butterflies. He dipped his head and pressed his lips to hers. The kiss was a delicious promise. Strong arms wrapped around her, and the fear of unworthiness that had held her back gave way. Her lips moved hungrily over his. Desire and heat pooled in her core as the kiss deepened. In this life, she wanted a partner, someone she could love and share a life with. She wanted a chance at something beautiful and real. That had been right in front of her for lifetimes, and now she wanted to give herself to this man. He'd protected their family fiercely for hundreds of years and loved her, even when she could not love herself. He had been patient and kind; he was a good man.

Chad's tongue rolled smoothly over hers, sending a shiver racing down her spine. Her breathing was harsh as he skimmed his lips over her neck, then up to her ear.

"Everything will be okay."

He kissed her ear gently, setting off more sparks of

desire, but then his hands left her body.

Well, that was anticlimactic.

Pulling in a breath, she shuddered and had to actually fan herself.

He came back because I needed him: how sweet! Okay, get it together.

She tried to think of something else, anything other than how Chad made her feel like *her*, and that she wanted to drag him off to a dark corner and have her way with him. Then, her stomach growled loudly, grumpy at having once again been ignored. She sighed and went for the destroyed pie.

"Nice choice." Chad popped the lid off the other slice in front of him.

She reached out a hand and stole it back. "I didn't say you could have that," she teased.

"I bought it, so technically, it's all mine." He raised a brow as he took it back, and she smiled weakly when he kissed her nose. "But I know how to share. You can have them both."

"Smart and cute," she said, shoving a large bite into her mouth.

As she devoured the first slice, she realized that Chad never flirted or teased in the past. She liked it. The weight of their past lifted for a moment, and she could see the Elapsed Seer for who he truly was: a man wanting to be loved and needed.

Rachel ate the second slice slower and relished the chocolatey goodness. It had been two days since she'd last eaten, and her body was not shy about letting her know how displeased it was. It gurgled and bubbled loudly, even as she took a bite of the cheeseburger. The salty contrast to the sweet was heaven in her mouth. Taking another bite of pie, and then a bite of the burger, she devoured the food in minutes.

Chad broke out laughing. "Man, you can eat."

Rachel dabbed daintily at her mouth with a napkin and then sipped her coffee, her stomach happy and full. She leaned back against the wall, lifting her feet to rest on the seat across from her.

Fat pants would be good about now.

Chad killed his cheeseburger in six big bites. When he was finished, he rested a hand on her leg. Her heart fluttered as he picked up his black coffee and held it for a moment.

"I saw the plan you have for Leora and Sapphire. Are you really going to take her child?" He inhaled slowly and looked more like the man he used to be: a father. "She's going to suffer more than ever before."

Rachel frowned, having forgotten that he wasn't there when she had the vision. "I've played the vision I had about it over and over again in my mind, and I don't see another way."

"Can I use my gift to see the vision?"

His green gaze held hers. She nodded, releasing her hold on the coffee cup so he could hold both of her hands in his. He didn't close his eyes, but watched her. A warm, buttery heat started at the top of her head and cascaded down her body, curling her toes in her boots; his energy was delicious. Seconds ticked by, and then he released her hands.

"I think we should tell her. She would understand, and then she would know that Sapphire is alive, even if she can't see her," Chad said.

"But the betrayal. How else would that come about?"

"You don't think keeping this information from her for this long isn't a betrayal?"

Rachel's mouth went dry. He had a point. Rachel's head hit the wall and she stared at the ceiling. Dropping her chin, she took a sip of her coffee. "We should talk to the others. I don't want Sapphire going with Marcus. I don't trust him."

She thought again about how she'd jumped into his perspective. It hadn't been a vision. It was something else entirely.

"Agreed." Chad sighed. He leaned back and rested one arm over the back of the booth.

"Are you here to stay?"

"Let's talk about something else."

She swallowed and pulled her legs off the seat across from her. "Like what?"

"Darron unlocked all of his power. He can take souls to Stephen and to the Creator now," Chad said. "I watched him from above. He steals souls."

He studied her face, but she wasn't surprised by this revelation. Shamus had called him a Soul Thief, and she'd watched Tabitha use his gift to take her father's soul out of anger and hurt. She had no doubt Darron could do the same if he chose to.

"It's unheard of to achieve such a thing, especially since his soul is still so young," Rachel said. "I don't think I've managed to tap into half of my own capabilities."

Chad shrugged. "Do we ever really know what we're capable of?"

He frowned as soon as the words left his mouth; he looked away.

Rachel placed a reassuring hand on his leg. "Don't. We have all had hard choices to make."

He squeezed her hand. "Thank you for that. I don't deserve it."

"Yes, you do." She rested her head on his shoulder.

"Darron should be proud of his gift, but he doesn't seem pleased," Chad said. She lifted her head and waited for him to explain. "He stole the souls of the Council members trying to stop you from returning to Leora. He captured them before they could return to their bodies and brought them to the Creator."

"No," she gasped.

Chad nodded. "They're awaiting judgment."

"How many?"

"There were four dozen and four Lost, so it looks like it takes twelve members to control one body with their diminished power."

"Holy cow. I can't believe it."

"I'm sure discovering their bodies will scare many of the others into rethinking their choices."

"I'll say." Relief swept through her exhausted mind and banished many of her fears. "I can't believe it…after all this time, Darron finally kicked their asses like he wanted to!" The cashier glanced up from scrubbing the condiment counter with a raised eyebrow. Rachel pretended to lock her lips and throw away the key. "Sorry."

Chad chuckled. "That he did. The best part was that they didn't even see it coming."

She stared at him for a long while. One life was all they needed to have forever as long as they kept each other safe. They were awakened, so they would not age, and they wouldn't get sick. They were not immortal, but with someone like Darron around, they could be healed if necessary. It was something to hold onto.

Peering at the clock on the wall, Rachel knew they had to get back to Leora and the others. "We'd better head back and check on everyone. They'll be surprised to see you."

Picking up the trash and the remaining items, they slipped out of the booth. With a coffee in one hand, he reached for her with the other. Excited, she took it, and they grabbed a few burgers, more fruit, and some cheesecake for the others.

Chapter Twenty-One

Rachel and Chad peered into Leora's room; everyone was asleep. A smile touched the corners of Chad's lips and Rachel paused.

"What's the smile for?" she asked.

He didn't answer right away, but placed the bag of food on a table by the door and closed it so they were still in the hall, but could talk without worrying about waking anyone. "Let's go for a walk."

"Where? It's snowing outside," she said.

"Then let's go sit in my truck."

"Your truck? You drove here?"

"Yes." He gently directed her down the hall.

"From where?"

"California. Now, come on."

She allowed him to guide her out of the lobby, tossing their coffees into the trash before strolling out to the parking lot. The air was crisp, and snow had accumulated fast. The thought of being alone with Chad both excited and scared her. The last two times they'd been alone had not gone well, even if parts of those experiences were not terrible either. The kiss they shared in the tunnel when Chad was wounded was hungry and needy. She'd never burned that hot for someone in this life.

She didn't know which truck was his, but as they passed Gavin's, she saw Marcus glaring at them from the front seat. Rachel couldn't help herself; just for fun, she gave Marcus two thumbs-up. He flipped her off. She laughed out loud, snorted, and then slapped a hand over her mouth.

"What's so funny?"

"Nothing."

She molded herself against Chad and rested her head against him. He slipped his arm around her shoulders and pulled her close. It felt easy, natural, like they had done this a thousand times, even though they hadn't. This was new: Chad wanting her, her wanting Chad, and seeing him for the man he had always been. She wrapped her arms around his waist and they held onto each other as they walked through the falling snow.

Chad strolled up to an old, blue Chevy truck that reminded her of a country music video.

"Where did you find this?" she asked as he opened the door for her. It groaned loudly.

"It's my dad's."

He closed the door, walked around to the other side, and climbed in. He started the engine and turned on the heater.

"Your dad's? You did mention that you still have parents in this life."

She picked at her jeans, thinking about her own parents and the beautiful moment they shared in the Two Tunnels. Tears burned her eyes as she recalled the love pouring from them.

There were so many other things they could talk about, but she wanted to get to know him. She wanted it to feel like it did at the Recovery Spring in the cavern, when they acted as if they were meeting for the first time.

She scooted over to him and lifted his arm so she could snuggle against him. It felt like home as he rested his head on top of hers. "Tell me about them. Did you return somewhere close to them after judgment in the sacred circle?"

"After Darron brought the Council members to the Creator, I found myself standing in front of their house. I should have just left, but I wanted them to know I was okay, even if I couldn't tell them what was happening. I just needed them to know I was still out there somewhere. My dad, Paul—family is everything to him. He was relieved to see me, and he didn't ask any questions. Told me some Marines had been by. They think I'm AWOL like Darron."

He turned off the truck's engine; the heater had made the cab piping hot.

"Will you go back?"

"We can't go back to our lives before our awakenings." He rested a hand on the steering wheel. "You know how it works. We protect Leora and Darron, and now the baby. We try to stay alive as long as we can. Many of the Council members will be judged, but Darron didn't get all those that are against us."

Snow piled up on the truck, blocking the world beyond from view. The heaviness of that truth weighed down on her.

"But this life is different. We're different." Rachel placed a hand over his chest where the destiny mark once was. "Tell me about your mother."

"Her name is Vickie. She's amazing, full of information, and always ready to help me or my younger brother, Sam, with any challenge. Nothing scares her. She's one of the strongest women I know." His voice broke. "I couldn't have asked for a better family. My brother cried when he saw me. I didn't know what to tell him except that I was sorry for making him worry."

There was sadness in his tone, but also love. She bit her lower lip as she considered her next words. As much as it would kill her to see him go, she had to think of him first. He deserved that much after all the pain she'd caused him.

"You don't have to stay here, Chad." She sat up to look him in the eye. "You can get your life back. The Council is weaker than ever. If something happens, I can find you."

He was quiet for a long time. Then, in a flat tone, he said, "I could pretend the last few weeks were all just a bad dream."

She leaned away from him as he stared at the snowy window.

"I was angry at my family for a long time after I awakened to my purpose and relived the past. I pushed them away. I didn't know what else to do. I knew I was going to have to leave everything behind," he said.

In a small voice, she asked, "Why were you angry at them?"

"Because they loved each other so well. My father and my mother loved each other with their whole hearts. My brother thought I was some sort of god, and I thought he was awesome in all the ways I wasn't. The love we felt for each other filled every room of our house. When I awakened, I felt *our* loveless bond pulling at me, and I just couldn't bring myself to live a life like that again—not after knowing what a family could be."

"I could say I'm sorry a million times, but I know it wouldn't change anything," she said.

"Don't you see?" He took her hand in his and his gaze searched hers. "I'm here, despite everything. When you forgave me in the sacred circle, the destiny mark was lifted, and I was given one last life. I was at peace with the choices I'd made, but before I knew it, I was standing on my parents' front porch. And then I understood what the

Creator was showing me. My family's purpose was not to cause me pain, but to remind me that love is always with us—if we choose to see it." He moved closer, and Rachel's body hummed. "I couldn't let Leora and Darron down. They need to see that love is unending, even in the worst of times." He cupped her cheek, caressing it with the pad of his thumb. "I have only ever loved you." He took her hand and placed it over his heart. "I give you this life."

His body was warm beneath her fingertips, and his heart beat strong and true. It was a rhythm she knew so well. She curled her fingers into a fist and he wrapped a hand over it, not letting her pull away. She looked everywhere but at him, and his hand fell away from her face.

Rip it off like a Band-Aid. Just do it.

"Stephen placed a destiny mark upon me after he learned of your judgment."

Chad stiffened. "Why would he do that?"

She ran a hand through her hair and bit her lower lip as she glanced out the side window.

He tilted her chin back toward him. "It's okay, Rachel. You don't have to tell me."

She shook her head. "No, you told me the truth. I can do the same." A tear ran down her cheek. "Stephen was furious you had been marked because of me. He said I'd ruined everything because I couldn't leave the past behind and heal. Darron judged me, and then I was able to walk from the circle and found myself by the bloodstones. This will be my last life too."

She locked eyes with Chad as he nodded. "Then we'll let it outshine all those that came before and begin again."

"Oh, Chad." She touched his cheek, and he kissed her palm. "I don't deserve you."

"Do you want to share this life with me?"

Rachel opened every closed door in her heart and a

soft, golden glow reached for Chad. He closed his eyes and sighed as she enfolded his entire body in her essence and savored the sensations. So much heat, so much need: she'd never felt as much from him as she did now. Her essence slid off his skin and formed a small ball floating in front of her chest, held there by a thread to her heart. She waited, offering herself to him.

A moment later, green fog flowed out and hovered over her skin, tasting her with gentle, heated kisses as smooth as rose petals. The light pulled away from her skin as he slid out from behind the steering wheel and settled in the middle of the bench seat. His hands traveled up her legs and to her lower back. Carefully, he lifted her onto his lap. The orbs of light touched and became brighter as she straddled him and rested her hands on his shoulders.

"Do you give me this life and our time beyond it?" Chad asked.

How had she not realized he was a romantic? Longing, tenderness, and desire mixed in and became a beautiful song.

"I will give you this life and whatever comes next." She pressed her forehead to his. "I am yours."

The two balls of light became one and encapsulated them. A bolt of lightning cracked, anchoring their hearts and souls together once again, only stronger and brighter this time.

Chapter Twenty-Two

Rachel pressed her lips to his, never wanting to let him go or hurt him. Time locked them together as the light exploded, and golden sparkles landed on their skin. This time, when the coupling bond was set, it didn't hurt or feel like she was being cut in two. She was more than she had ever been before. She reached further into the world because of him. It was amazing.

Chad's fingers tightened on her hips. She felt the heat of his desire pressing against her wet core, even through their clothes. Unable to resist the playful joy coursing through her, she rocked against him. His fingers began to massage her muscles and she shivered with delight. He grinned, and a light shone from within that she'd never seen before. She wrapped her arms around his neck, pressing her whole upper body against him. He growled, and her nipples hardened.

She smiled against his lips; they had never tasted sweeter. She leaned back and he quickly pulled off his sweatshirt, then tugged his T-shirt over his head, exposing his beautifully scarred body. Desire surged as she ran a finger over several scars on his ribs while he watched her. The thick, red-and-purple lines were evidence of the pain Chad had endured to escape the heartache of just the memory of their unfulfilled time together. She didn't want him to feel that ever again. She would kiss every scar and ease all his fears.

She shed her jacket and shirt, exposing her red, lace bra as she took him in. He'd never looked more beautiful than when he raised a trembling hand and rubbed his thumb over one of her nipples. Her head fell back with the pleasure of it. He kissed her shoulder and then her chest, just above her heart. He unclasped the bra with one hand, carefully sliding the straps from her shoulders, then dropped it to the seat as he took one of her swollen nipples into his mouth and flicked his tongue over it. She arched her back to offer him better access. His tongue moved smoothly from one breast to the other. Her hands ran through his curls as waves of ecstasy thrummed through her.

He unbuttoned her pants and reached into the back of them to cup her ass and pull her against his hardness. He groaned, and she smiled until he eased her up and off his lap. Then he laid her down on the old truck's wide seat. Her hands skimmed the hard planes of his stomach, and he growled low again. Her core grew wetter with the sound, and she opened her legs for him to settle perfectly between them. As his green eyes stared down at her and his perfectly chiseled body pressed against hers, she knew this life would be all that she needed to feel loved, wanted, and cared for.

·●○～○●·

Every muscle in Chad's body was so tense he thought he was going to come undone as he gazed down at his bonded offering herself to him, full of desire and perfectly lovely. It was a dream he'd had in many lifetimes. His blood ignited with desire, and he pushed a wave of it through their bond. It traveled easily between them, and he was in awe.

Never had their bond flowed so smoothly; there was no resistance, no barriers keeping him at bay. Intrigued, he reached for her current thoughts and found that she enjoyed the weight of him against her, though his jeans covering his shaft irritated her as she pressed firmly against him. Oh, he liked knowing her thoughts and feelings.

Rachel closed her dark eyes and arched her back as she rubbed against his bare skin. Seeing her in the thralls of passion hardened him painfully. He reached down between them to push at her jeans. Through the bond, she hit him with a wave of desire so hot he sat back, unable to breathe. Before he knew it, she had shed the remainder of her clothes and was unbuttoning his pants.

He laughed, allowing her need to drive him higher. Knowing that she wanted him so fiercely was the sweetest bliss he'd ever known. He pushed his jeans to his ankles, then kicked off his shoes. Her eyes were dark and hungry as her gaze swept over his body and his chest puffed out, knowing she yearned for him. Gently, he ran his fingertips down her side, over her hip, and down her leg. She shivered, and as much as he wanted to pull her on his lap and bury himself in her core, he didn't. This was his last life. He had to show her the love he'd always had for her. He ran a hand over her cheek and into her hair before laying her back on the seat once more so he could hover over her and then slowly rest his body against hers. Her hair was loosely draped over the seat like a golden cloak.

She kissed the palm of his hand as he caressed her beautiful hair, then her lips. He'd dreamed of those lips long before he awakened. He wanted—no, *needed* her to know how he saw her. Struggling to breathe, he rested his forehead against hers. As one, they closed their eyes. He stretched the bond, widening it so that it could contain his most cherished moments.

With his hands on her bare hips, he wrapped her in the heat of his power and pulled her with him through time. Tumbling back, she gasped at the sensation he was so accustomed to. His gift had always been a barrier between him and the ones he cared for. He had to always keep them at a safe distance so as not to invade their privacy. It was all too easy to disconnect from the world he wanted to hold onto.

His memory took her to the first moment he saw her in the Council room with Serena. Her pale-blue eyes had roamed over every face, chair, wall, and torch. Curiosity was alive in their depths. She wore a green velvet dress that hugged her body and skimmed the floor. Her red curls fell over her shoulders, making the light freckles over her nose and cheeks more noticeable. She'd reminded him of a Celtic queen he read about in one of Stephen's books on fairy tales. When he saw her, his heartbeat had been so strong he'd been confused by it. Emotions welled up in him that he didn't understand. Their gaze met and held for but a fraction of a second. She was so beautiful, he hadn't been able to breathe. He had wanted to smile, but he was afraid Stephen would sense a change in him while he stood at his side.

·●○↝○●·

Rachel's breath hitched; seeing herself through his eyes was strange. The way he saw her, curious and new to the Council, excited him. He took in every movement, every glance, and interpreted them so well. She remembered the moment his gaze had locked on hers. She had been curious about him, knowing he was a Learner like her, and that he, too, had never been beyond the cavern.

Another memory pushed forward. She sat in front of a

fireplace, playing with a squirming Darron. A round belly bumped against his small back as he showed her a toy truck. Her red hair seemed to be alive against the backdrop of the fire. She looked up at Chad and smiled; it was filled with love and joy. A wave of satisfaction, pride, and hope wrapped around her heart.

He really did think she was the loveliest thing, and he had always been there, just out of reach, waiting for her to love him back. She felt like such a fool.

"Chad . . . " She sniffled, trying to find the words to express how she felt, but there were none.

He pulled the memory back over the bond and claimed her lips. With his bare chest pressed to hers, every sense came alive. His kiss was possessive, and that was the only way she would have him from then on.

Their kisses grew hot with a passion she'd never felt from him. She gave herself over to it. Chad released her lips, leaving her aching for more. Unhurried, he placed feather-soft kisses down her neck to her collarbone. Her blood purred for more of his touch. Chad pushed up onto one hand and grabbed the back of the seat. He glanced around; they didn't have a ton of room. Before she knew what was happening, he had her upright and straddling his lap once again. Snow continued to fall and block the windows.

"I'm sorry. A truck in the middle of a parking lot is not ideal for making love."

Rachel laughed out loud at his distress and pressed her nipples against his chest. He clenched his jaw, watching her with fire in his eyes.

"It makes it more exciting," she purred. "Makes me feel like a teenager again."

Then she rocked her hips urgently against his hard shaft. He captured her lips hard and fast as she tempted him. She lifted up on her knees so her wet core hovered over his tip. Chad's hand seared a path down her abdomen to her thigh. He waited, caressing her skin. She sank down, and he filled her perfectly, stretching her walls so that she felt every curve of him entering her. She paused, but his tormented groan was a heady invitation, so she moved against him.

The scent of his soft flesh was intoxicating. His lips moved over hers, demanding more of her. He massaged the tip of one breast while suckling the other, his tongue twirling, his teeth nipping. Her world was spinning out of control. He urged her to go faster, harder. Both took what the other gave as they hurtled beyond the point of no return, and Rachel's body vibrated with liquid fire. She clung to his shoulders as he pushed her over the edge and a breathless cry escaped her lips. He pressed deeper, rocking with power and grace beneath her. The walls of her core gripped him hard, and he was carried away with her. Ecstasy wrapped her body in the softest blanket as her body slumped against his, satiated like never before. She bit her lip and caressed his side, and he kissed her shoulder.

"I'm yours forever. No matter what comes," she said, not wanting to move, afraid that by doing so, she would shatter the moment.

He ran his fingers down her spine and up again, dropping his head back on the seat. "No matter what comes."

She ran lazy circles over his chest and he tilted his head so his green eyes glowed intensely at her. She brushed his kiss-swollen lips once more.

"The past is gone, but the future is yet to come. Live here in this moment with me."

He tightened his hold on her and kissed her. She surrendered as he stoked her passion once again. The bond was so raw and real that she was lost to it. Despite the uncertainty of Sapphire's birth, in this moment, they were completely happy.

Chapter Twenty-Three

When Rachel and Chad strolled back into the waiting room, they saw Gavin talking to a doctor. Concern traveled through the coupling bond and she squeezed Chad's hand. He gestured for her to sit down, but Rachel wanted to hear what the doctor was saying, so she heightened her senses and eavesdropped.

"Her blood cell count continues to drop for some reason. We have to run more tests."

"She doesn't want any more tests. She wants to go home."

"I'm sorry, Mr. Jones, but that wouldn't be wise at this point. It's likely she will need to have a C-section, considering her condition. She'll be better off here, where we can monitor her."

Gavin's nostrils flared and the scar on his face twitched. The doctor took a step back, clearly intimidated. Rachel hid a smirk. Gavin was quite the male. Leora had done well in her choice of partner. And, despite his grumpiness, Gavin was great to have around. She really liked him.

She paused at those odd thoughts. The gloominess that had hovered over her since before she awakened was gone. Her hands covered her mouth as her grin widened. Chad stared at her and she shot him a wink.

When the doctor left, Gavin spun around. His eyes narrowed at Chad, but then he marched over and threw himself on the seat next to Rachel.

"Did you hear that bullshit?" He pinched the bridge of his nose. "Leora wants to leave, but I don't think it's a good idea since Darron can't help her." Gavin pointed at Chad. "Where did *he* come from?" He leaned forward, reached around Rachel, and hooked a finger on Chad's shirt collar so he could pull it down. "And where did these scars come from?"

Chad knocked his hand away. "Jealous I'm sexier than you?"

Gavin raised a brow and frowned. "Scars like that don't just appear."

She searched Gavin's face, but it was a mask of indifference as he waited for one of them to respond. "Do you really want to know, or are you just asking to be polite?"

Gavin stared at his hands as his fingers locked together, turning white from the pressure. "There's no time to care. I'm only thankful he's here for Leora's peace of mind. You should go see her."

He cast a glance down the hall, and Chad's green eyes lost their twinkling amusement as his mouth pressed into a thin line. A few nurses rushed past them, drawing his attention. To what, Rachel couldn't tell.

"Leora's awake." Gavin pushed to his feet. "I have to go check on Marcus in the truck."

Fear wrapped its icy fingers around her throat. She touched Gavin's arm, stopping him. "We need to tell Leora about the vision. Withholding it is a betrayal of sorts, just as the vision predicted."

"I don't know if she can handle the truth with everything that's happening."

The world seemed to grow dimmer and colder until

Chad leaned over and kissed Rachel's forehead.

"Let's go see our daughter. Then we can talk to the others." He held out his hand, waiting for her to take it.

When they entered the small room, Leora was rubbing her butt uncomfortably on the hospital bed. Her nerves were raw, and a sense of foreboding hovered in the room. Rachel could feel it snaking between Darron, Tabitha, and even Gavin. They were probably too worried about what was going on to notice the odd feeling.

When Chad's young face smiled in at Leora, she gasped.

"They saved you! I was so scared." Reaching out a trembling hand, she motioned for him to come to her and he strolled right into her arms. "I didn't know when I would see you again."

"How's my girl?" He squeezed her tight and kissed her on the forehead. "You're not supposed to be in here yet."

Leora sniffled a little as tears pooled in her eyes. "Sapphire . . . she tried to . . . "

Rachel hurried to the other side of the bed, shoving Darron's knees back as he stared at Chad with a bewildered look on his face and a cheeseburger hanging from his mouth. Tabitha's legs were draped across his lap as she munched on a grape, grinning.

"It's okay, Leora. You don't have to talk about it." Rachel brushed wild, red hair from Leora's face.

"It's okay." Leora patted Rachel's hand. "I need to talk about it. I went to look for Gavin downstairs when a sharp pain ripped through me. I felt angry, and then panic shot through me." She looked away and shook her head. "The emotions weren't mine. They were Sapphire's. I felt her heart beating faster." Leora caressed her belly. "The anger she felt was unbearable. I . . . am I crazy to know what Sapphire was feeling? I keep telling myself that it wasn't her, that I'm the reason I'm here, but . . . " Her voice cracked. "I know that's not true."

Chad and Rachel held her between them in their arms.

"It's okay. Everything will be fine," Chad said in a low, calming tone.

Rachel glanced at Chad and frowned, her eyes tearing up. She felt sick, and conveyed through the bond that they needed to tell her the truth. Things were anything but okay.

"What I don't understand is what made her so angry. She's not even born yet!"

Rachel glanced toward the door, thinking about Marcus and what she now thought was a connection between him and Sapphire. She had to find out what was going on.

Chapter Twenty-Four

Steam wafted from the shower, making the hospital room uncomfortably humid. Rachel handed Leora a small shampoo bottle from outside the shower, then leaned against the wall; her brow was so furrowed, she could have held a pencil on her forehead. Her frustration was aimed at her granddaughter, and even though the little thing hadn't even been born yet, she found herself wanting to have a stern talk with the little stink. There had to be more to what was happening to Leora, a piece of the puzzle they had all somehow overlooked.

"So, tell me what happened when you went to the cavern. Was it easy finding Chad?" Leora asked.

Rachel really didn't think talking about that was a good idea, so she changed the subject. "Darron stole a bunch of Council members' souls and sent them to the heavens. They're with the Creator, awaiting judgment."

Leora yanked the shower curtain back, her blue eyes round with disbelief. White foam she hadn't managed to rinse away yet ran down the side of her cheek. "How did he do that?"

Rachel stammered and fumbled for the right words as Leora closed the curtain again. "I'm not sure. It has to do with him tapping into all of his ability." She turned to grab a towel without really thinking about what she was saying. "I wasn't there, but Chad saw it."

"What was Chad doing in the heavens?" This time, Leora pulled the curtain open all the way. "Clearly, I am out of the loop."

Leora's words stabbed Rachel in the chest and she flinched, but then her jaw dropped at the sight of Leora there naked in front of her. Dark purple and blue splotches were all over the fair skin of her belly. What was Sapphire doing in there?

"Leora…" Feeling weak, she scrambled for the toilet and sat down.

Leora didn't look at her belly; instead, she reached out a hand for her towel. Rachel gave it to her, and she wrapped herself carefully. "Don't worry. I'll be fine."

Fear raged hot and loud inside her. "That's not fine. *You're* not fine." She stood and gripped Leora's shoulders. "That baby needs to come out of you before it kills you."

"Rachel." Leora's pale eyes darkened as she knocked her hands away. "It is not 'that baby.'"

"You said it yourself that she tried to kill you because she was angry. That's not normal, Leora, even for a gifted child."

Leora slipped on a sweatsuit that Gavin had brought and shoved past her to leave the bathroom. "When is anything normal about our lives?"

She wasn't wrong, but this wasn't okay. Rachel followed on her heels, jumping over Darron's outstretched legs from where he sat on the small sofa. She wasn't going to let a baby kill her best friend. If Leora died, they would have one chance to bring her back into the world, and Leora's birth only ever followed Darron's, so Darron would have to die, and Tabitha would suffer a loss she had never experienced before. It was too much to think about, starting over, praying they both made it through their awakening and coming into their power, and that the remaining Council members wouldn't come for them, and that Marcus wouldn't turn on them again.

"Will you stop being selfish for once and think?" Rachel cried.

Leora stopped and stared at her. "Selfish." She marched over to Rachel. "How so, Mother? Last time I checked, I was thinking only about giving my baby a chance to live, even if that cost me my life."

Darron sat up, suddenly interested in the world around him. Rachel didn't want to talk about this in front of him, but he had a right to be part of this conversation. The fire inside her didn't die; instead, it grew hotter.

"There's a lot riding on this lifetime. You can't sacrifice yourself for her."

Rachel balled her hands into fists and the air crackled around her. Darron placed a hand on her leg and tugged her back a foot.

"Why can't I sacrifice myself? You, Chad, even Darron have done it countless times for me. Why can't I do it for her?"

"Because you can't . . . not in this life." Rachel blinked, and red spots winked in and out of her vision. "If you die, what will happen? Think!"

Darron sat back on the sofa. Leora looked at him for a long while, and then turned her back on them and climbed into bed.

"What would have to happen, Leora?" Rachel pressed. "Say it out loud so we can hear it."

She lifted her chin, stubborn as ever. Even with her eyes closed, tears ran down her cheeks. "Darron doesn't have to take his own life right away for me to be reborn. He could live a hundred years with Tabitha first. It is not my fault the Creator chose the birth order that way."

"Oh, how kind of you." Rachel didn't want to be cruel, but she had to make Leora see that there were other things to consider. The steel of resolve straightened her spine. She wasn't Rachel in that moment, but the Seer, and she wouldn't back down. Leora didn't know about the destiny marks and Rachel didn't know how long her and Chad would have in this life. Now wasn't the moment to tell her. "Did you hear that, Darron? You don't have to kill yourself right away." Darron's gaze stayed on the floor as Rachel turned back to her daughter. "At least have the decency to look at him while you decide his future, Leora."

Leora didn't open her eyes, so Rachel continued.

"You know what it will be like for him this time, for Tabitha. You remember what it feels like to have your bonded killed, how the bond can almost destroy every part of you as they lay in your arms, dying. It's something I wouldn't wish on anyone, but especially not someone with a love bond. Are you ready to be responsible for that just so you can birth a child who has already tried to kill you?"

Leora snapped her eyes open. "I can't believe you. You want me to kill her to save myself?"

Rachel could see the fear in her sad eyes and knew this wasn't good for Leora right now, but it had to be done. She pushed on, her voice hard and unforgiving. "What about the souls that need to awaken? What will become of them while they wait a hundred years, maybe two, before you're reborn? You know what's happening to the Lost?"

"No," Leora whispered.

"The Council is possessing their bodies because their souls are so weak." She didn't want to go in for the kill, but there was no other way to get Leora to really think about what would happen without her. "You have your power. You could be out there right now if it weren't for Sapphire."

"That's enough," Darron hissed. "Leave her alone. What is done is done."

Rachel's vision went red. The secrets and the hurt caused by it all were overwhelming. Gold light crackled and hissed around her.

"I had a vision; Sapphire will kill you the moment she's born and you touch her with your love. Your love triggers her gift to erase time."

Leora flinched back, her jaw hanging open and her eyes wide.

Darron jumped up and put himself between them. "Stop, Rachel. Don't do this. It is not part of the plan."

Leora got up and went to his side, her face distorted by confusion and heartbreak.

"Sapphire will wipe every soul's memories. She will reset time. We will have no history together; we will not know each other. It will be a reset," Darron said.

Leora grabbed Darron's arm. "No."

He peered down at her. "It's true. That is why Gavin didn't know who you were after he drained Sapphire's energy to try and stop her from hurting you."

Leora shook her head. "No, no, no. Why would the Creator do this?"

"Because we have failed too many times," Darron said in a small voice.

Leora began to shake as she pointed at him. "You said her telling me wasn't part of the plan. What were you going to do?"

Rachel glanced at Darron, wondering which of them it would be. One of them had to tell her the truth.

Darron sighed loudly, knowing this wasn't going to end well for any of them. "We were going to take Sapphire and hide her from you."

"How could you do that? I can feel her!" Her blue eyes

darkened and her voice had a hard edge to it.

"The sacred circle would mask her from you . . . and we were going to tell you that she died," Rachel said, lifting her chin as if daring Leora to challenge her.

She was ready for the rage that was sure to come, and Rachel saw in Leora's expression when everything came together in her mind. She paled and backed away from them as if they'd punched her in the gut, wrapping her hands over her belly.

"Who? How could any of you leave to take her without me knowing?"

Darron straightened his spine. "Marcus can help her control her gift. He is strong enough to bind her."

That was Leora's tipping point; it had been for Rachel too. "You would give my child to a man who raped me and killed all of us countless times?" She pulled at her hair. "Does everyone know about this vision? Were you all part of this plan?"

Darron and Rachel didn't reply, but they didn't have to say anything for Leora to figure it out.

"Gavin knew?" She shook her head and screamed, "Get out!"

There was the promised betrayal. They had hit the mark.

Straightening her back like a steel rod, Rachel marched out of the room. Gavin and Chad were going to kill her.

She stormed down the hall, out of the hospital, and out into the snow. Her skin was hot as she marched across the parking lot to Chad's truck, and the snow that touched her steamed and evaporated immediately. She didn't bother to get into the truck, but threw herself down on the ground and leaned against the tire.

Anguish smothered her, and a sob exploded past her lips. What was she thinking? This wasn't the time to say anything to Leora, and this wasn't who she was. She had never been mean or hurtful, even when she was scared. That was her old self talking, and she didn't like that version of her very much. She threw her arms around her knees and cried into them. Trying to find a balance between who she was and who she used to be was proving to be even more of a challenge than she thought. The red in her vision spilled over to her mind, coating it like thick honey.

Then, she stilled. The world around her faded away to be replaced by another that was both new and familiar. She pulled in a breath, waiting for it to fully form, but then felt him hovering over her.

Marcus snarled, "Events record in the deepest part of my mind. Your little family is weak for letting their emotions rule them."

Rachel wrinkled her nose. He was not wrong; they were a mess. Images flickered before her like a poorly spliced movie.

"What do you think the odds are of me escaping this stupid bloodbond to my brother?" Marcus asked. She sensed him leaning away. "I just have to blink out faster than Darron can spirit himself."

The image in Rachel's mind glitched before it vanished entirely. That had never happened before. Something was wrong.

Rachel peered up at Marcus; he was looking over his shoulder at the hospital. She still couldn't move thanks to the paralysis that always lingered for a few minutes after a vision.

"I am so sick of that kid feeding off my power." He bent down to her eye level. "Want to know what I figured out?" He leaned in and whispered in her ear. "When I cut that little shit off from my power, she gets mad and I almost have enough energy to blink out of here." He leaned back and raised a black brow. "Want to see what happens when I do that?"

A wicked smile curled his lips, and Rachel's stomach dropped as a bloodcurdling scream rang out. She sprang to her feet, but then started to sink back to the ground; she braced herself against the old truck.

"You can't save her with this sad plan of yours. The bloodbond will not hold me, and it's not Leora's power that binds me. It is that child. She is a parasite. I don't want to care for a child. I want her to die," Marcus said, repulsed. "The Awakener dying is just a bonus. And now that I can see the Creator's little plan, I will see to it that Leora never gives birth to any child in any future life." He pinched Rachel's chin. "With you and Chad marked, I can make sure Leora and Darron are never born again."

He released her, and Rachel didn't waste any time rushing back to the hospital and down the hall to Leora's room, which was so full she couldn't get in. She pushed to her tiptoes to see what was happening. Between the heads bobbing around, she spotted Leora. Blood was everywhere, and she wasn't moving; she was so pale. Nurses shoved Rachel out of the way as they wheeled Leora out of the room. Darron, Tabitha, Chad, and Gavin ran around the corner to catch up with them. Darron reached down and tried to heal her. Tabitha rested a hand on his shoulder to amp up his power.

"Fuck." He yanked his hand back and waved it in the air as if he'd been bitten, then he hugged it close to his body.

"Shit balls!" Tabitha rubbed her hand as well.

"Out of the way!" one of the nurses yelled.

Gavin reluctantly moved aside. Rachel had never seen a man look more desperate.

"The little shit stopped me from healing Leora again! We have to let the doctors help her now," Darron said.

"They're going to take Sapphire out. We have to stick to the plan. Leora will hate us, but at least she knows." Darron rested a hand on Gavin's shoulder, but Gavin glared at him. "*How* does she know?"

"Rachel told her before you came back. That is why she wasn't talking to you."

Gavin grabbed him by the throat and lifted him off the ground with one hand. "She did what?"

Before things could escalate any further, Tabitha punched Gavin in the gut and he put Darron down, rubbing his stomach as he did.

"You can fight later. Right now, we don't have time for this," she said, always the voice of reason in a sea of chaos.

"Tabitha will project you two as nurses, and when the time is right, Gavin will drain Leora's power."

"The bond: she will feel me near."

"How close do you need to be to drain her and leave her unconscious?" Darron asked. Gavin's eyes turned black, and Darron patted him on the back. "Easy now. You know there's no other way."

Every muscle in Gavin's large body flexed as he closed his eyes. When they opened, the blackness was gone, and his shoulders slumped. "I need to be within two, maybe three rooms of her."

Then it hit Rachel. Marcus had said that the baby was feeding off his power, and when he cut her off, she got mad. Rachel didn't know why the baby needed or wanted Marcus, but he was a crucial part of this whether they wanted him to be or not.

"We need Marcus," she whispered. "This is because he's cutting her off." Rachel knew no one would understand, and she didn't have time to explain, so she started barking orders and figured she could fill in the gaps for them as they went. "Tabitha, go with Gavin. Darron and

Chad need to get Marcus. We need him here *now*."

Was he the only reason Leora wasn't already dead?

A hand clasped hers and heat rolled up her arm, warming her from within.

"It will be okay," Chad said.

She shook her head. "No, it won't. Not unless . . . "

Rachel peered over her shoulder and into the lobby. Darron and Chad took the hint and went after Marcus.

Chapter Twenty-Five

Chad peeled out of the hospital parking lot. The truck's back end fishtailed wildly.

Darron clutched his head. "That fucker is trying to get away. The base of my skull is burning."

Chad turned east, following wherever Darron pointed. His instincts told him they didn't have much time. He drove two blocks before he spotted Marcus rushing behind a building. Darron growled low, but Chad shouldn't have expected anything different from Marcus.

Now wasn't the time for a game of cat and mouse, but if that was what Marcus wanted to play, they would oblige him. Chad turned off his headlights and coasted down a dirt alley. Darron jumped out of the truck and headed around the corner of a gift shop without making a sound. A minute later, Chad saw Darron gripping Marcus by the shoulder. Darron's feet turned to mist, but then turned back. He narrowed his eyes at Marcus.

Chad parked and got out of the truck just as Darron asked, "Going somewhere?"

"Away from here," Marcus hissed as he knocked Darron away and stepped back.

"Hate to shit on your plans, but you're coming with me."

Red-and-black electricity shot to the ground from Marcus's palms. "When will you people learn? You can't make me do anything I don't wish to do."

"His power," Darron said, backing up just as Marcus vanished. He clutched the back of his head and looked around aimlessly. "Fuck, we don't have time for this shit. When did that asshole learn to blink? Time for a whole new manner of hunting, I guess." In a rush of darkness, Darron moved beyond this world, and Chad heard him say, "The hunt is on."

Alone in the alley, Chad didn't want to think of what Darron was about to face. But before he could think seriously of going back to the hospital to wait, Darron reappeared with his arms around Marcus's throat.

He yanked his head back and whispered in his ear, "I told you, Marcus. You can't hide from me."

Marcus struggled to free himself, but Darron's grip only tightened.

"Remember this moment when you start thinking you're going to try and run again. You can't—not from me. We're going to the hospital, and you're going to do exactly what we talked about. You'll take Sapphire to the sacred circle, and you'll care for her until she can control her power: not a day less. Do you hear me?"

He squeezed Marcus's windpipe so hard he heard the crunching of cartilage. Marcus wheezed and coughed up blood.

•●○༄○●•

Rachel sat in the waiting room on the edge of her seat, chewing her fingernails. So many thoughts rampaged through her tired mind, but she didn't have the strength to contain them. Everything was so unclear and off balance in so many ways. To make matters worse, a vision took root in her mind's eye.

Leora: gray and lifeless, her belly empty. Gavin standing beside her, holding a lifeless newborn. The doctor and nurses lay on the sterile floor, painted in their own blood.

She pulled in a ragged breath. The image dissolved and another took its place.

Leora screaming as Gavin holds her tight. Even when she hits him and catches on fire, he continues to hold her. Rachel's face is buried in Chad's chest as he embraces her. Darron wraps his arms around Tabitha before they turn to mist and disappear.

Rachel bit harder on her nail, praying the visions would stop shifting so she could know what was to become of them. Her sight shifted again.

Marcus standing next to a beautiful, young girl in the woods. Energy building around her to heights Rachel never knew were even possible. The girl's long, red hair lifts into the air. Her eyes are red, and when she screams, the tall pine trees are ripped from the ground. Marcus steps forward and pulls the power into himself, only to release it upon them all in the form of a lightning storm.

The image lingered for a long time, playing out the destruction of all mankind. Rachel stared at nothing on the floor.

Please, Creator . . . no.

The vision shifted again. She gasped as an arm draped over her shoulder, hugging her close.

"What do you see?" Chad asked in a broken voice.

A beautiful, young girl clinging to Leora. They are both crying and laughing. A large man that stands not far behind her. The girl reaches for him. He reluctantly takes her hand as she spins into him and rests her head on his chest. I can't see his face.

The vision stopped, and the fog in her mind lifted. Rachel trembled hard against Chad and sucked in a shaky breath.

"What did you see?" he asked again.

"Too many things. The future is not set, and it won't be for some time, I fear. Is Marcus here?" she asked, unable to move yet.

"Yes. Darron was struggling to contain him, but now that we are here, Marcus seems weaker."

"Thank the Creator," she said, finally able to turn and look at him.

"I don't know how, but he can blink even with his power bound."

Rachel stood, wanting nothing more than a strong cup of coffee. She could smell it from somewhere down the hall, probably in an employee area. Chad took her hand so easily.

"Leora doesn't have him contained. It's Sapphire. She's using him like a syphon."

"How do you know that?"

"Marcus said as much before he ran off, and I saw pieces of the truth when I was in his mind."

"Wait, you were in his head?"

She was too tired. She paused to sort out her thoughts and shrugged. "I think my gift is evolving. Anyway, when Marcus is too far away, Sapphire is cut off from his energy and she gets mad, then takes it out on Leora. Marcus has been trying to figure out how to stop her from draining his power. We have to keep him close until Sapphire is born, to keep Leora safe."

"Why didn't you let me know over the bond that you told Leora about the vision?"

She scrubbed a hand over her face. "I got upset. I messed everything up."

He squeezed her free hand and then kissed her forehead. "It is better that she knows the truth."

She touched his cheek and peered into those rich, green eyes. "There are many possible outcomes following Sapphire's birth. Some are beautiful, but others are laced with darkness and death. We have to pray the Creator is with us."

He kissed her lips softly. "Let's go."

Chapter Twenty-Six

Rachel and Chad found Tabitha and Gavin just outside the operating room. They could see Leora's profile; a blue cap covered her unruly hair, and a breathing tube had been shoved down her throat. A blue curtain separated her from the doctor as he worked to pull out the life Gavin and Leora had created, and who was now trying to kill her. Even with his hands at his sides, Rachel felt it when Gavin pushed his energy out through the wall and into the operating room, his power caressing Leora. Her energy level was no more than a whisper, and her heartbeat slowed.

A blue light shone bright as the doctor pulled her granddaughter free from her mother. Blue flames engulfed her tiny body and the doctor dropped her on Leora's torso before backing away, horrified. The nurses screamed and ran from the room, shoving everyone aside in their haste.

Sapphire cried as the blue flames darkened to red and then black. Rachel wanted to go in and comfort her, to hold her in her arms if only for a moment, but would she let her?

"Show the doctor that Sapphire is normal," Gavin told Tabitha. "Project that everything is normal. Then change us all into the nurses that left."

Tabitha nodded, and suddenly the doctor looked confused. He calmed down and rushed toward Leora and

Sapphire as Rachel, Tabitha, and Gavin entered the room. The doctor held the baby out to them, and Gavin took his daughter, since he was fireproof. The doctor didn't notice that Sapphire had burned his hands. He simply went back to work and closed Leora up.

All they had was this moment. Gavin stroked her little head. "Calm down, little one. Daddy has you now."

To Rachel's satisfaction, the flames eased to a soft blue and then dissipated. Sapphire blinked wide, new eyes at him, and tears rolled down Rachel's cheeks. Time, promises, secrets, and sorrow locked together as Gavin kissed her head and a lone tear ran down his cheek to land on Sapphire's soft head. It glowed white and sank into her skin. She cooed and wiggled in his arms.

"That's a good girl," he said.

He walked over to the station the nurses had set up and wiped her small body under the heat lamp. She watched him, studying him as he studied her. She had her mother's fair complexion, and damp, red curls flopped around on her little head, but her eyes were as bright a amber as his, although they each had a red dot resting in their centers. Her critical stare told Rachel that she was fully aware of what she was, even at such a young age.

"My precious, you have to go away until you can control your power. If you don't, we will all forget who we are."

Her little red brows pinched together. She turned her head toward Leora, and her bottom lip puckered out as she let out one single cry and tears gathered in her eyes.

"I know. I wish we could all be together too."

Swaddling her tightly, he looked over to see Tabitha doing her best to assist the doctor like a real nurse so as not to confuse him any further. She glanced at him and lifted her chin toward the window. Rachel followed her gaze, and there stood Marcus and Darron.

As Gavin gathered Sapphire into his arms, she gazed up at him and cooed. What would Sapphire do if Marcus tried to leave again now that she was out of the womb? Would she unleash her gift upon the world? Would Marcus want that? He would be reset too, and would probably lose his power. Rachel thought that perhaps that was why he was still there and not fighting for the moment. Was he afraid of what Sapphire could do if provoked?

Now that Leora knew the truth, could Rachel and Chad go to the sacred circle with them?

"Be a good girl and listen to Uncle Marcus. He's going to help you control your power so Mommy can come see you. And believe me, she wants to see you so badly." Gavin kissed her forehead. "I love you always, my little peanut."

She cooed again and then snuggled into her blanket, blinking sleepy eyes up at him. She wrinkled her nose and smiled as she fell asleep.

The next thing they knew, Tabitha was walking out with the doctor. Darron reached out and touched the man's shoulder to heal the hands that Sapphire had burned. Then, Darron walked into the room and stood next to Leora.

"We need to get her home. I can't heal her until Sapphire is gone."

Gavin cast a nervous look at Leora. Rachel peered at her too, wondering if she would continue to love them after going through all of this. Her heart ached for Leora.

A minute later, Tabitha reappeared, looking pleased. "We're in the clear. I persuaded the doctor and the nurses that there was never a Lily McMaster admitted to the hospital, and they're fixing the records now. So, let me see the little brat before she goes." Tabitha hurried over and pulled the blanket down to see more of Sapphire's face. "My first baby up close. She's so small." She lifted a tiny hand and spread it out on hers. "She's amazing, and she looks just like Leora. Darron, come look at your niece. She's so cute."

A smile tugged at Gavin's lips as Rachel joined them in admiring the newest family member. For many lifetimes, he and Leora had waited to see this little being come into the world and finally, there she was. Pride lifted Gavin's chest, but, just as suddenly, it deflated.

Darron looked down at the baby and barely held back a scowl. "Yes, she's cute. Now, can we get this show on the road? Leora is going to kill us when she wakes up."

"Yes, but she'll know Sapphire is alive."

Marcus leaned against the wall. His gaze never left Sapphire and an icy, ominous feeling trickled down Rachel's spine.

"Marcus," Gavin asked in his most controlled voice. "Can you take Leora and Darron to the house with your gift?"

Marcus pushed away from the wall, a dark storm brewing in his eyes as he studied Gavin. So, Gavin knew Leora's power wasn't holding Marcus. Rachel wondered if he knew it was Sapphire's.

"As long as that brat doesn't freak out because I'm gone."

Rachel sucked in a breath. Could Sapphire connect to him easier now that Leora's energy was not interfering with the connection, or did Sapphire not need him at all anymore?

"I'll explain later," Chad said, entering the room in response to Gavin and Darron's frowns, but then he shrugged. "That's if we still know each other." Rachel frowned, and Chad shrugged again. "What? Anything could happen at this point, right?"

"Darron, how long do you think it will take to heal Leora and for her to wake up?"

Darron walked over to Leora and touched her skin. "A few hours."

"We'll be at the house in two."

Marcus placed a hand on Darron and Leora. With a crack and a spark of light, they vanished.

Hot tears rolled unchecked down Rachel's face. "There has to be a better plan than this. What if Marcus tries to kill her because she hates Leora so much?"

Gavin shook his head. "I can feel Marcus's affection for me even after all these years. He will not do anything to break the bloodbond, and he knows I want to fix things between us. He will not hurt her."

"I hope you're right," Chad said, "because I still don't trust him."

Chapter Twenty-Seven

There was no time to waste. Tabitha, Chad, and Gavin all sprang from the vehicle. Gavin handed each one a list and they parted, sprinting off to different stores. Rachel stayed in the truck and held Sapphire; her small, round face reminded her of when Leora was born. So much love and joy swirled inside her that day. It would be many years before Leora would ever experience that feeling for herself . . . if ever.

She ran a hesitant finger over Sapphire's smooth cheek, wondering if she could wipe her memories with just a touch. What if she never learned to control her power, and Leora never got to see her? Her stomach rolled. Or what if Marcus used Sapphire to kill everyone?

No. She wasn't going to let her old self taint this life.

"Everything's going to work out, little one. You're going to be perfect in every way, just like your momma and Darron." She wrinkled her nose and then rubbed it against Sapphire's. "Well, Uncle Darron wasn't so perfect, but he tried hard to be."

She laughed to herself, and Sapphire wiggled in her arms. Her full lips pressed together, and then she blinked a few times and went back to sleep. Rachel hummed a soft lullaby she used to sing for Darron and Leora. After a few verses, Sapphire glowed a pale blue. It grew brighter before turning white, then blue again. Just as Rachel was about to stop humming, she realized Sapphire liked the song, and that she glowed in time with the tune: blue light on all the lower tones, and a brighter white when her voice got higher.

Rachel cuddled the baby closer and watched in amazement as she continued to hum. Her fears melted away one pulse of her light at a time. A soft heat, like a perfect bath washing over her skin, entered her chest where Sapphire's body was pressed against her. Unexpectedly, her own skin began to glow along with Sapphire. She sank lower into her seat, not wanting to draw any attention. Rachel giggled softly, and Sapphire once again wriggled in her arms. Stretching, she blinked amber eyes up at Rachel and smiled.

The red in her eyes glowed bright. It was off-putting, and gave Sapphire a sense of danger. Rachel just prayed she would be a happy girl despite what lay ahead. She had to believe Sapphire would learn to control her gift, and that Leora would see her one day soon. She had to.

•●○〜○●•

Chad didn't know how long he stood beside the truck. His hands were full of bags, and snow covered him like a light blanket, but he was completely mesmerized as he watched Rachel and Sapphire interact. The latter was only an hour old and already he could see the love transferring between his girls.

Then he thought about Leora, and sadness overwhelmed him. She wouldn't get to experience a mother's love for her daughter for a long time. Sagging miserably, he opened the door and climbed inside the cab. Dropping the bags at Rachel's feet, he pulled out his list and glanced at the haul to make sure he'd got it all. Babies sure needed a lot of stuff.

He met Rachel's dark eyes and saw they were full of tears. Her anguish suffocated him. He slid across the bench seat and wrapped his arm around her shoulders as he listened to her sniffles. Sapphire stopped glowing, and her bottom lip pouted as her face scrunched up. She looked ready to cry as well.

He ran a finger over Sapphire's round cheek and said in a soft, soothing tone, "Everything will be fine. If you are worried about Marcus, I can go and set up camp inside the circle with them."

"You would do that for me?" She lifted her head and gazed deeply into his eyes.

"For you, I would do anything. I want her to be safe too. I don't know what Marcus's intentions are yet, but it would be my pleasure to watch him and find out. Besides, we have to finish rebuilding the cabin sometime."

"This feels awful. Leora's going to be devastated, and I don't know if I can help her through this."

He ran a hand up her neck and then over her cheek, loving the feel of her. She nuzzled his hand, and his chest tightened. "If there is anyone who can help her, it's you. You have lost your children countless times. Think about what helped you get through it."

A tear touched his thumb and he wiped it away. The sorrow in her eyes was almost too much. He wanted to take it away, but was unsure of how to do that. Brushing his lips over hers, he sent his deepest love for her through their bond, and she sighed against his lips. He would never tire of that sound.

Just then, Sapphire cooed up at them. She was smiling brightly and glowing . . . literally. *What a bright little girl.*

He chuckled at his own joke and took the baby from

Rachel so he could hold her up and they could look at each other. "Oh, we haven't forgotten about you."

Sapphire smiled again, and he kissed her on the nose before placing her on his shoulder and gently patting her on the back.

"Rachel, grab her a diaper and the outfit I got her from that bag."

As Rachel rummaged through the bags, he absorbed as much love as he could from Sapphire and gave it right back.

"Chad . . . really?" Rachel asked, giggling.

He took the diaper and rested Sapphire in his lap, unwrapping her. Together, he and Rachel dressed Sapphire up, laughing all the while. Her pink outfit had a built-in tutu around the middle and read, "Grandpa rules."

Their laughter slowly grew silent and a weight settled on his chest. He swaddled Sapphire once more, holding her close while waiting for the others to get back.

"I love you, little one. Always remember that Grandpa and Grandma love you."

Sapphire glowed brightly and closed her eyes, falling asleep in his arms.

"It is a little weird hearing that," Rachel whispered. "I mean, I haven't even been pregnant in this life."

Chapter Twenty-Eight

Rachel rested her hand on Gavin's shoulder, sending him some of her energy and strength, as did Tabitha. His shoulders shook sadly as he cried, holding his daughter on the sofa in his home.

"We are all broken souls trying to find our way. You and Leora will make it through this, and you'll all be together again. Time is just the rise and fall of the sun, nothing more," she said, wanting to believe her own words even as her own heart broke too.

"Gavin, it is time to let her go. We are already taking a risk by having Sapphire this close while Leora is healing."

"I know, but how do I do this? How do I let her go?"

Tabitha squeezed his shoulder. "By remembering that you must—for her own good."

"Tabitha, get Marcus and gather everything we bought for Sapphire. Make sure he can take it all with him," Rachel said.

Tabitha eyed the boxes in the living room. "Did anyone get him a tool kit?"

"Yes," Gavin said, lifting his head to suck in a deep breath.

Tabitha climbed over the boxes to reach the ones near Gavin.

"You must take her from me," Gavin said to Rachel.

"It will be okay." There was a hitch in her voice, and she prayed Gavin didn't hear it.

She reached out her hands. Gavin looked at them until the screen door slammed, causing him to jump. He stared at his brother for a long while, and Marcus didn't look away. Rachel sent a prayer to the Creator.

Please save us all.

"This is the only way, Gavin, or we'll never know each other again."

He stared into her eyes as she took Sapphire from his arms, and then his jaw locked.

"Go to Leora. She's going to need you." Rachel held Sapphire tightly to her chest, fear rolling in her gut over and over as she walked over to Marcus. Gavin didn't move.

"Can you take all of this with you?" Tabitha asked, indicating the boxes of supplies.

He stared at the child and nodded. Meanwhile, Rachel studied Marcus's face. His emotions had long been tinged with hate and pain. There had to be some part of the boy he once was in there. Against her better judgment, she held Sapphire out to him. He hesitated for only a second, then carefully took her in his arms. His eyes lightened for the first time to a golden amber color that matched Gavin's. Her breath caught as hope sparked in her chest.

It lasted only a moment, and then the blackness she recognized consumed his eyes once more. A wicked smile curled his lips and then they were gone, along with all of the stuff they had bought for Sapphire.

A sob escaped her, and Chad pulled her into his arms. What had they done? She buried her face in his chest. A scream tore through her like a thousand shards of glass had ripped her open. She tried to stop it, but she couldn't.

"We will go to the sacred circle as soon as we know

Leora will be okay."

A strong hand squeezed her shoulder as heat pooled in the center of her chest. She turned just in time to see Darron walk into the room. Tabitha followed him with tears running down her cheeks.

"She's going to wake up shortly," Darron said, his voice solemn.

He looked at Rachel and then at Tabitha before he forced Gavin to stand and hugged him; it took a few seconds for Gavin to hug him back, but when he did, he wrapped him in a fierce embrace and they stayed that way for a while.

"I am sorry, brother," Darron said, taking a step back and letting his arms fall to his sides.

"As am I."

Darron took Tabitha's hand and followed Gavin upstairs to Leora. When they were gone, Rachel wiped her face.

"I can't go up there."

Chad lifted her chin. "You can, and you will, because you love Leora, and you know she needs you."

Marcus's wicked smile was etched into her mind. Sapphire was gone, and there was no going back, but together, she and Chad climbed the stairs to the second floor.

Gavin sat beside Leora on the edge of the bed, stroking her wild, red hair. Her skin was paler than usual and covered with a fine layer of sweat. Dark circles underlined her eye sockets. Carrying Sapphire had taken a toll on Leora—had brought her to the verge of death. Rachel wished she could understand it all and why it had to be this way, but there was just too much to think about.

The corners of Leora's mouth pulled up slightly and then she wiggled a little. Gavin lifted her hand and kissed it softly. Her lashes fluttered open and a confused, sleepy look spread over her face.

"There's my girl," Gavin said, drawing her attention.

"Home," Leora breathed.

She tried to sit up, but Gavin gently pushed her back down. Rachel watched as panic built within Leora once she really started to get her bearings, but the words wouldn't form on her tongue. She shot a glance at Darron and Tabitha, who were sitting in the corner of the room, and silently implored one of them to say something.

"Rachel," Leora whimpered. "Where's Sapphire?"

"She's gone," Darron said, staring at the floor so he wouldn't have to meet his sister's eye.

"What do you mean?" Leora's voice broke and became a whisper as she pulled at Gavin's arm. He looked away from her, and Leora began to cry. "No . . . please, no. Babe, tell me she's okay."

"She's gone," Gavin said, meeting her heartbroken stare with his own damp eyes. "It's not for forever. It is just for now. We have to find a way for you to be together and not trigger her gift."

Tears quickly dampened the sheets. She carefully touched her stomach as if there was some chance she'd find something still there. "Why? Why is the Creator doing this?"

She sank back onto the bed and curled into a ball, sobbing. Gavin lay next to her, molding himself against her back and holding her tight.

"I love you," he whispered in her ear.

She rolled over and faced him so she could rest her head on his chest. "Did you get to see her?"

"Yes."

"Was she beautiful and perfect?"

"Perfect."

Chad sat beside them and placed a hand on both of

them. "Show her your memory through the bond. I will help her see it."

Gavin nodded and closed his eyes. After a few tense seconds, Leora gasped and then began to cry fresh tears. "She is perfect."

Rachel rose and went to Chad, placing a hand on his shoulder. As she watched Leora's heart break, a familiar, cold emptiness filled her. There were no words that could be spoken to heal a mother after the loss of a child.

Whenever Rachel had lost Leora or Darron in the past, she had been bonded with Chad, but there was no love between them. She had essentially grieved on her own in the woods, in her room, in the sacred circle, and countless other places. Rachel glanced at Chad. She could feel his pain and knew he, too, had grieved alone for his children in the past. A knot formed in her throat. How had she ever thought Chad wasn't grieving for their family?

She squeezed his shoulder. Never again would they be alone in their loss, or their love.

Rachel watched Leora and Gavin and the love they shared and knew they would be there to help each other through this. Together, they were stronger.

She kissed Chad softly, and in that moment, his love eased some of her pain, just as she hoped her love eased his. Together, they would make this life better than all the others. They had each other, and they had love. They all did. They had all found what they needed, and that would see them through all the darkest days and nights to come.

"She is perfect, and I will see her again," Leora whispered.

The End

About the Author

R.E.S. Tidmore is a defective writer who writes. She has a BA and MFA in creative writing. Being dyslexic, she never  thought she could make a living from writing. Writing isn't only about dotting your i's and crossing your t's. It's about storytelling, and doing it in all the best ways. She loves Jane Austen, tattoos, sarcasm, quick wit, CrossFit, gardening, all things Harry Potter, being a writing coach, and a happy ever after.

Check out her other adult romance series: The Verbecks of Idaho, Managing Mayhem, and her new young adult novel D is for Defective.

For more on the characters you love from all her series, visit her website and click on EXTRAS to see posts.

Please help her reach new readers by writing a review of this book at the retailer you purchased it from. Your support is the greatest asset an indie writer could have. Thank you.